A Potluck of Murder and Recipes

A Hot Dish Heaven Mystery

Also by Jeanne Cooney

Hot Dish Heaven: A Murder Mystery with Recipes

A Second Helping of Murder and Recipes

A Potluck of Murder and Recipes

ഇ ര

A Hot Dish Heaven Mystery
(Book 3)

Jeanne Cooney

NORTH STAR PRESS OF ST. CLOUD, INC.
St. Cloud, Minnesota

Printed in the United States of America

Published by
North Star Press of St. Cloud, Inc.
St. Cloud, MN

www.northstarpress.com

Dedication

This book is dedicated to my granddaughters, Brooke and Molly. I hope your lives are rich in mystery and humor and, one day in the very, very distant future, even a little romance.

Acknowledgments

Once again I must thank my sister Mary Cooney for brainstorming ideas and reviewing drafts. I also want to thank my sister Teresa Cooney and my niece Amy Hennen, who, along with Mary, provided critiquing that immensely improved the final manuscript. Thanks also to my daughter, Elizabeth Young, for overseeing my Facebook page, and my niece Haley Cooney, who designed and continues to monitor my website. And, finally, thanks to my publisher, North Star Press, for all that is done by its staff, from editing and cover design to overseeing printing and distribution.

Part I

Post a Potluck Sign-up Sheet

Chapter One

RUSHED THROUGH the back door of the senior center, stomped snow from my boots and skidded down the hallway. I was an hour late for the bridal shower. From what I could hear, a couple drinks behind everyone else, too.

"I'm not sure which one I like better, the Gimlet or the Gin and Tonic." I recognized the voice, even though it sounded a tad shaky. It belonged to Margie's niece Little Val. According to Margie, the combination bridal shower/bachelorette party was to be Little Val's first solo night out since giving birth to her son two months ago. "I'll have to drink . . . umm . . . at least one more of each to decide for sure." *Hiccup.* Evidently, she planned to make the most of it.

"Oh, come on now, you've had more than enough and then some." I rounded the corner to find Vivian, Little Val's mother, scolding her married daughter as if she were a child. "Ya sure as heck don't wanna pass out and miss all the games and such."

"Games?" I silently prayed I'd heard wrong. "Please don't tell me we're playing silly shower games."

Vivian whipped her head around, her eyes bobbing between me and the door I'd just closed. "Brrr," she uttered, rubbing her arms.

I felt no sympathy for her. It was the end of December in northern Minnesota, and she was wearing a thin, sleeveless, v-neck top. Even indoors, sweaters were the order of the day. For normal people, anyhow.

"Well, Emme," she said to me, "it's about time ya showed up."

I faked a smile. As anyone might have guessed, I didn't care for Vivian. She thought a lot of herself and not much of anyone else. On top of that, she was like a static-laden song on the radio—grating and nearly impossible to understand. In a screechy voice, she regularly misused idioms, mixed metaphors, and generally jumbled her words—"a fate worse than a dog's bark." Still, she was Margie's sister, and Margie was one of my dearest friends, despite being thirty years my senior. So I made an effort to be kind. Or at least act the part.

As for Little Val, she seemed nice enough, although I didn't know her well, notwithstanding the fact I'd witnessed her give birth to her son. That's right. I saw her deliver baby Brian with an "I," not a "Y." But that was a whole other story.

Little Val staggered my way, reaching out with arms clad in a red pullover sweater, a cartoon moose appliqued on the front. "Hi, Emme," she slurred as she embraced me, the alcohol on her breath warming my cheeks and providing me with a contact buzz. "Glad to see you." Her antler headband slipped down over her face. "Though you've seen way more of me than I have of you." She giggled as she pushed the headband back up on her head.

"Oh, Heavens to Betsy, there you are!" From the other side of the room, Margie hurried my way, shouting over the jukebox sounds of Dean Martin and Martina McBride, as they stated the obvious in their duet, "Baby, It's Cold Outside."

Reaching me, she sandwiched Little Val between us when she leaned in with a hug of her own. Like always, she smelled of vanilla.

"'orry, I'm 'ate," I sputtered into her neck. After she let go, Little Val continued to hold on tight, her nose nestled in what little cleavage I had developed in my twenty-six years. "With all the blowing snow, I had a hard time seeing where I was going." My tone sounded edgy, even to my own ears.

"Uff-da, I was startin' to worry."

"I called but couldn't get through."

"Oh, yah, that's par for the course up here, 'specially durin' bad weather." Margie grabbed Little Val, spun her around, and propelled her in the direction of her mother. "But, you're here now, so let's get ya a drink. Somethin' to calm your nerves, there."

I shrugged off my navy pea coat, as she snatched a hanger from the coatrack.

"We'll shovel some food into ya, too. We've got plenty." She eyed me from head to toe. "And, by gully, ya need it. You're so skinny that if

2

your sweater were yellow, I'd swear ya were a No. 2 pencil." With a chuckle, she then escorted me to the center of the room.

The place was decked out in streamers and balloons in purple and gold, a-la the Minnesota Vikings. The tables along the outside walls held gift bags, bottles of booze, and two crock pots, one filled with Potato Hot Dish, the other, Chicken Crescent Hot Dish. Margie informed me that both had been prepared by her friend Bonnie Johnson, who, at the moment, was chatting with several other white-haired ladies in the open kitchen behind us.

Next to the hot dishes rested a three-tier dessert tray overloaded with bars. And on a card table sat a four-layer cake with a creepy paper-mache bust of a bride on top. No doubt, Vivian's doing. As were the life-size, wooden cutouts of the Precious Moments bride and groom propped up close by. I'd seen them before. Believe me, those two got around.

Margie raised her hand to the fifteen or so women scattered about, all balancing martini glasses, luncheon plates, and gold paper napkins in their hands. "Hey, everyone!" She motioned for someone to lower the volume on the music, and within seconds, Dean and Martina faded away. "Pipe down, I've gotta young lady here I wancha to meet. Her name's Emerald Malloy, though everyone calls her Emme. She's a newspaper reporter from Minneapolis. She's the one who wrote those real nice articles about me and my recipes last year, don't ya know." Margie playfully yanked one of my long, red curls, surely causing my face to turn the same color. My dad used to call it the curse of fair-skinned, Irish women. We blushed easily. Very easily.

"Anyways," Margie proceeded to say, "when I told her I was marryin' John, she said she wouldn't miss the weddin' for the world. So, even with the poor weather and Christmas just gettin' done with and all, here she is." She flipped her large hands like she was the Midwest's answer to Vanna White. "Now, if ya didn't meet her when she was here before, come on over and introduce yourself. But not until she's chowed down some."

She bent over and lowered her voice. "For sure ya gotta try that Chicken Crescent Hot Dish. It's out of this world." To everyone else, she added, her volume cranked all the way up again, "The rest of ya gotta keep on eatin' and drinkin', too. We've got enough food and booze here to choke a horse."

"Yoo-hoo. Yoo-hoo." Vivian wiggled her perfectly manicured fingers. Her nails were red, like her lipstick, her flimsy shirt, and the Christmas ribbons threaded through the French roll that was her mustard-colored hair. "Margie, you, yourself, oughta take it easy with that there food and whatnot. Remember, ya hafta fit in your weddin' dress the day after tomorrow."

Margie sent her sister the stink eye.

"I'm only tryin' to help." Vivian adjusted the frameless rectangular glasses perched on what I presumed was a surgically sculpted nose. "Ya know the old sayin', 'Middle age is when your age starts showin' around your middle.'" She laughed, then snorted.

A few of the ladies chuckled at that—the snort, not the joke—while Margie rubbed her chin with her middle finger, although her cryptic message seemed lost on Vivian.

❧ ☙

ASIDE FROM MARGIE, Vivian, and Little Val, I recognized very few of the women at the party. I knew Barbie Jenson, the local newspaper editor. She saluted me with her martini glass from several tables over. Janice Ferguson, Kennedy's city clerk, was also there, visiting with another woman, whose name was Sandy. Her husband, Ed, was the sheriff's deputy who planned to run against the current sheriff in the next election.

No one else struck me as familiar, though, until I caught sight of Henrietta and Hester Anderson, Margie and Vivian's crazy octogenarian aunts. They and their sister, Harriet, had been embroiled in a mess that had come to light during my first visit to town. As a result, they'd been "sent away" for a while. Margie had failed to mention their return, despite informing me of Harriet's recent passing. I guess Harriet's distress over being far from home had proven too much for her heart. I couldn't help but feel guilty for my role in the trio's demise and, ultimately, Harriet's death. Then, again, guilt's a perpetual burden of mine. That's correct, I'm Catholic.

Margie barely glimpsed at me before answering the question I hadn't yet asked. "They got back a couple days ago," she whispered. "I didn't have time to call ya."

4

"What about Rosa?" I was referring to Margie's other niece, the daughter of Ole, her deceased brother. She, too, had been tangled up in that earlier mess.

Margie handed me a plate. "She's got a few months to go."

Relief washed over me, and I quickly turned so Margie wouldn't see.

I zeroed in on Henrietta and Hester. They didn't look any different from the last time I'd seen them. Like then, they wore dark, belted, shirt dresses and orthopedic shoes, with white sweaters hanging from their shoulders. Henrietta was large framed, with a head covered in tight gray curls, while Hester was tiny, her hair pulled into a bun at the nape of her neck. Both possessed faces reminiscent of overripe fruit—spotted and wrinkly—with straw-thin lips. Currently, they were "discreetly" plucking bars from the dessert tower and stuffing them into oversized purses. Some things never changed.

The reminder of that fact prompted me to return my plate to Margie. "I'm going to start with a drink," I informed her. "And I probably won't stop at one."

"I'm really sorry I didn't get a chance to warn ya."

"Don't worry about it." I massaged my forehead to stave off the headache loitering around my frontal lobe. "I've just had a really long day. With the heavy snowfall, my drive took closer to eight hours rather than the usual six. Then, seeing those two . . ." I nodded at the old ladies, who seemed confident their thievery was going undetected. "Plus . . ."

I let the word trail off. It was neither the time nor the place to discuss Boo-Boo, my old boyfriend. True, I needed to talk to someone about him. But Margie was getting married over the weekend, so it wouldn't be right to saddle her with my Boo-Boo-related problems. Besides, she wouldn't be much help. No, I had to take up the matter with someone else, fully aware of whom that had to be. I just wasn't thrilled at the prospect of a conversation with him about an old flame. "Well . . . umm . . . I guess I was . . ."

She finished my sentence for me. "Hoping to see Deputy Ryden before the party?"

I didn't respond, choosing instead to reach for a bottle of Solveig gin, an award-winning liquor produced by Far North Spirits, a local distillery.

The gin was made from rye grown right here in Minnesota's northern Red River Valley. But, at that precise moment, I didn't care about the origin of the rye. I was far more interested in the alcohol content. The greater the better. Because of my arduous trip, coming face to face with Henrietta and Hester, and the whole Boo-Boo thing, my anxiety level had risen like a flame, and I needed a few drinks to douse it. Following Little Val's example, I'd start with a Gimlet. After that, I'd probably go with a shot or two of Far North's rum. A Dark and Stormy Daiquiri seemed apropos.

"Randy stopped in a few hours ago," Margie explained, "when Vivian was decoratin' the place." She rolled her eyes at the word "decoratin'." "He was gonna wait around for ya."

I gave her an "And?" look as I splashed gin into a metal drink shaker.

"And," she obliged, "he got a call on his police radio and tore out of here like a bat out of hell. Didn't say how long he'd be."

I added a couple other ingredients, along with some ice, covered the top, and shook the cylinder, letting my angst do the mixing.

After arriving in town, I'd spotted a missed cell-phone call from Randy. Since I never heard it ring, I figured it must have come in while I was driving through the boonies, where reception was iffy at best.

What was I talking about? This entire area was "the boonies." Sure, I liked it, but that didn't alter the fact that Kittson County, in the northwest corner of the state, was desolate by most standards. Kennedy's population had fallen to 193. And Hallock, the nearby county seat, now claimed fewer than 1,000 residents.

I poured my drink into a glass and immediately downed most of it. I'd returned Randy's call before entering the senior center but only got his voicemail. Truth be told, I wasn't altogether disappointed.

Don't get me wrong. I truly liked the guy. I'd met him here in Kennedy in August, at a benefit dinner in the Hot Dish Heaven Café. The newspaper I worked for in Minneapolis had sent me in search of the best hot dish, Jell-O, and bar recipes for a feature it was doing on country church cuisine. You know, the food eaten in rural church basements after funerals. And I'd ended up here, in a tiny, Scandinavian, Lutheran farm town.

Yep, a master's in journalism from Northwestern, and I was chasing casserole recipes and writing blurbs about small-town cooks. I wasn't happy about it then and still wasn't sure what to think, regardless that my assignments had led to kudos from my editors, something akin to a mother-daughter relationship with Margie Johnson, the owner of the Hot Dish Heaven Cafe, and a budding romance with the aforementioned Randy Ryden, a local sheriff's deputy.

℘   ℘

RANDY AND I BECAME friendly soon after Margie introduced us, though not as friendly as either of us would have liked. We were ready to remedy that during my second visit to Kennedy, this past October, but our timing was off. Randy got called out of town on police business, while I got caught up in a murder investigation that involved Margie's way-too-handsome nephew, Buddy Johnson. Then I got caught in a lip-lock with the guy. By none other than Deputy Ryden.

It was more than a month before Randy accepted my apology. Time and again I insisted I wasn't really attracted to Buddy. True, he was gorgeous and sexy and loads of fun . . .

Granted, my apologies may have been better received if I hadn't repeatedly mentioned all that. Oh, well.

Finally, in early December, Randy and I found our way back to each other when we met for lunch at Mama's on Rice Street in St. Paul. He was in the Twin Cities for a law enforcement conference. And over the best spaghetti and Italian fries in the state, I once more pleaded my case, swearing that Buddy and I had merely gotten swept away by the moment. A moment that had ended in a single kiss. Nothing more. I didn't want anything more. I wanted a relationship with him, Randy Ryden. Not that a relationship with him would be nothing. I was certain it'd be more than that. It'd have to be, right? How could it be less than nothing?

Yes, when nervous and frustrated, my mouth tended to run amuck, usually followed by my tears, then my nose.

Thankfully, on that day, Randy took pity on me. Or, perhaps, he simply couldn't stand the sight of a women mixing her tears and snot with to-die-for marinara sauce. Whatever the case, he scooted his chair closer and cleaned my cheeks with his napkin. Then, he hugged me, admitting that he, too, wanted us to be together. He just believed we should take things more slowly.

I wasn't sure how much slower we could go. We hadn't even had a sleepover. But, believe it or not, I didn't say that. I simply nodded, delighted for a second chance with someone who might actually be a keeper.

From then on, we e-mailed back and forth and talked on the phone. I also spent Christmas Day with him at his parents' house in Minneapolis. It was all very nice, but I was ready for more. A whole lot more. And I preferred to get it before Rosa, the woman Margie referenced earlier, returned to town.

See, in addition to being Margie's niece, Rosa was Randy's ex-girlfriend. She was dark, curvaceous, and the one who'd ended their affair. Not that I was insecure or anything. I just favored being comfortably involved with the guy before encountering her. Developing decent-sized breasts and exchanging my freckles for exotic features wouldn't hurt, either.

But first things first. I had to tell Randy about my afternoon. I needed to give him the lowdown on Boo-Boo. As a law enforcement officer, he'd know what to do.

I twisted my hair while pretty much doing the same with my thoughts. Hopefully, communicating with my ex-boyfriend wouldn't create more relationship obstacles for Randy and me. Admittedly ironic, given my concerns about Rosa. But, hey, this is my story. Even if I had no control over the outcome.

Chapter Two

FOLLOWING A HEARTY HELPING of Chicken Crescent Hot Dish, I set my plate on a table covered in purple tulle and switched my attention to the women around me. With any luck, their conversation would distract me from the goodies on the dessert tower, although I soon had my doubts.

Their discussion focused entirely on the upcoming hot dish cook-off, with some of the ladies arguing for more "sophisticated judges" because "the simplest recipe always wins," and others contending that there's "nothing wrong with your basic hot dish." As for me, I remained mum since I'd presumed all hot dishes were merely ground meat mixed with a can of cream soup and potatoes, noodles, or rice. And how much simpler could it get?

With no one clearly winning that particular argument, the ladies went on to debate the merits of actually regulating the hot dish entries. And while most strongly opposed the idea, one woman insisted that something had to be done to stop certain people from participating. "I don't know about the rest of ya," she complained, "but I didn't taste any of the entries last year, and I won't this year either if Booger's allowed to register."

"Booger?" I absently echoed the name while ogling the dessert tower.

"Yes, Booger," she replied. "That man picks his nose constantly, and since the entries are set out for sampling without referencing the cooks, you have absolutely no clue what you're eating."

I shuddered before assuring myself that one or two bars probably wouldn't do me any harm. As I stepped toward the dessert tower, however, Janice placed a fresh drink in my hand, and I immediately gulped down most of it. After that, I congratulated myself for avoiding the sweets.

ℰℴ   ℭℛ

OF COURSE, MY DRINK'S rich flavor was primarily due to the incredible rum, yet I also had to tip my imaginary hat to Janice Ferguson. She was no slouch when it came to mixing drinks. True, she got plenty of practice. See, while serving as Kennedy's city clerk by day, she often worked nights as a bartender at the VFW here in town and at the Eagles in Hallock, just up the road. From what I gathered, she needed the extra money. She played Bingo. A lot of Bingo. But she wasn't very good, though I never understood where skill entered into it. Either you had N-14 or you didn't, right? It wasn't like you could bluff.

"Okay, I have another joke," Janice announced, tilting her head, her unnatural, pitch-black beehive doing its best to remain atop her head. "My friend Jeanne Reff Bates told me this one, but I altered it some." Her long, skinny fingers, tipped with black dagger nails, jetted back and forth to punctuate her words. "Ole and Lena were driving down the highway one day when they hit a family of skunks. So, right away, they pulled over to check them out. And, wouldn't you know, the mother skunk was dead." Janice surveyed her audience. "Figuring he had no other option, Ole put the baby skunks in the car, while Lena fretted, 'Oh, my goodness, oh, my goodness, dey look awfully cold, Ole. What more can we do for dem?' But rather than answering, Ole gave her the once-over, his gaze finally settling on her big, flabby arms."

Janice cocked her head. "You know, the arms with so much fat hanging down it'll slap you right across the face if you're not careful." She regarded her own arms. Despite being wrapped in a thick sweater, they remained Q-tip size.

"Anyhoo," she continued, clearly disappointed she couldn't demonstrate the arm-flab waggle, "Ole told Lena, 'I suppose ya can stuff da baby skunks under dose humongous arms of yours. Dat should keep 'em warm.' Lena scrunched her nose. 'Oh, I don't know, Ole. What about da smell?' And Ole answered, 'I'm sure da skunks will get used to it. I know I have.'"

Barbie harrumphed. "That was bad, Janice. Really bad." She sounded far more disgusted than warranted. It was only a joke. Crude, perhaps. And not all that funny. But a joke, nonetheless.

"Oh, come on, Barbie. It was damn funny, and you know it." Janice adjusted her turtleneck. Because she was cadaver thin, it was way too big for her. And, in spite of an abundance of makeup, she pretty much resembled one—a cadaver, that is. "You're just a sourpuss." She glanced between Sandy and me, obviously waiting for us to concur. When we didn't, she mumbled, "Well, you are." She sucked down the remainder of her drink and smacked her lips. "Come to think of it, you've been in a foul mood for over a month now. What gives?"

Barbie fisted her hands against her broad hips and set her feet shoulder-width apart. "Just because I don't find you all that funny doesn't mean I'm in 'a foul mood.'" Barbie was dressed in a thigh-length, green, knit tunic with matching leggings, all trimmed in fake white fur. With her spikey maroon hair, dramatically made-up eyes, and ample bosom, she reminded me of a plus-size Betty Boop. At the moment, a Grinch-type Betty Boop. But Betty Boop, just the same. "Maybe I simply have a more developed sense of humor than you."

Janice coughed, giving evidence of her two-pack-a-day habit. "You're more developed, all right." She examined Barbie. "In fact, you've 'developed' quite a weight problem."

Barbie got in her face. "What was that?"

"Hells bells," Margie muttered as she stepped behind Barbie, snaked an arm around her waist, and eased her backwards. "We're supposed to be havin' fun here."

"Well, she started it," Barbie grumped.

"She's a grouch," Janice countered. "And even if no one admits it, that joke was funny." She jabbed a rigid finger in Barbie's face. "And whether I say it out loud or not, you're fat."

"Who you calling fat?" Before Barbie could haul off and smack the woman, Margie yanked her back a few more feet.

"You," Janice repeated. "You're fat. You've always been big, but lately you've become downright fat."

Barbie strained against Margie's grip. "Well, if I had a dog as ugly as you, I'd shave his ass and make him walk backwards."

"Oh, for goodness sake," Sandy uttered to no one in particular, "my glass seems to be empty." She spun on her heels and hurried toward the

11

refreshment table, undeniably eager to distance herself from the pending brawl. I decided to follow, but Margie squelched that plan with a menacing look that implied I'd sorely regret leaving her to handle the situation on her own.

"Janice," Margie said after apparently assuring herself I'd remain rooted where I was, "why don't ya go on and join Sandy, there. That'd be best for everyone."

Janice opened her mouth but held off saying anything, even though the combative expression on her face spoke volumes. For her part, Barbie puffed herself up and narrowed her eyes until they were mere slits. And the tension grew.

I scanned the room in search of one or two women who, if necessary, could hold their own against these World-Wrestling wannabes. Margie was a big-boned Scandinavian, but I questioned whether she alone could restore peace if Barbie and Janice tore into each other.

The other women were clustered in cliques, all captivated by the main event. A few near the kitchen spoke but only in hushed tones. For some reason, I watched as they whispered behind their hands. Then, they dug into their pockets and purses to retrieve money—bills as well as coins—and discreetly exchanged it among themselves.

My mouth fell open, and I felt my eyebrows slap against my hairline. I could hardly believe what was happening, and if the hostility between Barbie and Janice hadn't been so unnerving, I would have laughed out loud at the absurdity of it all. Here I was in the Kennedy Senior Citizens' Center, attending the wedding shower of a menopausal, first-time bride, and the attendees, prim and proper Swedish and Norwegian protestant women ranging in age from twenty to ninety, were wagering on which of two female guests would win a "knock-down, drag-out."

"Go on, now," Margie repeated for Janice's benefit.

After a few more uncomfortable moments, during which the would-be warriors did nothing but glare at each other, Janice pivoted in the direction of the booze bottles. "I'm leaving but not because of you," she shouted at Barbie as she walked away. "I just need a refill."

The gamblers by the kitchen groaned in disappointment. I guess they really wanted to see a fight. And, naturally, that surprised me. Then, again, I'd never before been to a Kennedy bridal shower. Perhaps wagering on brawls was commonplace. If entertainment choices were routinely limited to that or silly shower games, I could understand why.

ဢ ᘑ

"LET ME GO," BARBIE whined as she wiggled out of Margie's grasp. "You're hurting me."

"It's your own gall-darn fault," Margie scolded.

"I wasn't really going to hit her." Barbie smoothed the front of her tunic. "And while I admit I'm getting heavier, I can always go on a diet." She pointed an accusatory finger at Janice. "But, no matter what, she'll forever be a witch."

With some trepidation, I waded in. "Barbie, I thought you and Janice were friends."

"We were. But not anymore."

"Why? What happened?"

Margie blew a strand of wayward gray-blonde hair from her forehead before quietly answering on her friend's behalf. "Janice can be a real pain in the keister. And, at times, she's totally inappropriate." Margie dropped her head toward mine and further lowered her voice. "Last month, right around Thanksgiving, a bunch of us went to a fundraiser in Crookston, for Alzheimer research, don't ya know." She worried her bottom lip. "More and more folks 'round here are gettin' that disease. Elma Carlson, one of the smartest people I've ever known, just got diagnosed. It's the darndest thing."

Barbie cleared her throat, signaling Margie to get back on track. "Anyways," she said, doing just that, "Janice spent most of the night chasin' rich-looking widowers. And when none of them took notice, she went after the married men with sickly lookin' wives. Ya know, women pullin' oxygen tanks and such."

I shrugged. "That's not all that unusual for Janice, is it?"

"Well, Barbie was on the plannin' committee, which was a pretty big deal. So, naturally, she was humiliated when one of the men Janice had been stalkin' complained to the other committee members that Barbie's guest was makin' lewd suggestions to him." She bracketed her mouth with her hand. "She made snide comments to his ailin' wife, too."

"That's right," Barbie confirmed. "As if being tethered to an air tank wasn't bad enough, that poor woman had to put up with Janice's big mouth. She actually said that the candles on the old lady's birthday cake were the leading cause of global warming."

"Yah," Margie continued, "ever since that hullabaloo with her boyfriend last fall, Janice has been lots harder to get along with. She feels as if life's been unfair to her." She nodded to emphasize her point. "Not long ago she let it be known she was gonna start doin' whatever she wanted regardless of who got hurt by it. Oh, for sure, she'll settle down. But it might not be for a while, yet."

Margie draped her arm across Barbie's shoulders. "And while she can be as ornery as all get out, she's not wrong about everythin'. Fact is, when it comes to you, Barbie, I hafta agree with her. You've been real nasty lately." She pulled her closer. "These days, when someone ticks ya off, I halfway expect ya to knife 'em in the back, then have 'em arrested for carryin' a weapon." She grinned, plainly aiming to coax a smile out of her friend with that remark. It didn't work. "Come on, honey, spill the beans. What's goin' on with ya?"

Barbie finished off her drink. "Nothing's going on. Nothing at all."

"I don't believe ya." Margie's tone was ripe with concern.

"Well, I'm not about to discuss it with you tonight. This is your bachelorette party! As you said, we're supposed to be having fun."

Fun? Really? If that was true, why was anxiety itching beneath the surface of my skin? Granted, I'd just witnessed a near brawl, and the Anderson sisters were glowering at me from across the room. I also had major Boo-Boo trouble. My trip from the Twin Cities had rivaled a journey through hell. And I'd arrived too late to see Randy. Nevertheless . . .

I decided I needed another drink and started for the refreshment table, debating if I should ask Janice to do the mixing for me. I wanted a good cocktail. She was a master mixer. And since she wasn't upset with me, she might consent to serving as my personal bartender.

Almost there, my eyes pulled toward the dessert tower. Specifically, the Raspberry Squares. No question about it, if I didn't opt for another drink, I'd eat one or ten of them. They looked scrumptious. And, as I alluded to earlier, I had a weakness for sweets, particularly when agitated.

I nudged closer to Janice, waiting for an opportunity to interrupt her conversation with Sandy. Yep, one more drink, expertly made, and I'd offer my excuses and head off to bed. A few delicious cocktails, followed by a good night's sleep, and I'd be far more relaxed in the morning, making tomorrow a much better day.

Don't count on it, Emme. The foreboding words were murmured somewhere in the recesses of my brain. *Don't count on it.*

Chapter Three

ARBIE POKED HER THUMB and forefinger between her lips and whistled, the shrillness sending shivers down my spine. "Hey, everybody, it's time for Margie to open her shower gifts!"

The women clapped and shouted and, without being told twice, dragged their chairs across the worn carpet and staged them in a circle in the center of the room. I had no idea what was bothering Barbie, but I hoped all notions of fisticuffs could be set aside for Margie's sake. Janice was seated between two Amazon women on the opposite side of the circle, well beyond Barbie's reach, so, perhaps, we'd be spared a fight, at least for a while.

Margie claimed her chair beneath a bunch of balloons tied to the ceiling fan, and Vivian crowned her with a sparkly tiara. That prompted almost everyone in attendance to do a joint eye roll. Being a nice person, Margie refrained. She also left the goofy crown on top of her head.

"Everybody! Everybody!" Vivian flailed her hands as she squawked. "Prior to gifts, I have a few games I wanna play." A number of women, excluding Margie, who was plainly bucking for sainthood, booed while throwing their wadded-up napkins in Vivian's direction. It was quite a sight. It made me laugh, which felt really good.

Vivian plopped down next to her sister and kicked at the napkins that buried the toes of her stilettoes. "If that's how you're gonna be," she whimpered through pouty lips undoubtedly aided in their poutiness by a double dose of collagen, "we'll just go ahead there and open gifts." That announcement was met by a round of cheers, which led Vivian to attempt a frown. It was an exercise in futility, however, given her regular botox routine. Yep, Vivian was a plastic surgeon's dream—a nightmare for most other people—but a plastic surgeon's dream. "Just let it be said that I never overlooked a gift horse. I also hafta tell ya one and all you're actin' childish and ill-mannered, and when it comes to other parties and progressin' them and what not, I'm gonna have an axe to grind my teeth on."

The room fell silent. I was pretty sure everyone was using the quiet time to decipher what the woman had said. I suppose, though, it was possible they were contemplating whether or not to feel bad for hurting her feelings. After all, she had organized the party. Yet, she was seldom nice to anyone, so why feel sorry for her? And, don't forget, she'd planned shower games!

Regardless of the reason for the silence, it didn't last long. In short order, it was disrupted by a string of burps. Yep. Burps. A whole lot of them.

Right away I peeked at Little Val, presuming she was the culprit, but her mouth was otherwise occupied—taking in more liquor. That left me to scan the rest of the group, practically coming full circle before reaching Hester Anderson, the smaller of Margie's elderly aunts, who met me with a belch that would make any trucker proud.

Given the old lady's glazed eyes, I suspected dessert bars weren't all she'd been sneaking. Sure, the cloudiness affecting her corneas may have been the result of cataracts, but odds were far greater she'd gotten too close and personal with the gin.

My suspicions were confirmed when she slid off her chair, as if her bones had turned to Jell-O. Right away Margie leaped to her feet and grabbed her under the arms. "Sorry," Hester muttered to her niece once she was propped back in a sitting position, "must of been somethin' I ate."

"Late?" her sister, Henrietta, trumpeted from one seat over. "It's not late. The party's just gettin' started. Ain't that right, Margie?"

"That's right." Margie raised her voice in an effort to push through the near century of sounds clogging Henrietta's ears.

"Ya don't hafta holler, dear." Henrietta patted Margie's shoulder with her gnarly fingers. "Since I got this new hearin' aid, I don't miss a thing." She pointed to her right ear. "Sure, it was a bit spendy. To be exact, $4,000. But it was worth every red cent."

Bonnie Johnson leaned forward. "What kind is it?"

Henrietta checked her watch. "Nine-forty-five."

ℴ   ℞

AN HOUR LATER, I was having a great time, with no more plans to retire early. Barbie and Janice were whooping it up, too, although in separate areas of the room. As for the Anderson sisters, they occupied chairs in the far corner, where Henrietta dozed, while Hester elbowed her every now and again to keep her from tipping onto the floor. And Margie? Well, she celebrated like never before.

After two martinis, she agreed to model the black negligee and robe Barbie had given her. That, in turn, led Janice to ask about the edible underwear she had gifted.

Margie replied, "I'll never get drunk enough to model them."

Of course that delighted Hester, who was munching away on a pair, her earlier indigestion seemingly no longer a problem.

It was the first time I'd ever seen Margie with her hair down, literally or figuratively. She'd removed her customary ponytail while changing into her new nightgown, leaving her hair to sway as she danced in wool socks to Kelly Pickler's version of "Santa Baby."

When the song ended, she bowed and stated in an alcohol-laced, ceremonial tone, "Thank you, ladies. That concludes our evenin' wear competition." She wagged her index finger. "And I guess we'll hafta forego the bathin' suit event since none of ya remembered yours." She tipped her martini glass, licking the last drops from the rim. "But, I expect to see ya all back here on Saturday for the talent contest, when I'll not only get confirmed bachelor John Deere to admit his undying love for me publically, but I'll also get 'im to dance!" We applauded, and Margie bowed once more before heading off to change back into her street clothes.

When she returned in jeans and a UND Fighting Sioux sweatshirt, she oversaw a brief cleaning frenzy. And once the dishes were dried and put away and the floor vacuumed, she shooed her guests from the building, leaving behind just the two of us, along with Vivian and a very drunk, rubber-legged Little Val.

ℴ   ℞

WHEN THE FOUR OF US made our way outside, Vivian insisted she needed her sister's help in heaving Little Val into the back seat of her extended-cab pickup, which posed a problem. And not just because Margie was a bit wobbly. Vivian, you see, had no intention of doing any heavy lifting. And I was unable to determine how best to lend a hand since I, too, was slightly impaired.

To further complicate matters, Little Val refused to let go of the life-size Precious Moments bridegroom. Clasping him around his wooden waist, she swore he was her soulmate and insisted on taking him home. Vivian tried to reason with her as only Vivian could, explaining that Wally, Little Val's husband, wouldn't appreciate another man in their house, "even if he is wood and such." She also mumbled something about Little Val needing to follow the lead of "the rich and famous and do some of that there 'unconscious uncouplin'.'"

Little Val wasn't listening or had given up trying to interpret her mother's words because she spoke over them, saying to the wooden cutout with the rosy cheeks, "My soul saw you, and it kind of went, 'Oh, there you are. I've been looking for you.'" With unfocused eyes, she then glanced in our general direction. "I read that on a poster somewhere. Isn't it beautiful?"

"Oh, brother," Margie mumbled as she yanked the fake groom away from her niece and tossed him into the truck bed.

Little Val whimpered, "What do you mean 'Oh, brother'? Don't you believe in soulmates, Aunt Margie?"

Margie tugged on the cuffs of her jacket. "No, I don't."

"How can you say that?" Little Val acted as if Margie had committed blasphemy. "You're getting married on Saturday. Then, you and John . . . will . . ." Her voice petered out, and a vacant expression overtook her face. She had lost her train of thought. Considering she was slightly green around the gills, I prayed she wouldn't lose her supper, as well.

"I'm sure John and I will get along fine," Margie informed her, being far more patient than I would have been. "But I seriously doubt I'm the only woman in the world who could make him happy. Or visa-versa. It just so happens we both live here and—"

"That's not the least bit romantic." Little Val blinked back tears as she began to sway.

"Oh, brother," Margie repeated, catching the girl before she fell into the snowbank that bordered the street. I clumsily stepped over that same mound to open the back door of the four-door truck. Then, with a grunt, Margie boosted Little Val onto the seat. It wasn't pretty, but she got the job done.

"Now, close your eyes and shut your mouth," Margie ordered. "And don't throw up!"

Little Val followed her aunt's instructions and passed out, mere drool dribbling down her chin.

At the same time, Vivian continued to fret out loud about how she was going to explain her daughter's condition and "the man in the truck" to her son-in-law. Margie assured her she'd come up with something, although, truth be told, she didn't sound as if she truly cared one way or another. She just wanted Vivian and Little Val to be on their way.

"Yah," Vivian mumbled in resignation while climbing in behind the wheel, the hood of her parka pulled over the tiara that now sat on her head. "I suppose, like always, it'll be up to me to get us through this sinkin' ship, though I don't have a paddle." She put the pickup in gear. "Oh, well, I suppose I'll just hafta jump off that bridge when I come to it."

∞   ∞

AFTER VIVIAN AND LITTLE VAL LEFT, Margie and I boxed up the shower gifts and schleped them down the snow-covered sidewalk to the Hot Dish Heaven Cafe, an old, two-story, clapboard building along the highway that served as the main street of the tiny town. I was staying in one of two bedrooms above the café, and Margie was spending the next couple nights in the other since the interior of her house was getting painted. John was scheduled to move in with her after the honeymoon, but he didn't care for her pastel wall colors and had asked that they be changed. According to Margie, he'd actually alleged that her pink bedroom caused him "performance" problems.

"So," Margie said, stuffing the last present into her bedroom closet, "care for some coffee and a snack? I'm cold from our time outside, and I'm too keyed up to sleep."

I snickered. "Keyed up? Is that what you call it?"

A blush pinked up her cheeks far more than the outside air had. "Okay, okay, I'm still a bit tipsy, and I could use some coffee."

"Yeah, I'll join you. I'm a touch 'keyed up,' too." I headed for the hallway, halting before I got there. "First, though, may I see your dress?"

Margie smiled shyly as she backtracked to retrieve the purple satin gown from the hook behind her bedroom door.

"Margie, it's stunning!"

"Really? Ya think so? Vivian wanted me to go with white or beige, but neither's particularly flatterin' on a middle-aged, full-figured bride with pale skin and gray-blonde hair. And John really wanted Vikings' colors, and I didn't care."

I wasn't sure about a Minnesota Vikings' wedding theme, but the dress was beautiful. It was like something from a 1950s movie. A-line and ankle length with three-quarter sleeves. It gathered slightly across the bodice, a cut-glass pin catching the fabric just below and to the left of the waist.

She returned the hanger to the hook on the door, pausing to appreciate the garment for an extra moment. "I've never had such a pretty dress. Never had the occasion to wear one."

"Weren't you in Vivian's wedding?"

"Uff-da, the dress she forced me to wear was ugly. Orange taffeta with a green bow. Folks kept mistakin' me for a pumpkin. I was afraid if I stopped movin', someone would stick a burning candle in my cleavage." She waited a beat. "I'm pretty sure that was her plan all along."

"To light your boobs on fire?"

She swatted my arm. "No! To make me look like a giant pumpkin, while she got to be Cinderella. That's where she got the crown she stuck on my head tonight. Her weddin'. She wore it that entire day."

"Well, now's your chance for revenge. Are you making her wear something hideous on Saturday?"

Margie sniffed. "Nah. I'm almost sixty, and though she'll deny it, she's not far behind. It's time we stopped bickerin'."

I gave her a hug. "You're a good person. I'm very happy for you."

She slipped her arm through mine. "I'm glad you're here. Now let's go raid the refrigerator, Vivian's dieting rules be damned!"

"I'm game. I didn't eat a single bar at the party. I didn't have any cake, either."

"What's wrong with ya?"

I cringed. "That cake was too scary looking. And, as I said earlier, I'm attempting to fix some of my bad habits, my addiction to sweets being the worst."

"How's it goin'?"

"My consumption of sweets is down, but now my alcohol intake has spiked."

"I suppose that's not what ya were aimin' for."

"No, not really, but what's a girl to do?"

℘   ☙

WE SAT AT THE METAL PREP table in the café's kitchen. In addition to the table and usual commercial appliances and countertops, the space featured an old Hoosier cabinet, the sole piece of furniture with any personality. Given the characters who frequented the place, however, personality was never really in short supply.

We were enjoying a cup of coffee and a few Salted Caramel Brownies. Margie's friend Rachel Korkowski had provided her with the recipe, and with my first bite, I was grateful Rachel believed in sharing. After my second, though, my spirits fell as a voice in my head reprimanded me for consuming "too much sugar."

Yes, I'll admit I hear voices once in a while, yet I'm not crazy. Not certifiable, at any rate. And, quite honestly, I usually ignore them. Although, in this instance, I did one better by closing my eyes and drowning them out by loudly moaning over the sinful taste sensations oozing across my tongue. It was then, when my eyes were shut and I was mid-moan, that a knock at the back door almost startled me right off my seat.

"Who in the heck would drop by at this hour?" Margie squinted at the schoolhouse clock high on the wall. "Oh," she added with a chuckle, "must be John. The bachelor party's probably over. When you're our age, ya can't party real late."

"You guys aren't that old."

Margie scoffed. "I don't know about that. I often find myself wishin' I was home before I even get where I'm goin'. That's a sign of old age." She made her way toward the door. "And the other night John told me some guy at the bar asked if he'd like a joint, and before he realized what he was sayin', he told the man he wouldn't refuse a new hip."

Margie opened the door. "Well, I'll be." She stepped back, allowing Deputy Randy Ryden to enter. "What are ya doin' here?" She fluttered her eyes at me. "As if I didn't know."

"I have to talk to Emme." Randy stomped snow from his boots and peeked over Margie's shoulder. Spying me, he lumbered across the floor, causing my stomach muscles to contract. Regrettably, it was the only exercise they'd gotten all week.

As he moved closer, Margie concocted some phony purpose for leaving the room, but I wasn't exactly sure what she said because Randy had a way of distracting me. See, he was extremely good looking, especially in uniform.

At well over six feet, with broad shoulders, and lots of muscles, he came across as somewhat menacing, which often made my pulse run ragged. Yes, I'd always been drawn to bad boys. I was positive I had a genetic predisposition for them. But I was doing my best to change. To mature. And since Randy was a law enforcement officer who only came across as dangerous, I assured myself I was headed in the right direction.

When he stopped in front of me, even the pheromones in the air swirled with desire. And understandably so. He was very sexy. His hair was dark, wavy, and a tad shaggy. His eyes were a warm brown but morphed to black whenever he was amorous. And his smile was usually crooked, as if he was up to no good. At that moment, though, his eyes were cold, and his smile was nonexistent. "What was your old boyfriend's name?"

Huh? I was baffled. Not that I had a lot of old boyfriends. That wasn't the case. I was merely caught off guard. I was expecting a "hello" of some kind. "You mean Boo-Boo?"

"Yeah, Boo-Boo." His tone was colored with impatience. "What was his real name?"

My chest tightened. "Owen. Owen Bair. Why?"

"When did you last see him?" His features were hard set, not at all what I pictured when I dreamed about him.

"Well, it's been over a year since I actually saw him." Irritation radiated off him like heat, making my lips go dry. And while my pulse remained rapid, its tempo no longer had anything to do with Randy's charisma or my bedtime fantasies. "Why do you want to know?"

"What do you mean 'over a year' since you 'actually' saw him?"

"Randy, what's going on?"

His face was like granite. Just a bunch of plains and edges. "He's dead, Emme. His body was discovered at Lake Bronson." He was referring to the town and the state park a dozen miles east of Kennedy.

"Dead?"

"Yeah." He scratched his whisker stubble. It sounded like sandpaper. And, for some peculiar reason, that sound was the only thing I heard as I grappled with the words, *Boo-Boo's dead.*

Chapter Four

"I T WAS MURDER," RANDY explained just prior to catching me as I fell off my stool.

I had a habit of fainting whenever I received shocking news. The tendency first came to light following my parents' death in a car crash when I was thirteen. After I began coming to Kennedy, I discovered I also blacked out whenever someone tried to kill me. Not exactly surprising, but disconcerting nonetheless. To date, it had happened twice. You might think it would have convinced me to avoid this town. Yet, I was drawn to it like a moth to a flame.

"Boo-Boo was murdered?" I must have misunderstood.

"Yeah." He settled me back on my stool and patted my shoulders, as if that would ensure I'd remain upright. "Emme, I have to ask where you were around four o'clock this afternoon."

"What?" His meaning slowly dawned on me. "You think—"

"Of course not." His voice and expression had softened but only a smidge. "That's why I want to establish your alibi. So we can move on."

"Umm." My head rattled. "Four o'clock did you say?"

"Yeah."

"Well . . ." My brain misfired, forcing me to try again. "Well, I guess I was almost to Thief River." I had to concentrate really hard just to get my words formed. "I was . . . umm . . . running late, but I needed to stop for gas."

"Did you?"

"Huh?

"Stop for gas?"

"Yeah, I—"

"Pay at the pump?"

"What?" He had me at a disadvantage. At best, my mind was operating on only one or two cylinders. "Why does that—"

"Emme, think. Please think."

I closed my eyes and put all my energy into answering him. "Yeah, I paid at the pump."

"Did you get a receipt?"

The question confounded me. How could it be pertinent to Boo-Boo's death? Then, again, I probably wasn't the best judge at that particular minute. "Yes. I needed a receipt to get reimbursed. The paper agreed to cover my expenses if I returned with more of Margie's recipes."

"Where is it?"

"The receipt?" I motioned toward the row of pegs behind the back door. "In my purse."

He crossed the room in three long strides. "I'll give it back, but I have to take it for a while." He delivered my purse to me. "That receipt will prove you couldn't have shoved Owen Bair off the observation tower in the park."

My stomach roiled. "Is that how he died?"

He grunted in the affirmative as I handed him the slip of paper.

"Are you sure he was murdered, Randy?"

At the sound of my trembling voice, he bent over the corner of the table and clasped my hands. "It wasn't an accident, Emme." He looked as if he'd finally grasped the extent of my shock. "He was too short and the tower ledge was too high. Plus . . ." He hesitated, seemingly deliberating whether or not to say anything more.

"Keep going, Randy. I can take it."

His expression implied he wasn't so sure. "His shirt was torn, and his neck was bruised, suggesting a struggle, so we know it wasn't suicide, either."

He twisted his lips. "We just can't figure out why he was there." His volume rose as his exasperation became more apparent. "He lived in Minneapolis, for cripes' sake. What on earth was he doing at Lake Bronson State Park in the middle of winter?"

I slowly breathed in and out, praying the effort would help me gather my wits or, in the alternative, give me the energy to make a break for it. True, I had already decided—albeit reluctantly—to talk to Randy about Boo-Boo. But, now, with him dead—murdered no less—that discussion seemed like a terrible idea, particularly in light of Randy's frustration over the situation.

Even so, I knew I had no choice. Absolutely no choice. I had to tell him. "Well," I mumbled to my feet, not daring to meet his eyes. "I was supposed . . ."

He dropped my hands. "What?"

Keeping my head down, I spoke a few decibels louder. "I was supposed to meet him at the park at four."

"Huh?"

"Not at the tower. But outside the Visitors' Center. The building with the native bird and animal displays." I hunched my shoulders before going on to explain—again to my feet—"But I was late. I didn't get there until five-thirty. Still, I waited until well after six. He never showed."

Randy clasped my chin between his thumb and the knuckle of his forefinger, lifting it until we were eye to eye—in the physical sense only. His manner suggested we'd never truly see eye to eye on this particular subject. "Why were you meeting your old boyfriend?" he wanted to know.

Oh, man, this wasn't good. The tenderness he had shown earlier had vanished, and his tone was so icy I had to rub my hands up and down my arms to refrain from getting frostbite. "Didn't I mention that Boo-Boo had been calling and texting me?"

Randy canted his head and carefully enunciated, "No, you never said a thing." From past experience, I knew that the angrier Randy got, the more succinctly he spoke. At this point, I gauged him to be pretty damn mad.

Who could blame him? I hadn't been much of a girlfriend. He'd caught me kissing one guy, and now I'd failed to inform him about setting up a meeting with another. One who just happened to be an old boyfriend. Yep, if I were Randy, I'd probably walk away, which made me really glad I wasn't him. Hopefully, he was way more understanding than me.

"It's not like we were communicating." I wrapped a clump of my hair around my index finger. "The truth is, I refused to answer his calls, and I erased his voicemails and text messages without ever checking them.

I assumed he wanted to get back together. And I didn't want any part of that. I wanted . . . I want to be with you."

Randy closed one eye while concentrating on me with the other. "Then how'd you end up scheduled to meet with the guy?"

"He got a different phone. I didn't recognize the number and answered his call by mistake."

He opened both eyes. And I didn't like what I saw. Anger, of course. But something else, too. Was it distrust or simply a boatload of disappointment? Whatever, it sucked. It gave me the sinking feeling that Randy wasn't as understanding as I'd prayed he'd be, which meant just one thing. He'd had enough of me messing up. As a result, by the time this conversation was over, more than likely, we would be, too. Yep, we'd be done as a couple. *Kaput*, as Margie might say.

The air in my chest escaped me, leaving my heart feeling heavy and unsupported. I was certain all further attempts to explain myself would serve no purpose. My motivation for meeting Boo-Boo, regardless how innocent, wouldn't matter. Randy was fed up. And our relationship was doomed.

My shoulders slumped before involuntarily rising again as I inhaled. *If you have nothing left to lose, why not speak your mind?* That question was a mere whisper in my head. The ones that followed were louder and more insistent, fueled by my intake of oxygen and, quite possibly, my naïveté. *What's the worst that could happen? He'll dump you like garbage. But, if you're lucky, you'll say something to convince him to reconsider.*

Relying on that dubious logic, I spilled the rest of my story. "He was scared, Randy. He was in trouble and needed my help." I contemplated that. "At least that's what his last call was all about."

"His last call?"

Oops.

"How many calls were there?" He clinched his jaw.

"None. No others." I'd tangled my hair around my finger so tightly it had turned blue. My finger, not my hair. "That's not right. Like I said, there were lots of calls." I unspooled my hair and wiggled my finger to get the blood flowing. "And texts. Lots of texts. But I didn't respond to any of them, and I only took that one call. A couple days ago. Tuesday. Yeah, that's right. I spoke with him on Tuesday."

Randy stood a little taller, his shoulders pulled back a little farther, his countenance stern. Once again he was in full cop mode. "What exactly did he say?"

I tucked my fingers under my thighs to keep from wrapping my hair around them. If cutting off my circulation would have guaranteed a halt to Randy's interrogation, I would have bound all my fingers and all my toes. But, in view of his unyielding demeanor, I suspected that nothing would prematurely end it.

"He begged me to hear him out," I explained. "I insisted I was done with him. And that's when he claimed he wasn't calling for personal reasons. He said . . . umm . . . it was more of a professional call." I addressed Randy's bewildered expression by providing him with one of my own. "I don't know. He said he was working in the area and got himself into a jam. He wasn't sure where to turn."

"He didn't specify the kind of 'jam' he was in?"

"No. When I told him I was coming up this way, he said he'd rather talk in person. That's when he asked to meet with me at the park at four o'clock today."

"Emme, didn't that strike you as odd? Your old boyfriend requested a clandestine meeting but refused to provide any details?"

"Well, when you put it that way—"

"There's no other way to put it! You were stupid to agree to get together with him!"

Stupid? That made me angry. He'd made his point. It wasn't necessary to resort to name calling. "He was scared, Randy!" I slid off my stool. This time on purpose. "I'd never heard him sound that way before."

Randy's eyes showed he regretted his rudeness, yet he failed to apologize, though he did curb his tone. "I can't believe you didn't call me, Emme. I'm actually trained in law enforcement, remember?"

"At the time, I had nothing to tell you because I hadn't yet met with him." I vacillated, but in the end, I laid the rest of it out there. "And since things were just getting good between us again, I didn't want to chance ruining them by bringing up my old boyfriend unless I had to."

"Unless you had to?"

Another *oops*. "Well, the truth is, I was hoping I wouldn't have to mention it at all."

"Nice, Emme. Great way to build a relationship." Like me, Randy appreciated sarcasm and didn't pass up many opportunities to use it.

"Don't get all self-righteous. I didn't want to say anything because I was afraid you'd react like this." I waved my hands in exasperation. "And I was right!"

He glared at me but said nothing.

Okay, casting blame in his direction was totally unfair, and I immediately adopted a more conciliatory approach. "When he didn't show up or answer his cell phone, I got worried. And that's when I decided I had to talk to you. Get your advice. Ask for your help."

"With your old boyfriend?" The cords in his neck strained against his words.

"I'm not . . . I mean I wasn't interested in him romantically. You know that. But I didn't want anything awful to happen to him, either."

When Randy inhaled his next breath, he practically sucked all the oxygen out of the room. In fact, it took me a while to locate enough of the stuff to fill my lungs to make my final point. "In any case, it wasn't my fault he was murdered."

He chewed his bottom lip. "That may not matter. If you recall, the sheriff doesn't take kindly to you. You've upstaged him twice over the past five months by solving murders he couldn't."

"So?"

"So, he'd like nothing better than to cause you trouble."

"And?"

"And now he might get his chance."

"How?"

He rested his large hands on his hips, the fingers of his right hand absently tapping his holstered gun. "We found a piece of paper in Owen's jacket pocket. It had your name on it, and the notation, '4:00 p.m., Thursday.'"

I gave myself a moment to put two and two together. When I came up with five, I raised my hand. "If you already knew about my meeting with him, why all these—"

"I wanted to hear directly from you." He caught my gaze with those piercing dark eyes of his. "Even though I knew better, I guess I was hoping there was another Emme out there. See, I didn't want my Emme caught up in another police matter. Especially one concerning her ex-boyfriend's death."

He sounded disheartened, which made me feel bad. On the flip side, he had called me "his Emme," which felt really nice. Not surprisingly, those conflicting emotions couldn't co-exist and ended up colliding somewhere between my head and my heart, leaving me bewildered.

With no idea what to say, I went with my old standby. "I'm sorry."

"Yeah, I know. You always are."

Okay, that was harsh. "What?"

He rubbed the back of his neck. "It's never easy with you, that's all. You're constantly nosing around where you don't belong."

The sympathy I had momentarily felt for the guy was kicked aside by a big boot of furious. "Well, if I'm too difficult—"

"That's not exactly what I said."

"It's what you implied."

"Emme." He splayed his hands in front of his chest. "Let's stop before we say something we'll regret."

"Too late for you."

He reached for me, but I stepped away, avoiding his grasp. "I can take care of myself, Randy. I've been doing it for years. I don't need your help. And, as I said, if I'm too much trouble, just stay clear of me."

Tears gathered behind my eyes, threatening to undermine all my tough talk. To steel myself, I closed my hands and dug my nails into my palms. I wasn't about to buckle. I'd come too far. I'd made too much progress. I was growing stronger and more self-assured every day. At least that's what my therapist routinely wrote on the bottom of my monthly counseling bills. "If Sheriff Halverson has questions for me, tell him to bring them on." I stiffened my spine and, with any luck, my resolve. "I have nothing to hide."

Randy pinched the bridge of his nose. "Of course you have nothing to hide."

Detecting some affection in his tone, I let go of my anger. "Mighty big of you to believe in me." I guess a bit of snarkiness replaced it.

He offered up a throaty chuckle and pulled me into his arms. "You're lucky I like sassy women."

This time I willingly snuggled against him. "I'm sorry you're upset, but I'm not sorry for offering to help Boo-Boo."

He gently rubbed my back. "Was that an apology?"

"As near as you're going to get."

I felt him smile against the top of my head. "Emme, I only got angry because you didn't come to me. I don't want anything bad to happen to you, especially if I can keep you safe." He hugged me tighter. "I don't want you to keep secrets from me, either. I understand that for most of your life, you haven't had people you could confide in, so you're not used to doing it. But, you've got me now. And you have to be open and honest with me. It's the only way our relationship will work."

A few of the tears I'd been holding back spilled down my cheeks. Randy was overprotective, but he truly cared for me. Boo-Boo, on the other hand, only cared about himself. He'd treated me poorly while alive and continued to cause me problems in death.

"Boo-Boo wasn't a nice person, Randy. Even so, he didn't deserve to be murdered." I quickly added, "Contract a painful sexually transmitted disease? Yes. But not murdered."

I sniffled against Randy's chest, as images of my happy times with Boo-Boo flickered through my brain. Because there were so few of them, the same couple of pictures played over and over again. He in his Twins' uniform, grinning through his closely cropped beard as he motioned to me from the field following a home game. Then, he in a tux, winking at me while we slow danced at a charity gala at the Walker Art Center.

Despite my best efforts, a few more tears fell, turning an area on Randy's tan shirt a wet, dark brown. "I was terribly naive when I met him." My voice was hushed, as if I were talking to myself alone. "When he looked at me, I felt like the only woman in the world. And, my God, every time he kissed me, my knees practically buckled."

With his arms still wrapped around me, Randy spoke into my hair, "Hey, when I said we needed to be open and honest with each other, I didn't mean we had to share all the sordid details of—"

"I loved him so much. At least I thought I did." I was lost in ruminations, oblivious to the words I was uttering out loud. "I believed he loved me, too."

"Emme, please don't tell—"

"I'll admit that after he cheated on me, I dreamed about doing him in. A couple nights Jose Cuervo and I even concocted some plans. Not for murdering him, mind you. Just hurting him like he had hurt me." I peeked up at Randy. "I did a few things I'm not very proud of." I grimaced at the recollection of puncturing his car tires. "But I never did him any bodily harm. I wouldn't do anything like that."

Randy cupped my cheeks. "Emme, you don't have to explain. The truth is, I'd rather you didn't."

As if in a trance, I continued. "Eventually, I got over him."

"Emme . . ."

"Regardless, for a long time, I—"

"Emme!" he shouted, and I jumped.

It was only then, as I gaped at him, that I realized what I had done. "I'm so sorry. I didn't mean to go on like that."

"Everything will be all right." He brushed my wet cheeks with his calloused thumbs. "To be on the safe side, though, you may want to avoid mentioning any of that 'getting even' stuff to Sheriff Halverson."

"You're sure he'll question me?"

He tweaked the tip of my nose. "Your name was found on the murder victim, and since the sheriff genuinely dislikes you, odds are you'll get a visit from him. You can also count on him giving you a lot of grief. Remember, you've exposed his incompetence. Given that, he probably blames you for having an opponent in the upcoming election."

I eased myself from his arms. "He has an opponent because he's ineffective at his job, and he's a first-rate ass."

"There you go again with that mouth of yours."

I shrugged.

"Don't worry." He patted his breast pocket. "This receipt is your 'get out of jail free' card. Even if the sheriff refuses to believe you were physically incapable of committing the crime, he has to agree that the receipt exonerates you. It puts you fifty miles away at the time of death."

"You're convinced about when he died?"

"Yep. The body was discovered by a cross-country skier at 6:25 p.m. He'd already been dead for more than two hours."

I had to swallow a few times to digest that information. "Randy, regardless of the receipt, I had no motive to kill Boo-Boo. I let go of my anger a long time ago. And I certainly didn't want him back."

"I know." He took my measure. "And even if you did have a motive to murder him and were strong enough to commit the crime, you wouldn't have been dumb enough to leave a note implicating yourself. You're too smart for that."

I stared at him. "Thanks, I think."

While Margie had disappeared right after Randy's arrival, she was back again, now that the yelling and crying were over. "You two need another cup of joe?" In her hands, she held a tray with a fresh pot of coffee, a few clean cups, and a plate of homemade peanut clusters. "I pulled this together out front."

"No, thanks." Randy zipped his jacket. "I should go. I have to get back to work. We have a long night ahead of us."

I offered him my best big-girl look. "I'm not afraid of Sheriff Halverson. Go ahead and tell him where he can find me. Although, if he actually wants information, I have no idea what I can offer."

"Well," Randy began, his brain clearly percolating, "someone must know why Owen Bair was up here."

Margie set her tray on the prep table. "Oh, I can help ya out there."

Randy wrinkled his forehead. "Really?"

"Ya betcha." She motioned for us to sit down and join her.

I hesitantly returned to my stool. What on earth did Margie Johnson know about Boo-Boo?

I'm not sure you really want to find out, a voice whispered from the back of my mind.

Chapter Five

ARGIE WAS BAFFLED, so I took another stab at clarifying myself. "Boo-Boo and Owen Bair are—or were—one and the same person. And he was found murdered earlier today in the park in Lake Bronson."

"Well, I'll be." Margie sank down on her stool. "Emme, I had no clue the guy I knew was your Boo-Boo."

"He wasn't 'mine.'"

She ignored my point of clarification. "To me, he was just Owen Bair, a former baseball player." Randy poured coffee all around before pulling up a stool for himself. "Because I'm not into that sport," she added in his direction, "I didn't realize he was connected to Emme." She fussed with her coffee cup. "Baseball's just too slow for me. And there's way too much crotch scratchin'."

The corners of Randy's mouth twitched, but he didn't smile. He was Margie's friend, but first and foremost, he was a cop. And, at that particular moment, he was investigating a murder and wanted information. "Go on." He rolled his hand, motioning her to get on with it.

"Well, he came into the café here a few times during the last several months. Said he'd retired from baseball and was workin' with some investors to start a wind farm up here. Said it would be part of a network of wind farms across the state. And he asked if I was interested in gettin' in on it."

"What did you tell him?" Randy tossed a nut cluster into his mouth.

I did the same. I couldn't get past the fact that Boo-Boo had been to the Hot Dish Heaven Café and hoped some sugar might improve my brain function.

"I said that from what I understood, the wind blew too hard 'round here for a wind farm to operate effectively. It's so flat, and there are so few trees . . ." She didn't finish the sentence, obviously presuming we understood where she was headed. "Anyways, he said they had that worked out. I then asked how he and his buddies were gonna harness the excess energy that the turbines would generate." She swiveled her head in my direction. "Otter Tail, the local power company, only has to accept so much, don't ya know." She refocused on Randy, her pale blue eyes sparkling. "See, I'm not just another pretty face. I've got some smarts." She tapped her right temple with her dry, red, index finger. This time a smile ghosted Randy's lips. "But the guy had an answer for that, too. Somethin' about havin' a long list of commercial customers to ensure there'd never be excess energy."

She huffed. "He had a ready reply for everythin'. Made me suspicious. I hate to say it, Emme, but I got the feelin' he wasn't an honest person." She smoothed her hair away from her face. "Before long, I got the sneakin' suspicion he wore that beard of his mainly so no one could call him a bare-faced liar."

"Margie, you aren't telling me anything I don't already know. It just took me a while to see him for who he truly was."

Randy filled his mouth with a second nut cluster, then a third. He clearly didn't appreciate talk of my relationship with Boo-Boo, but there was no getting around it.

"Margie?" he asked, clusters stuffing his cheeks. "Did you end up investing in the venture?"

"Oh, no, not me, though lots of other folks did. Most gave $5,000 or $10,000. But, from what I gather, the President invested a heck of a lot more." She stared off in the distance, apparently viewing something through her mind's eye. "One day several weeks back he came in here and announced to everyone that if we were gonna save this county from becomin' nothin' but a half dozen ghost towns, we had to be willin' to risk some of our own money on the deal."

She eyed me directly. "He's on the city council now. Moved here from Hallock a couple months ago. Said an executive at the canola plant offered him so darn much money for his house he couldn't turn him down.

Personally, I think he just wanted to get closer to Vivian." For some strange reason, the President was obsessed with Margie's sister, "strange" being the operative word to describe the obsession as well as the President and Vivian. "Anyways, a month or so back, he took Burr Nelson's spot on the council."

Margie's features highlighted her contempt for the President, yet that contempt appeared to be at war with some other sentiment. Amusement, perhaps? "Burr was ice fishin' up at Lake of the Woods," she went on to inform me. "His truck fell through the ice, and he dove in after it. Uff-da, what an idiot." She shook her head. "Shortly after that, he gave up his council seat, and the President was appointed to serve out his term."

Randy cleared his throat, the universal sign to return to the subject at hand.

"I'll go quick," Margie assured him, "but I hafta tell Emme another story 'bout Burr. It's a doozy."

Randy unzipped his jacket, evidently resigned to the reality that Margie would explain what she knew about Boo-Boo in her own time. And this was not the time.

"Anyways," she began, "one day, a few years back, when Burr came in for lunch, I asked if he had read somethin' or other in the paper. And he answered that he hadn't because the truth of the matter was, he couldn't read very well. His actual words were, 'I'm pretty much *illegitimate*.'"

"Wait a second," I said on the back side of a snicker. "You just told me he was on the city council."

"Oh, yah, that's right. But don't get me goin' about that now." She snuck a peek at Randy. "I hafta hurry." She thumbed in his direction. "He's gettin' antsy."

Randy restated the obvious, as if a reminder was called for. "I'm investigating a murder, Margie."

"Exactly. The guy's dead. He's not goin' anywhere."

Randy glowered.

And I took that as my cue to wrap things up. "So, what happened to him in the end, Margie?"

"Well, someone pulled him out of the water and took 'im to the Tradin' Post in Warroad. And the sales' clerk there put 'im in dry clothes and filled 'im up with hot coffee before sendin' him on his way. He was fine, yet he left the council. Said he had to take it easy. But I don't know . . ."

"Burr," I repeated, letting my mouth get a feel for the word. It surely wasn't the man's given name. It was too unusual. What's more, half the men in these small towns went by nicknames. "Is that how he came to be known as Burr? He fell through the ice a while ago?"

Margie worked to keep her chuckles in check. "Actually, that was his third go-round in the lake."

Randy broke in. "The first was three or four years ago, when he drove his snowcat right into a big patch of open water."

"Snowcat?"

"You know, snowmobile. Yeah, every year he's determined to be the first person out on the ice."

Again, Margie took over. "Which means, more often than not, he's also the first to break through. Oh, yah, even with this year's record cold temperatures and the extra early start to winter, he went out there just a little too early."

Both of them chuckled.

"You people are brutal," I scolded. "The poor man almost drown. Three times."

Margie sighed. "And now the President's on the city council. From what I gather, he's itchin' to run for mayor next, God help us." She glimpsed at me knowingly. "You'd expect that gettin' caught in that sex scandal last fall would of caused him to crawl back under his rock, but he doesn't seem the least bit bothered by his shenanigans. Ya know, I get the impression he believes he did absolutely nothin' wrong." She tsked. "Some folks have no shame."

The President's real name was John Hanson. Folks called him the President because his claim to fame, limited as it might be, was that his namesake and great, great, great, grandfather, or something like that, was president of the United States under the Articles of Confederation. The current John Hanson spent an inordinate amount of time petitioning every group around to pressure the powers that be into demanding that history books be rewritten to recognize his ancestor as the true father of our country. Yeah, he was a pompous ass. Scary, too. Not too long ago, I had learned all of that along with far more about his sexual peccadillos than any human being should have to know. Since then, the mere mention of the man gave me the willies.

"Let's get back to the whole wind farm thing," Randy suggested.

After one last shudder, I agreed.

"Margie," he said, "did you hear of anyone else who might have invested a lot of money in that deal?"

Margie bit down on her thin bottom lip. "I'm not sure off hand. I'll hafta think about it."

"You do that." He stood, and we did the same. "I guess that's it for now."

"Emme, why don't ya walk Randy on out?" A sly smile played across my friend's lips. "I'm goin' to hit the hay."

Randy ambled toward the door only to circle back around. "One more thing, Margie. Did Owen Bair ever tell you who he was working with?"

Margie leaned against the wall, arms crossed over her chest. "Oh, for sure. He mentioned to everyone that the man in charge was Greg Rogers."

"The Minneapolis billionaire?" I was surprised the guy was involved in a project this far from the Twin Cities. Then, again, what did I know? I occasionally skimmed the paper's Business section, but I wasn't an avid reader of it.

"Oh, yah," Margie answered, "I got the impression he expected all of us to jump at the chance to invest with someone like Rogers."

"I understood he was contemplating some kind of project around here," Randy said, "but I never heard any details."

"No disrespect," Margie stated, "but I doubt any of ya guys in law enforcement were high on his list of possible investors. With what ya get paid, he probably didn't see any point in talkin' to ya."

"I suppose you're right. But I should have heard something 'in the wind,' so to speak."

I groaned at his attempt at "wind farm" humor.

"It's not surprisin' ya missed it," Margie assured him. "With all your traipsin' back and forth to Williston this fall, ya were busier than a one-legged man in a butt-kickin' contest."

Before he spoke, Randy saluted Margie, the queen of quips. "But I'm done out there for now," he then said, referring to the booming oil fields in western North Dakota, where law enforcement officers from across the region were assisting the local police. Randy was the primary representative from this area. "I've got no excuse. I better check into it right away." He fixed his eyes on me. "It could very well be tied to murder."

୨୦   ୯ଛ

I LAY IN BED, the radio on the nightstand turned low, the D.J. playing songs to "help you through a cold, winter night." Bob Dylan and Johnny Cash were singing "A Girl from the North Country," and even though the sounds were soothing, reflections from the day horned in on any prospective sleep, much to Otto's dismay.

Otto is my dog. A two-year-old Maltese-poodle mix. I more or less adopted him during my last visit to Kennedy. He'd been abandoned, and we took an immediate liking to each other. Margie adored him, too. That's why he was welcome to stay with me above the cafe.

Icy snow pellets pinged against the window, as Otto repositioned himself in the crook of my knees. At the same time, Dylan and Cash sang, "Remember me to the one who lives there. She was once a true love of mine."

The song prompted ruminations about my relationship with Randy. I was pretty sure we were okay. He had given me a mind-blowing kiss before leaving the café. But since all his kisses blew my mind, they probably weren't a good barometer.

Emme, he never even suggested that you gather your stuff and join him back at his place, now did he? With those words uttered by a cruel voice in the back of my head, a twist of doubt tied itself to my insecurities and formed a pretzel-like knot in my stomach. *So maybe you're not "okay." Maybe he's waiting to see if you'll muck up your relationship again by reconnecting with Buddy Johnson or butting into another murder investigation.*

Curling into a ball of neuroses, I mumbled under my breath that Randy had nothing to worry about on either front. Buddy Johnson was old news. And, while curious about Boo-Boo's death, I'd promised Randy before he left that I was done poking around in police business. Not only

40

had it proven hazardous to my love life, it had jeopardized my personal safety on more than one occasion. Plus, as the deputy had noted, Sheriff Halverson would undoubtedly take every opportunity to badger me, and I wasn't about to make it easy for him.

Sure, I still had dreams of becoming a big-time investigative reporter. It was something I'd envisioned ever since my parents' death, which, in my opinion, was caused by negligence on the part of the Minnesota Department of Transportation. Yet, to my dismay, the state accepted little responsibility for the accident. As a result, I wanted to do right by my folks and become a reporter who'd ferret out wrongdoing and write about it to affect real change in our justice system.

To date, however, the two times I'd gotten involved in police investigations, I was left feeling conflicted and more than a little disillusioned. Consequently, I'd decided to avoid delving into any cases of life and death for a while. Instead, I planned to concentrate on my job as a food reporter while, at the same time, encouraging the editors at the paper to assign me stories about less serious community issues, like snow removal. But, given my curious nature, I was struggling with my decision.

୧ ୨

As I PULLED THE COVERS up around my neck, another picture of Boo-Boo invaded my mind. It was followed by an array of images, all of them from the last time I'd seen him. I didn't relish reliving that day. It was one of the worst of my life. Yet, I couldn't seem to prevent my head from going there.

I had only wanted to surprise him. The Twins were in the middle of a long road trip, and when they stopped in Chicago to play the White Sox, I flew down and rushed to Boo-Boo's hotel room in hopes of catching him before he left for the ballfield. And catch him, I did. He was there with two women, all three of them naked. He and one of the human blow-up dolls were in bed, tangled up in sheets, while the other stood next to me. She had answered the door, presuming I was room service.

At the sight of them, I actually vomited a little in my mouth, but I didn't let that deter me. Swallowing the bile and pushing my humiliation aside, I allowed my rage to take over. I must have looked crazed because the women seemed so scared they didn't move a muscle, and believe me, in view of their state of undress, I would have noticed.

Of course, Boo-Boo started fast talking—making excuses and telling lies—but I paid him no mind. Rather, I gathered their clothes, along with the hotel robes and towels, opened the window, and tossed everything outside, watching it fall to the ground, several stories below.

Turning around, I found the three of them slack jawed, apparently stunned by my actions and more than a little nervous over the prospect of what I might say or do next. But I didn't speak. I couldn't find my voice. And since I wasn't able to think of anything else to do that wouldn't land me in jail, I simply left the building.

As I walked across the hotel courtyard, I spotted a bald man sitting on a bench, waiting for the airport shuttle. He pulled a black bra off his head and dangled it in front of his face, examining it closely before popping open his suitcase and stuffing it inside. I also saw a couple homeless men sifting through Boo-Boo's belongings, while a female hotel worker, possibly on break, scrutinized a trampy slip of a dress as she sucked on a cigarette.

I managed to wish them all "good hunting" before returning to my rental car, where I cried until there were no more tears left in me. Then, I ate the complimentary chocolates I had snatched from the dresser in Boo-Boo's room.

With that memory thankfully waning, I flipped over, and Otto growled. "Sorry," I mumbled, "I can't sleep. True, Boo-Boo was an ass. Even so, I want to know what he needed to talk to me about. I also want to find out who killed him. And why?"

Otto lowered his head and closed his eyes. Either he didn't care about Boo-Boo, or he was content to leave the investigation to the police.

How about you, Emme? Are you willing to let the authorities handle the case without interfering?

"Yep," I muttered. "I have no desire to get involved." I gave that some more thought. "No desire whatsoever," I repeated, as if I might need additional convincing.

Chapter Six

I WOKE BEFORE EIGHT O'CLOCK, sunlight filtering through the sheer curtains that covered the only window in my room. I brushed my teeth and showered, doing my best to keep my hair from getting wet. With it being long and curly, it took forever to dry and comb.

I pulled on a pair of skinny jeans and a baby-blue, fitted sweater, along with my red, high-top, tennis shoes. After that, I added a bit of mascara to accent my emerald-colored eyes and swiped on some pale-pink lip gloss before bounding downstairs, Otto in my arms.

Margie was already in the kitchen, listening to Chris Stapleton on the juke box. Like me, Margie wore jeans, but hers were topped with a blue, long-sleeved, Hot Dish Heaven baseball jersey. Her hair was pulled back, as usual, and she was makeup free. She never went for much makeup, but this morning her face was conspicuously absent of any, leaving her thin lips and pale brows virtually invisible.

She poured me coffee, while I donned my jacket and hooked Otto to his leash. I retrieved my mug from her and led my dog outside. When we returned a cold minute later, she exchanged the mug for a small plastic container of water and another with Otto's food in it.

"What's on your agenda for today?" I asked while settling Otto down for breakfast by the back door.

"Well, first of all, I wancha to taste this British Pasty."

"What's a British Pasty?" I shucked off my coat, hooked it on a peg by the door, and blew on my hands to warm them.

"It's like a turnover, only filled with meat and vegetables. My dear friend Mary Beth Welter gave me this here recipe. Most folks eat pasties for supper. But, as far as I'm concerned, the crust makes them a good breakfast food, too." Slipping on a kitchen mitt, she pulled a cookie sheet

43

from the oven. The "pasty" resembled a turnover, though much bigger. She cut it in two and placed each steaming half on a separate plate. "Now, let me know what ya think, there."

With my plate, utensils, and cup in hand, I moved to the metal prep table, claiming the same stool I had the night before. Margie followed, sitting kitty-corner from me.

My fork and knife at the ready, I inhaled the aroma of beef and potatoes. "Smells good."

Margie slapped the table. "Good? Why that pasty dragged 'good' out back and smacked it around until it cried!"

A giggle bubbled up inside of me. "You're right. It smells way better than 'good.'" I cut into the crust and stabbed some meat, blowing on it until reasonably sure I wouldn't burn the roof of my mouth. I then slid it between my lips. "Mmm. It's delicious. Utterly delicious."

Margie winked at me before checking the time. "We better eat up. Barbie will be here before we know it. She's gonna trim and highlight my hair, paint my nails, and give me some makeup tips for the weddin'."

"Can you believe it, Margie? Tomorrow is New Year's Eve, and you'll close out the year by getting married."

"Honestly? I kinda wish tomorrow was over and my life was back to normal. I don't like all this . . . hoopla."

"Margie, your life will never be 'back to normal.' Come the New Year, you'll have a husband."

She must have mulled that over while we ate because some time later she said, "Yah, I'll be married, but doggone it, I don't want things to change a whole heck of a lot. I'm happy with my life the way it is. John is, too." She wiggled her eyebrows. "But I'm lookin' forward to havin' him to snuggle up against on cold nights."

"Trust me, I know first-hand, you two do far more than snuggle."

Margie slapped my forearm. "Eat your breakfast!"

For several minutes, we did just that. Then, she said, "Wanna get your hair fixed, too? How 'bout havin' your nails done? I know Barbie would be happy to do both."

I fisted a clump of my curly, red hair. "Barbie may be tough, but even she's not tough enough to tackle this." I dropped my hand. "I'm open to getting my nails polished, though." I sipped my coffee.

"How do ya feel about a bikini wax?"

My coffee went down the wrong way, leaving me to sputter.

"My sentiments exactly," she replied. "But Barbie's really pushin' it."

I cleared my throat. "A good wax job takes some skill, Margie. And . . . umm . . . it's kind of intimate. I wouldn't let just anyone do it." I couldn't help but tease, "Unless you and Barbie are way closer than you let on." She flicked her finger against my shoulder, and I added, "That might come as a surprise to John." She flicked me again.

ⁿ ⁞

OUT OF WISECRACKS, I went back to my breakfast, my taste buds pleased with what I was sending their way. At the same time, my mind jumped from thoughts of bikini waxes to Boo-Boo's murder and the investment project possibly tied to it. Yeah, I know, some mighty big leaps, but that's how my mind works. "Margie, tell me more about the wind farm operation. That whole deal seems unreal to me."

She reached over and squeezed my forearm. "I can only imagine, sweetie."

"Why would a Minneapolis billionaire develop an industry way up here? It doesn't make sense."

Margie cuffed the sleeves of her baseball jersey. "I don't know about that. For the most part, folks up here have a strong work ethic. But since farm equipment is gettin' more sophisticated every year, the demand for workers keeps decreasin', which means young people keep leavin'. Long term, these little farm towns will die unless other businesses move in."

"You're talking stores and restaurants?"

"Oh, ya betcha, we could use some more of those." She tapped her index finger against the table. "I had to go 125 miles to find a guy to re-finish the hardwood floors upstairs. And those of us who live in Kennedy can't buy milk or bread without drivin' all the way to Hallock, and if you remember, that's practically ten miles away."

"Then, why don't you advertise for people to relocate here and start some of those businesses?"

Margie rubbed the tip of her thumb against her index and middle fingers. "Even small operations take money. And life up here isn't for everyone. It's pretty quiet, not to mention darn cold durin' the winter." She rested for the count of two. "Plus, those types of businesses alone won't save us. We gotta have companies that can employ a fair number of people."

She bobbed her head to the north. "The canola plant's a blessin'. So's the sugar beet plant over in Drayton, there. But most folks are of the mind we hafta diversify. And, supposedly, that's where Greg Rogers, or people like him, come in." She set her elbows on the table and balanced her chin on her fists. "The fact of the matter is, we can't put all our eggs in one basket, so to speak. If every company around is related to agriculture, a few bad farm years strung together could ruin an entire town."

"Which makes the wind farm a good idea, right?"

"In theory. But, in spite of what Greg Rogers, the President, and your Boo-Boo—"

"He wasn't 'mine!'"

She tittered. "Ya know what I mean."

I regarded her intently. "You sure have negative feelings about their project."

"Well, somethin's felt off about it from the start." She rose, her stool squeaking as it scraped across the vinyl floor. "And now one of the guys involved is dead. Murdered."

₭ ℂ

MARGIE SAUNTERED TO THE REFRIGERATOR, speaking over her shoulder. "John called earlier, and I asked 'im about the bachelor party. Not surprisingly, the death of your Boo . . . I mean the death of Owen Bair came up. He said Randy phoned him last night to let him know he wouldn't make it to the party because of work. The murder and all. Then, later, he dropped by anyways to question some of the guests."

"He must have gone over there right after he left here."

"Yah, I reckon. John said the party lasted 'til the wee hours of the mornin'. Way later than intended. So he's gonna sleep most of the day. I won't see him 'til tonight."

I swallowed the last of my coffee, returning my cup to the table. "What did he learn about the murder?"

"Not a whole heck of a lot. Though the President supposedly knew a few things."

"Of course he did." I couldn't keep the derision out of my tone.

"He claimed Greg Rogers only gave Owen Bair a job because he felt sorry for the guy. Called 'im a 'has-been jock.' Said he—the President, that is—did most of the work up here over the last couple months, findin' investors and all. He also said he's been 'personally' workin' with Greg Rogers to secure the money needed to break ground this spring." She opened the refrigerator door and scrutinized its contents.

"Isn't Boo-Boo's death going to delay things?"

"The President doesn't think so. He said Owen Bair wasn't much more than a goffer, runnin' money and paperwork from here to Rogers' people down in the Cities."

"In light of what he told you, that doesn't sound right."

"Well, remember, the President's full of hot air much of the time." She rummaged through the pans and bowls, obviously on a mission. "He was pressurin' everyone at the bachelor party to cough up cash for the project. I guess he went so far as to accuse John of not bein' loyal to the community if he didn't give a minimum of $100,000."

"Yawza! That's a lot of money."

"The President supposedly gave $250,000."

I whistled.

"But, as I said, he's a blowhard. Maybe he ponied up that much. Maybe not."

"Is John going to invest?"

"No. He told the President, at his age, he doesn't do any long-term investin'. Said he doesn't even buy green bananas."

Margie claimed an orange, oblong Tupperware container and closed the fridge door. "I guess a couple guys at the party also tossed around a theory about Owen's death."

"Why doesn't that surprise me?"

"They called him a big-time womanizer and said he most likely got killed by a ticked-off husband or boyfriend. He evidently stayed at the Motor Inn in Karlstad whenever he was up here, and he picked up women in the Maverick Bar in Lake Bronson. Supposedly, he didn't care if they were attached or not."

"Interesting."

"What's that supposed to mean?"

"Nothing."

"Uh-huh." Margie's expression was one part amusement and two parts circumspection. "Randy's a smart man, Emme. So are most of the other deputies. They'll figure out what happened in the park."

"I'm sure they will."

Margie pressed her lips together until the corners of her mouth resembled question marks.

"What?" I asked defensively.

"Ya don't hafta get involved, ya know."

"I never said I planned to."

"Well, it's obvious you're thinkin' along those lines."

"Am not." Her pinched features made it clear she didn't believe me. Probably for good reason. "Well, thinking isn't doing."

With a shake of her head, she broke eye contact with me to admire the bars she had uncovered. "Emme, we only have a few jobs today, and none of them concerns police business." She motioned to the pan. "First, we need to make sure these bars taste good enough to serve at the reception tomorrow. They're Almond Bars. Helen Kolden made them. She's a very good baker, and these are one of her specialties."

"So, why do they have to be tested?"

"Because I'm . . . umm . . . really cravin' 'em."

Utensils clanged as she rummaged through a nearby drawer. "For Pete's sake, I can never find what I'm searchin' for."

"Calm down. You'll get your sugar fix soon enough." I leaned against the counter. "When did you become such a sweets' eater?"

"I dunno." She plucked a pizza cutter from the drawer and addressed my notable confusion by explaining, "A pizza cutter's the best way to cut certain kinds of bars. Leaves real nice edges." She went to work, vertical slices followed by horizontal ones. "I suspect I have all these cravin's because Vivian has warned me every day for the past six weeks to avoid sugar. And fat. And anything else that tastes good." There was a gleam in her eyes. "Besides, with ya becomin' a health nut and all, someone's gotta pick up the slack."

I lightly hip-checked her. "Health nut? I'm hardly a health nut. Since I arrived in town, I've had more than my share of sweets."

"But ya sure as heck aren't eatin' 'em like ya used to."

A second hip check, this one hard enough to bump her away from the pan. "Well, let's see what I can do to change that."

ᔥ　ᔧ

MARGIE'S PHONE RANG, the ring tone Kenny Chesney's song, "She Thinks My Tractor's Sexy."

Borrowing one of her favorite lines, I uttered under my breath, "Oh, brother."

She put the phone to her ear and left the room, and for that, I was grateful. I had no desire to listen in. Doing so might upset my stomach, and I wanted to finish the Almond Bar I'd just started.

Again, don't get me wrong. I liked Margie's fiancée. John Deere was one of the good guys. But I'd heard more than enough from Margie and him during my last visit. See, they'd spent the night together in the bedroom Margie kept upstairs, above the café, and apparently presumed the wall separating that room from the one I was in was thicker than it was. Now I couldn't listen to Marvin Gaye music without becoming slightly ill, which was a shame because I'd always enjoyed Marvin Gaye.

ᔥ　ᔧ

A KNOCK ON THE CAFÉ's back door put an end to my stroll down memory lane, such as it was. Naturally, I hoped the person on the other side was Randy Ryden. We had arranged to spend the day together, although those plans got waylaid after Boo-Boo's murder.

After a pat on Otto's head, I opened the door, and my stomach sank so low I had to press my knees together to keep it from crushing my toes. It wasn't Randy. Not even close.

"Sheriff Halverson," I squeaked as my throat constricted. "I'll get Margie."

He trudged past me, not waiting to be invited inside. He didn't wipe his feet, either.

49

Obviously disturbed by the guy's lack of manners, Otto barked fe-rociously. At least ferociously for a ten-pound dog.

Right away I swept the little guy into my arms so the sheriff couldn't drop-kick him across the room. Not that he had threatened to. I just took him for that kind of person.

"I'm not here to see Margie," the man barked, sounding much like a dog himself. "It's you I've got business with."

Okay, I had expected that all along. I was merely doing what I could to delay the inevitable. And who could blame me? The sheriff was a big meanie. I'd been subjected to his wrath on a few occasions and didn't wish to experience it again.

On top of that, he was the President's lackey. He did the President's bidding in return for financial support at election time. Just another reason to keep my distance. But how could I do that with him standing right in front of me?

I couldn't, of course, which left me no choice but to hike up my big-girl panties, metaphorically speaking, and deal with the situation. "What's on your mind?" I asked, as if I didn't know.

He propped himself against the Hoosier cabinet. He was an impos-ing figure, reminiscent of a bulldog. Squat with broad shoulders, clipped hair, and a considerable underbite. "Why were you scheduled to meet Owen Bair at the state park in Lake Bronson?"

He watched closely as I pushed the sleeves of my sweater up to my elbows. I was trying to create an air of toughness I didn't feel.

"I asked you a question," he sniped when I didn't answer fast enough. "Why'd you meet with Owen Bair?"

Otto was scared. His tiny heart pounded against his chest, which, in turn, thumped against the palm of my hand. Not surprisingly, his fear fed my anger. "I didn't meet with the man," I growled.

"You were scheduled to."

"Yes, but he never showed."

"How long did you wait?"

"I don't know. Around an hour. Didn't Randy tell you?"

"Yeah, he told me, but I wanted to talk to you myself." His gaze roamed over me. "Mighty convenient that you have that gas receipt."

"What can I say? I needed gas. It's impossible to travel all the way up here from Minneapolis on one tank. Impossible in a Ford Focus, at any rate."

He stared at me, but I refused to blink.

"What were you two planning to discuss, Miss Malloy?" He shifted his considerable weight until the Hoosier loudly complained.

"I don't know."

"You set up a meeting with the man but don't know why?" He was the second person to find that strange.

"He said he'd explain everything when we got together." It made perfect sense to me.

"At the Visitors' Center in the park?"

"Yep." We seemed to be talking in circles, which, I sensed, was causing deep wrinkles in my forehead. For a split second, I imagined I resembled one of those Klingons from Star Trek. And I smiled.

"What's so funny, Miss Malloy?"

"Nothing." I applied a more serious face. "Absolutely nothing."

He folded his arms. "What led you two to break up in the first place?"

"Huh? We broke up a long time ago. And what does that have to do with—"

"He found someone better?"

"What?" The question bugged me. As you may have gathered, while no longer in love with Boo-Boo, I remained sensitive about the circumstances surrounding the end of our relationship.

"Did I hit a nerve, Miss Malloy?"

I refrained from slapping the man, but I do believe I snarled at him. I'm also pretty sure Otto grinned at me when I did.

The sheriff sneered, and I ordered myself to take a mental step back before I did something stupid. He was merely attempting to rile me, and he'd succeed only if I let him. "As I said, that was a long time ago."

The sheriff followed up with a few more questions, and from what I could tell, none of them served any purpose other than to bait me. Even so, I answered each one, although I may have offered up more than a little attitude along the way.

When he was done, he plodded past me before wheeling back around. "How long do you intend to stay in town, Miss Malloy?"

"Through the weekend."

"Do you really think that's a good idea?"

"What do you mean? I'm here for Margie's wedding tomorrow afternoon."

He glared. "It might be smart to leave before then."

"Huh? You're asking me to 'get out of town'? Isn't that a bit dramatic?"

"Well, you know the old saying, 'Out of sight, out of mind.'" He peered down his nose at me. "I'm going to charge someone in the death of Owen Bair, and I'm going to do it sooner rather than later. Now, if you stick around, I may be inclined to consider you, regardless of that receipt of yours."

He pulled the door open and stepped outside. "Think about it, Miss Malloy. And, in the meantime, stay out of my way. Don't get involved in my investigation. If you do, I'll haul you in on obstruction charges."

I didn't respond.

"I'd also hate to see Deputy Ryden in trouble—maybe even lose his job—because of his association with you. But it could happen, especially if I discover you've been snooping in my business."

I had to grind my molars to keep from telling him to go to hell.

"There's always trouble when you show up." He sucked his teeth, that disgusting slurping noise punctuating his remarks. "Why do you suppose that is?" With the door open, cold air swirled into the kitchen, sending shivers up my spine and down my arms. At least I told myself the gooseflesh was due to the cold and nothing else. "Makes me wonder about you, Miss Malloy. Really makes me wonder."

As soon as he left, I hugged Otto to my chest before squaring my shoulders and collecting all the composure I could find. Holding onto those few scraps, I then mumbled something about how the man didn't frighten me. Not much, at any rate. I also said something about being able to take care of myself. Again, I didn't catch it all because my pulse was pounding in my ears.

Chapter Seven

ARGIE MADE HER WAY back into the kitchen. Since there was no point in causing her distress the day before her wedding, I decided to stay mum about the sheriff's visit. And to keep her from detecting that I was hiding something, I made a beeline for Gail Larson's famous Frosted Fudge Brownies. I figured the best way to avoid answering questions or looking guilty was to stuff my face.

As I swallowed the last of my brownie, Barbie came through the back door. She kicked snow from her boots, and my pup, who had Margie's permission to laze around the café since it was closed, lifted his head and sniffed. Apparently, he was befuddled by her appearance and taken aback by her odor. I couldn't blame him.

Her hair was smashed against the side of her head, and her eyes were puffy. Most of her usual makeup was missing, and what was there was smudged, as if left over from the previous day. The yoga pants and Kittson Central Bearcat tee-shirt that peeked out from beneath her unbuttoned jacket were badly stained, like they had served as pajamas, and more, for several days running. And, on top of all that, she smelled like dirty socks.

Weighted down with bags, she trudged to the prep table, where she dumped out everything. Combs, brushes, scissors, a blow dryer, two boxes of hair dye, and at least a half dozen bottles of nail polish clattered as they scattered across the metal surface. "Okay, let's get this over and done with." She sounded like she was about to undergo a mammogram rather than spend a day playing "beauty parlor."

Margie didn't pick up on her tone. She was too caught up in her own nervousness, as demonstrated by the way she approached the table. She moved with trepidation, as if sitting near Barbie might truly cause her pain. And given Barbie's mood, I considered it a strong possibility. "Now take it easy with all that stuff there," Margie warned. "Ya know I'm not much for a lot of fuss."

"I'm well aware of that." Barbie tossed her jacket on a stool but continued to slog around in her heavy boots, leaving small slush puddles wherever she walked. "But you're almost sixty, Margie. It's time to give up the ponytail. It's the only thing your sister and I agree on."

"A ponytail's perfect for work. Keeps my hair out of the food."

"Oh, for crying out loud." Barbie rolled her eyes so hard I saw nothing but the whites.

"All I'm sayin' is ya gotta watch what you're doin'."

"Yeah, yeah."

"I mean it, Barbie. I don't like gettin' all gussied up."

"Can I trim your hair or not?"

"I suppose." Margie sounded less than excited by the prospect.

"If you don't want my help, just say so, and I'll leave." Barbie's tenor rose, a mix of exasperation and petulance riding her words.

"It's not that. It's just—"

Barbie slammed her comb on the table. "You're impossible some-times, you know that?"

"And you're downright testy."

"No, I'm not."

"Yah, ya are."

"Am not."

"Are too."

It was my turn to yell. "Enough!"

"I was only—" Barbie began before I interrupted.

"Enough!" I repeated.

I spun in Margie's direction and asked in a calm manner, "Now, what are you serving at the wedding reception?" Not a subtle segue by any means, but it did the trick. It ended the bickering, and that was my goal.

You see, I get extremely tense when people I care about argue. I'm not used to it. As the sole child of parents who truly loved each other, I was rarely subjected to it. And even after my folks died, the aunt and uncle who took me in seldom raised their voices. Consequently, I never grew accustomed to verbal sparring and routinely attempted to circumvent it by changing the subject. Yeah, total avoidance, as my therapist loved to remind me.

"Well," Margie started, fully aware of what I was doing and slightly embarrassed for her role in the tiff that had led to my unease, "the ceremony's at four o'clock, at Maria Lutheran, over there on the west end of town. The reception's in the middle room, beginnin' right after the weddin'." The middle room was the space that bridged the Hot Dish Heaven Café and the VFW bar. "Supper's in the middle room, too, at six. We're servin' pan-fried walleye, and we're smokin' a pig. All side dishes will be potluck. Folks 'round here insist on feedin' me on my weddin' day since I've fed them for years."

"That's nice." I made tracks to the refrigerator, opened the door, and perused the contents. My resistance to treats had taken a nosedive since coming to town. I wasn't sure if it was because I faced more temptation here than at home or because anxiety had been nibbling away at me ever since I'd left my Minneapolis driveway. In any event, I craved sugar—big time—and the Frosted Fudge Brownies were all gone.

I selected a cake pan with a tin top. I had no hint as to what was inside, but my spidey senses suggested it was sweets of some kind. I set the pan on the counter and slid the top off. "May I?" I was well aware of my sheepish expression. After all, I'd complained ad nauseam about my sugar addiction.

"Go ahead. Have one." Margie sounded like the devil herself. "They're M&M Bars," she added, prodding me with her virtual pitchfork. "Shawna Hennen made them. She's one of the women who brought food early. And since there's no way we'll eat everythin' tomorrow, you might as well have whatever ya want today."

"Sit still," Barbie scolded as she swatted Margie's shoulder. "I'm cutting hair here!"

"I hardly moved. Yep, I'm sidin' with Janice on this one. You've been so bitchy lately, Jesus couldn't live with ya."

"I'm not hard to live with! And I'm not bitchy!"

"Yah, ya are. At first, I chalked it up to menopause, but it's way more than that. You're a big crab."

"Am not."

"Are too."

"Stop!" The bar in my mouth slid down my throat, making me cough uncontrollably.

Barbie whisked to my side and pounded my back. "Are you all right?"

I gasped, "Will be." Leaning over, I clutched my knees. "Just give me a second." I peeked up at her and wheezed, "And for God's sake, get rid of those scissors."

She slapped me some more, scissors still firmly in hand. "I'm sorry, Emme. I know how much you detest bickering. And here I am, sniping at everyone."

I flapped my hands in the air. "No problem. I just—"

She hit me again, way harder than necessary.

"Hey, stop!" I hollered, inducing yet more hacking.

She gave me another whack, and Otto lifted his head and growled like a much bigger dog. That got her to step away.

"I'm sorry," she whined. "I'm truly sorry."

I straightened and repeatedly cleared my raw throat. "It's . . . fine. You . . . just caught me by—"

"No, it's not fine." Tears leaked down her cheeks.

"Oh, Barbie, don't cry. I didn't mean to yell." I swallowed several times. "It's just—"

"It's not that." She covered her face and broke down. "It's . . . it's . . . the rest of . . . my life. It's . . . turning to . . . sh-sh-shit."

Margie removed the scissors from Barbie's clutches and wrapped her in a bear hug. "Oh, there, there, now." She spoke on a whisper. "Everythin's gonna be okay. But this has gone on long enough. If ya expect to go the rest of the day without tellin' us what's wrong, ya got another thing comin'." She guided Barbie back to the work table, planted her hands on her shoulders, and gently pressed her down onto a stool. "Now, out with it."

℘   ℂ

WE WAITED FOR BARBIE to catch her breath. After she more or less had, she wiped her runny nose with the bottom of her shirt and aimed her watery gaze at Margie. "It's really hard to take you seriously," she said through a bad case of the hiccups, "with your hair all crooked like that." *Hiccup.*

She was right. Margie's hair was nearly two inches shorter on the left than the right. "Nice try, kiddo," Margie replied, "but you're not changin' the subject. Now, out with it. What's happenin' with ya?"

Barbie had the sudden urge to inspect her cuticles. "Well . . . umm . . . it's not me." *Hiccup.* "It's . . . umm . . . Tom." She was referring to her husband.

Margie cocked her head until her hair was just about even. "What about 'im?"

"Well, he's not doing well."

"Is he sick?" I asked.

She served up a fatalistic shrug.

Margie's manner changed from confused to alarmed. "He's not . . ."

Barbie bobbed her head. "His medicine quit working." Her words were barely audible. "And he won't go to the doctor."

"How did that happen?" Margie demanded to know. "How'd his medicine give out? He's been managin' pretty darn well for what? Thirty years?"

"About that." A belated hiccup. "But he's not doing well now. Hasn't been for the past couple months." Barbie swiped at her runny nose with the back of her hand. "He doesn't eat or sleep. He's in a foul mood. And he bought an old car online. Supposedly, he's going to restore it."

Hesitantly, I asked, "Is that so bad? Lots of people work on old cars."

"The car cost $40,000, and Tom can't change a tire!" With that, another crying jag took hold, and I handed her a napkin in hopes she'd use it in place of her clothes or her limbs.

Then, while she sobbed, I stirred the gray matter in my head in an effort to come up with some memory to help me better understand the situation. I had a vague recollection of Barbie informing me that her husband struggled with mental health issues, but I'd never seen any sign of trouble and couldn't recall any of the details she had shared.

"That's . . . not . . . the worst of it," she said once she again found her voice, shaky as it was. "He invested $75,000 in some deal he thinks . . . is . . .

is going to make us rich. All things totaled, he cleaned out our life savings. And he did it without even consulting me."

"What kind of investment?" A sense of dread settled in me.

Barbie rubbed her eyes, smearing old mascara toward her ears. "A wind farm of some sort. He bought a promissory note. He was supposed to earn at least twenty-percent interest, starting right away, but he hasn't received a dime."

Margie gaped at me, her eyes practically bugging out of her head.

"A baseball player talked him into the deal," Barbie informed us. "Some guy by the name of Owen Bair. I told Tom that when a deal sounds too good to be true, it usually is. And I threatened to leave him if he didn't get our . . . our money back." She took in a settling breath. "I got the car guy to void that transaction, but I didn't know how to get hold of the baseball player. And since Tom wouldn't tell me, I gave him forty-eight hours to get the money or else."

"And?" Margie and I uttered in unison.

"He was to meet with the man yesterday."

"And?" We repeated, our tone climbing right along with our apprehension.

"He came home last night drunk. Drunk as a skunk."

Margie raised her hand. "Wait a minute. Tom's been sober for—"

"Thirty years!" Barbie threw both used napkins onto the table. "Yet, he was drunk last night. He passed out on the couch. Right after telling me he didn't get the money." Her voice fell to a hush. "It was a couple hours after I heard on the police scanner—the one I use for work—that Owen Bair was found dead." Her lips quivered, giving notice that more tears were on the way. "Last week I was afraid he'd lose his teaching job because of calling in sick so often lately. Now I'm . . . I'm afraid . . . he'll go to prison for . . . for murder!"

Margie grabbed another napkin for her friend, while I stood by, feeling like a jerk for ever getting involved with Boo-Boo Bair.

"Barbie," I said, desperate to ease her pain and, if possible, my own guilt, "from what I've heard, lots of people invested in that venture. And some, or at least the President, parted with far more than $75,000." I waited while Barbie blew her nose. "He supposedly invested $250,000."

She stared at me, clearly in the dark about where I was going. "My point is that since other people had far more to lose than your husband, it's a mistake to assume the worst of him. In fact, the President is a much more likely murder suspect."

Barbie reached for my hand, and despite her need for comfort, I wasn't inclined to give it up. I had never been a germaphobe, but she was on the verge of converting me. Yep, she was one snotty mess.

"I'd like to believe you, Emme." I grudgingly let her give my fingers a brief squeeze. "But I have an awful feeling about this. Besides, the President has money to burn. It wouldn't make sense for him to do anything drastic. Not for $250,000, at any rate. But Tom blew everything we've worked for. Without that money, we have nothing." She appeared terrified. "He was desperate."

After adding her snot-filled napkin to the growing pile on the prep table, she rose from her stool and plodded to the counter next to the refrigerator. There, she pulled a loaf of Rhubarb Bread from a clear plastic bag, grabbed a knife, and cut a huge chunk. "Now you know why I've gained weight over the past couple months. I've been using food to try and appease my fear about Tom." She slathered on a generous amount of butter. "Every time my hips recommend I skip dessert, my angst overrules them."

I made a mental note to avoid the Rhubarb Bread.

Chapter Eight

ARBIE, WHY ARE YA EVEN HERE?" Margie asked. "Ya should be at home."

Barbie swallowed a mouthful of Rhubarb Bread. "I didn't want to be there when Tom woke up. I'm not sure I want to be around him ever again."

Margie pointed a finger at her. "He needs ya."

"He was dishonest!" Once more Otto raised his head.

"He wasn't thinkin' right," Margie argued.

"I don't care!" Neither did Otto. He laid his head down and went back to sleep.

Margie marched over to Barbie and grabbed her arms. "Listen here. I love ya, and I love Tom, and I want the two of ya to be happy. And together."

Barbie tipped her nose into the air. "Well, in the words of Mick Jagger, 'You can't always get what you want.'" She shook off Margie's grip. "What's more, I love you. And I promised to make you beautiful for your wedding. And that's what I'm going to do." She shoved the last of her bread into her mouth and talked around it. "Why 'ouldn't I? You 'idn't deceive me. You're 'oyal and trustworthy and—"

"Ya make me sound like a dog."

"A dog," Barbie repeated the words as she strode to the front of the café to pour herself a cup of coffee. "Maybe I should get a dog," she said upon her return. "At least then I'd have . . ." Her voice stalled as she settled her attention on Otto.

"Oh, no!" I stepped between her and my four-legged buddy. "I'm sorry you're hurting, Barbie, but Otto's mine."

Margie leaned against the counter. "Although, if ya demand perfection, ya might hafta limit your companions to the four-legged variety because people make mistakes. And some of 'em are far worse than piddlin' on the carpet."

"Exactly!" Barbie exclaimed. "Some mistakes can't be forgiven."

"Oh, for land sake, there's no rulebook for relationships. How ya react is all up to you."

"What are you saying, Margie? Am I supposed to pretend that everything's 'hunky-dory'?"

I leaned in. "Barbie, we don't know for sure what happened in the park."

"You're right. But I do know that Tom blew all our savings. He admitted as much. Even so, Margie thinks I should act as if everything's fine."

"No, sir-ree. I didn't say that. But I will say ya have lots of options between actin' like nothin' happened and kickin' your husband to the curb." She waited for Barbie to meet her eyes. "I just wancha to keep that in mind. Ya don't wanna go and do somethin' ya might regret down the road."

"Yeah," Barbie responded. "Whatever."

"Barbie!" Margie scolded.

"Oh, all right. I'll think about it." Once again she wiped her nose with the hem of her tee-shirt. "For the next few hours, though, I'm not going to dwell on Tom or the mess he's made of our marriage. Understand?" Margie and I nodded. "I'll just highlight your hair—"

"No!" Margie pulled her uneven hair out to the sides, Pippi Longstocking style. "First, you'll finish cuttin' it. Right after you wash up."

Barbie attempted to paste on a smile, but it slipped right off. Because of her mood or the messy state of her face, I wasn't sure which. "Okay, I'll go wash. Then, I'll cut your hair. And when I'm done, I'll add highlights and paint your nails."

"Ya hafta paint Emme's, too."

"No problem."

Margie wagged a finger in front of Barbie's face. "But it's a no-go on the bikini wax."

"Fine," she replied. "I don't care."

"Yah, ya do."

"Well, maybe a little, but not enough to fight about it."

"Emme doesn't want one, either."

The repeated sound of my name had me tuning back in after taking a short break to ponder what Margie had said about relationships. Since I was a black-and-white thinker, her advice to Barbie that she consider forgiving Tom was hard for me to understand or accept. Sure, I'd messed up with Randy, and he had forgiven me, but our relationship wasn't as serious as Barbie and Tom's. We hadn't taken any solemn vows. They had. That made Tom's behavior far more egregious, didn't it?

Totally confused, I tabled my notions for another day, when I had more time to think. Presently, I had other things to do, the first being to come clean with Barbie about my relationship with Boo-Boo. She was my friend and deserved to know the truth. Granted, my association with the guy wasn't directly tied to her husband or his actions, but I still felt somewhat responsible for their trouble. After all, I couldn't help but suspect that Boo-Boo's primary motivation for participating in the wind farm project was to reconnect with me.

Yes, that sounded egotistical, but why else did the man get involved in a business venture way up here? Why else did he repeatedly drop by the Hot Dish Heaven Café? Strangers didn't just happen upon this town or the café. Don't forget, it was on the far side of "no man's land." Located at the intersection of Highway 75 and the edge of the world.

"Barbie?" Being completely honest with her would be difficult, but I had no choice. I had to divulge everything. If she hated me afterwards, I'd simply have to deal with it. "Well, you may not want to be so quick to include me in your spa day." I swallowed over the lump in my throat. "Umm . . . in truth, after I'm done explaining what I know about Owen Bair, you may never wish to speak to me again."

With that ominous declaration, I repeated the entire Boo-Boo Bair saga, starting with how we met and ending with what I knew about the murder. I left nothing out, not even the Chicago hotel debacle.

For her part, Barbie worked on Margie's hair while she listened, stopping only occasionally to offer up an "Oh, my God," or "You've got to be kidding."

When I finished, I held my breath and waited patiently for her to say something. Okay, that wasn't true. I wasn't the least bit patient. Desperate for her to speak, I twisted my hair around my fingers and chewed my thumbnail.

Either Barbie failed to notice my discomfort, or she enjoyed watching me sweat. In any event, she took her time with Margie's hair. She checked it over, snipping here and puffing there before setting her comb and scissors on the table and handing Margie a mirror. It was then that my hair twisting and nail chewing gave way to tongue clicking. And it was that irritating sound that finally prompted her to look my way.

"Okay, you used to go out with the guy," she said, stepping directly in front of me and gripping my wrists. Right away I feared she was about to shake me to death. "That doesn't mean you're responsible for him being up here. And it's certainly not your fault he did what he did." Apparently, she wasn't going to do me in, after all. With that realization, I released the breath I'd been holding and made an effort to relax. "Believe it or not, Emme, the world doesn't revolve around you."

"Uff-da!" Margie huffed. "That's kinda harsh."

Barbie let go of me. "I only meant that it's not difficult to see how Boo-Boo—or Owen Bair or whatever his name was—ended up around here. And, most likely, it had nothing to do with Emme. But she's going to blame herself because that's what she does. And she's got to stop it." She swung my way. "You've got to stop it."

She then continued. "Let's consider the situation logically. There's money to be made around here. And it stands to reason that a big-time investor like Greg Rogers would come up with a plan to get some of it for himself. It also makes sense that he'd hire people who could help him." She poked me in the arm. "You said yourself Owen Bair was handsome and charismatic. And that, along with his background as a member of the Twins, made him the perfect pitch man. Who better to entice folks to part with their hard-earned money? Hell, people like my husband were probably thrilled to give the guy whatever he wanted just to say they'd spent time with him. That they were 'friends.'" She added the air quotes.

I was almost convinced.

"I will admit, though," she went on to say, "I'm surprised you got involved with him to begin with. I never met him, but I have every reason to believe he was a major scumbag."

Margie slapped her arm. "Hey, give the girl a break. She's young. She's gonna kiss a few frogs—or scumbags—before she finds a prince."

Barbie studied the tiled floor. "Yeah, you're probably right." She faced me straight on. "Sorry. I guess I am kind of touchy these days."

"Don't worry about it." I was thrilled she was speaking to me at all. "You're right. He turned out to be a scumbag."

"And even though I didn't know him, I really hate him." Barbie hitched her shoulders, a gesture that implied she couldn't help herself. "To be fair, though, I pretty much hate all men right now."

In view of everything she'd been through, I wasn't about to pass judgment. Instead, I hugged her briefly—the only way Scandinavians preferred to be hugged—and thanked her for being so understanding.

She waved off my appreciation in favor of rifling through her shoulder bag. She removed a brush, a water bottle, a can of mousse, sunglasses, three mismatched gloves, and a pair of slippers before recovering her wallet. Opening it, she withdrew several dollar bills and scuffed her way to the jukebox, while Margie and I hung back.

She fed the bills into the machine and announced, "Now, as therapy, I'm going to play every man-bashing song I can find on this thing." She then called out song titles as she pressed the corresponding buttons. "First up, B-52, 'Mamma Get a Hammer, There's a Fly on Papa's Head.'" She glanced at us, a devilish expression on her face. "After that, B-71, 'I Would Have Writ You a Letter, but I Couldn't Spell Yuck.'" She ran her finger up and down the glass, scanning the rows of song offerings. "Oh, here they are." Again she glimpsed in our direction. "I can't have a man-hating, good time this afternoon without G-16, 'My Give a Damn's Busted,' and G-33, 'Did I Shave My Legs for This?'"

Margie and I exchanged glances but said nothing. Barbie needed to vent and playing socially inappropriate music was a harmless way to do it. *Far better than slashing car tires,* a vindictive little voice echoed from inside my head.

₧   ₨

OVER THE NEXT FEW HOURS, as Barbie painted our nails and waxed our brows and upper lips—yeah, we compromised on the whole waxing thing—she sang along to the jukebox. And when she wasn't singing, she was sharing horror stories about her husband and every other man who had done her wrong, as well as some who had merely made the mistake of crossing her path.

"I shouldn't belittle Tom," she said at one point, when talking about her husband. "He's really smart. But his brother's a whole other story. You know, one day his wife got furious with him for being a slob and told him he'd have to do his own laundry. So, he pulled his dirty clothes together and carted them to the laundry room, only to holler back to her, 'Hey, what washing machine setting do I use for my sweatshirt?' Frustrated by his ineptness, she replied, 'I don't know. What does the sweatshirt say?' To which, he answered, 'University of Minnesota Football.'"

I squinted. "You made that up."

"No, I didn't. He's that dumb. But he comes by it honestly. His dad was so useless even his wife got sick of him."

Fully aware I was being strung along, I nevertheless said, "Tell me more."

"Well," she began, struggling to keep a straight face, "a while back his wife took him to the doctor. And following the exam, the doctor pulled her aside and said, 'Your husband's very sick and unless he's kept calm and happy at all times, he'll die. Therefore, you must make him good meals every day, do most of the farm work, and avoid complaining to him about anything. If you do all that, he'll live and, perhaps, even regain his good health. But only if you do everything I've instructed.' The woman nodded, exited the room, and met her husband in the lobby. 'Well,' he said, 'what did the doctor have to say?' And she answered, 'No doubt about it, you're going to die real soon.' Which he did."

Margie admonished her. "Barbie, that's enough, there!" It wasn't particularly effective since she was laughing as she spoke. "No more makin' fun of men. I happen to like 'em. In fact, I'm marryin' one tomorrow."

Barbie scoffed. "They don't need you defending them, Margie. Truth is, they don't need any woman defending them. They've got it made. The entire world's their urinal. Their sleep is never disrupted by hot flashes or night sweats. And when it comes to chocolate, they can take it or leave it."

"Yep," Margie countered, still chuckling, "like Janice said, you're in one foul mood." She threw her hands up, as if afraid Barbie might attack. "I understand why, considerin' everythin' that's goin' on with ya and all. But still . . ."

"I already admitted I've been bitchy. What more do you want?"

"I'm just givin' ya a hard time."

Margie grabbed two potholders and pulled a hot dish from the oven. "Now let's have some lunch. That'll make us all feel better." She set the casserole dish on the counter. "This here's called Gertrude's Hot Dish. It's just hamburger and canned soup for the most part, but it's still real good. My friend Candice Homstad made it, but it's Gertrude's recipe. She's Ole Homstad's wife. They used to live in Lancaster, don't ya know."

The food looked wonderful. But if I had known the predicament I'd end up in by remaining with Margie and Barbie that afternoon, I would have left that very moment, regardless of the great eats.

Chapter Nine

W E LOADED UP OUR PLATES and sat down at the prep table, but only after forcing Barbie to dispose of her filthy napkins and wash the table twice with anti-bacterial soap. We also made her douse her tee-shirt with the perfume Margie kept upstairs.

Since we were lunching late, I ate heartily. Yet, Barbie outdid me by consuming everything on her plate with what could only be described as "a religious fervor all ministers prayed for but few ever attained," as Margie's friend Father Daley liked to say.

After finishing her meal, which included a substantial second helping of hot dish, she went digging in the fridge for dessert. Naturally, she found an assortment of wonderful goodies, including left-over Raspberry Squares from the bridal shower. Doing my best to be gracious, I tasted one or two of them, but I'm pretty sure I didn't eat four, as Margie later claimed.

While I nibbled on those decadent bars, Barbie provided a litany of makeup tips, most of which, I was certain, neither Margie nor I would ever use. Around four o'clock, when I was about to nod off, visions of concealer, glitter shadow, and lip liner dancing in my head, she announced, "That's it. Stick a fork in me. I'm done. I'm going home for a nap."

"What about Tom?" Margie asked.

Barbie didn't respond.

"Ya know ya can sleep upstairs," Margie told her. "I wancha guys to stay together. But you're my friend, Barbie. And if you're not ready to face Tom, you're welcome to stay here 'til ya are."

Barbie patted Margie's hand. "Nah, that's all right. I'll head home. We've been married for close to thirty years. He's the father of my children. And, as you know, even though they're grown and on their own, they pop in on a regular basis. I can't hide what's going on forever. I almost drove myself crazy pretending everything was fine at Christmas. I was so stressed that before anyone else got up Christmas morning, I ate an entire pumpkin pie topped with ice cream. I nearly convinced myself it was like eating health food since the ice cream was full of calcium, and the pie was made of fruit." Barbie packed up her cosmetic bag. "Or is pumpkin a vegetable? I always get that mixed up."

Margie took hold of her shoulders. "Promise me ya won't do anythin' rash."

"I won't. There's no food in the house."

"That's not what I meant."

"I know." Barbie flicked her eyes from Margie to me and back again. "In my heart of hearts, I'm positive Tom didn't kill that guy. He'd never physically harm anyone." She hoisted her bag onto her shoulder. "But the circumstances really scare me. The sheriff will be hell-bent on a speedy resolution. With the election less than a year away, he can't afford to drag his feet. That makes me afraid he'll zero in on Tom. In his present condition, he's an easy mark."

Barbie hesitated, then set her bag on the floor. "I've been thinking. What if those guys at the bachelor party were right? What if Owen Bair's death had nothing to do with his job?"

Margie rubbed her chin. "In that case, the death wouldn't be linked to Tom's investment, which, in turn, would rule Tom out as a suspect. Is that what you're gettin' at?"

"Yeah. That about sums it up."

I raised a finger. "Barbie, while I appreciate what you're attempting to do, you have to remember Boo-Boo confessed to me that he got himself in a jam while working up here."

"Did he specifically say the 'jam' was job-related?"

"Well, no, I guess not. But—" She didn't allow me to plead my case any further.

"Maybe those guys were onto something. Maybe Owen Bair got killed because of how he played around." She dipped her head at me. "You admitted he was a hound, so it stands to reason he could have been killed for stepping out with some guy's wife or girlfriend." She must have seen the doubt registered on my face because she quickly added, "The possibility is not that far-fetched."

She lifted her coat from where it was heaped on the stool next to her. "Yep, the more I think about it the more convinced I am that some guy in the Maverick Bar heard about his wife or girlfriend getting it on with Owen Bair and decided to do something about it. He followed him to the park, confronted him, then threw him off the observation tower." She slipped her coat on while directing her next comment specifically at me. "As you said, he was a small man, despite being an athlete. And since we grow them big and burly around here, a local guy could have tossed him from the tower without any trouble whatsoever."

While the notion of Boo-Boo getting killed because of his philandering wasn't hard to imagine, it flew in the face of what he'd revealed to me on the phone. At least I thought it did. "Barbie, even if we dismiss what Boo-Boo told me, there are other problems with what you're suggesting."

"For instance?"

"Well, he was found by the observation tower. Why there?"

Barbie buttoned her coat. "That's easy. The killer probably stalked him. Possibly for days. And when he saw him enter the park to meet you, he decided it was time to act. After all, what better place to kill someone than a state park that's practically deserted in the winter?" She slid her tongue across her teeth. "Most likely he had a knife or a gun."

It was Margie's turn to poke some holes. "Why follow 'im anywhere if he had a weapon? Why not stab 'im or shoot 'im right where he found 'im?"

"Like in his motel room or in the bar's parking lot?" Barbie was incredulous. "Too many potential witnesses. Plus, the tower served as the perfect backdrop for an 'accident' or 'suicide.'" More air quotes.

"Boo-Boo put up a fight," I reminded her. "His body was bruised. Consequently, his death didn't bear any resemblance to an accident or a suicide."

"True," Barbie granted. "But I'm sure the killer didn't expect a physical confrontation." She nodded, as if agreeing with herself. "I imagine it just sort of happened."

I wanted to support my friend, but she had to deal in reality. "Barbie, you aren't even—"

"Yep. To my way of thinking, your old boyfriend left the motel and stopped at the Maverick before your scheduled meeting. Maybe he needed some liquid courage before seeing you again. Or, maybe, he just needed to kill some time." She sucked her breath. "Oops, bad choice of words." She momentarily pressed her fingertips against her lips.

"In any case," she proceeded to say, "when he left the bar, the spurned husband or boyfriend followed, waiting for an opportunity to strike. As I said, the park was the perfect place. But since there'd be fewer red flags if the murder looked like an accident or suicide, the guy pulled a knife or gun and ordered Owen to the top of the observation tower. And, there, he pushed him off."

My mouth fell open, and Margie reached over and shut it with a lift of her finger. "With all due respect," I said, not all that respectfully, "you made up that theory without one shred of evidence to support it."

Barbie fluttered her eyelashes. "It makes more sense than your theory that the President killed him. Why in the world would he have it in for your Boo-Boo?"

"He wasn't 'mine!'"

Barbie's eyes got saucer-sized. "I just realized something." She offered us a self-satisfied smile. "Since Owen Bair's body had bruises from his struggle with the killer, the killer must have bruises, too!" She practically bounced with excitement. "That means we just need to find a guy with unexplained marks, and he could very well be the murderer."

"You've got to be kidding."

"Oh, come on, Emme. My premise is a good one, unless you want to confront the President regarding your suspicions about him."

"I never want to talk to the President again!" After mixing it up with him during my last visit, I had no desire to come face to face with him.

"In that case, we'll begin with my plan."

"Begin what?" I grew uneasy merely asking the question.

"Our investigation."

"Oh, no."

"Come on, Emme, let's just visit the Maverick and nonchalantly search for bruised men."

Margie chuckled. "For goodness sake, Barbie, you're talkin' about the Maverick Bar. Odds are every guy in there will have bruises."

"Very funny."

"The Maverick's on one side of the street," Margie informed us, "and the Legion's on the other. By last call, folks at both bars are often in the road, fightin'."

"Margie," Barbie squealed, "that's a great suggestion!"

"Fightin'?"

"No, checking out both bars." She momentarily pressed her lips together. "We should start with the Maverick, though, since that's where Owen Bair spent his free time whenever he was up here."

"Says a couple drunks at a bachelor party," I protested.

"Drunk or not," Barbie argued, "they'd have no reason to lie about that."

She instantly raised her hands to keep Margie from speaking. "I know you're in no position to help, with the wedding and all, but . . ." She flashed me doe eyes.

"I already said no!"

"Oh, come on, Emme."

I shook my head back and forth really fast, as if that would better demonstrate my steadfastness. "I won't go. Those places sound way too rough."

"They aren't that rough. In fact, the Maverick can be a lot of fun. Anyhow, we're journalists."

What did that have to do with anything? "So?"

"So, we can handle ourselves in sticky situations."

Margie piped up, "And I imagine just about every gall-darn surface in those two places will be sticky."

Barbie glowered at her. "You're not helping."

Margie pretended to zip her lips, but her eyes kept right on smiling.

"I'm not getting involved," I reiterated. "I may have been interested in doing some snooping initially. But now that I know the sheriff is out to get me, I'm keeping my distance from him and his investigation."

"Emme, the sheriff expects us to do a little digging. It's our job. And he respects that."

Margie snorted.

Once more Barbie glowered. "Okay, he doesn't respect it. Truth is, he's a male chauvinist pig. But it's our job, damn it!"

"Maybe it's your job. But it's not mine. I'm only a glorified errand girl for the Food section of the Minneapolis paper. I write about recipes, when I'm lucky enough to write at all."

Barbie propped her hands on her hips. "Then how do you explain solving those other murders?"

I rubbed the back of my neck. It was getting stiff. With any luck, I was coming down with the flu and would be confined to bed very shortly. "There's no decent explanation. I just stumbled upon the killers."

Barbie stomped her foot. "We have to help Tom. If we don't, he could get arrested for murder. You don't want that to happen, do you?"

"Of course not."

"Well, in his current state, he can't do much for himself. Therefore, we have no choice but to step in." While I wasn't so sure about that, I kept quiet. Barbie didn't. "True, I'm furious with him. And I'm not sure what I'll do when this is all over. But I won't be able to look myself in the mirror unless I've done my best to clear his name."

She scratched her head thoughtfully. "Emme, if you won't go with me, I'll go by myself." Evidently, she was doubling down on the guilt she was laying on me. "But I don't understand why you'd let me go alone if you truly believed it was dangerous. And if it's not dangerous, I don't see why you won't go with me."

She searched my face, clearly attempting to discern if she was getting to me. "I also find it odd you aren't more intent on tracking down Boo-Boo's killer. Granted, he turned out to be an ass. But he was your first love. In many ways, he shaped who you are today."

Margie snorted. "Ya had me until ya got to 'he shaped who you are today.' That was just way too corny."

Barbie bent her head, her features displaying faux innocence. "I was only saying . . ."

I knew exactly what she was saying. And doing. Nevertheless, I felt my resolve crumble.

While I doubted that I owed Boo-Boo anything, I wanted to support Barbie, even if she was delusional to presume we could find "the real killer" in a bar in Lake Bronson. What's more, in spite of what my common sense said, I couldn't kowtow to a bully, and that's what Sheriff Halverson was. A big bully. And kowtowing was exactly what I'd be doing if I avoided the investigation solely because he had ordered me to steer clear. Finally, there was a little part of me that wondered if this might be the case that finally changed my career path. Propelled me from lowly errand girl to actual investigative reporter. "Oh, what the heck," I grumbled. "I'll go with you for a quick look around. But that's it. That's all I'm doing."

"I'm not asking for anything more."

Barbie's eyes showed a triumphant gleam, whereas mine, I'm sure, reflected wariness, not only because of our ridiculous plan but because of the impact that plan might have on my fragile relationship with Deputy Ryden. "Randy," I said under my breath, "please understand."

Randy, hell. You've just declared war on the sheriff and a cold-blooded killer.

Part II

Make Sure You Offer a Little Bit of Everything

Chapter Ten

$\mathcal{A}$FTER WALKING AND FEEDING OTTO, I gobbled down some Meatball Hot Dish for my own supper. The masking tape on the cover of the casserole dish indicated the meal was made by Bernice Erdahl of Morris, Minnesota. I didn't know how it got way up here, near the border of Canada and North Dakota, but I was glad it did. It was great!

When done eating, I changed into black jeans and ankle boots along with a gray fitted sweater and a short quilted jacket, maroon in color. Barbie insisted that we look "somewhat threatening" when visiting the bar, but this was as "threatening" as my outfits got. To compensate, I applied an extra layer of mascara as well as some of the eye liner Barbie had given me. I did my utmost to follow her earlier instructions but ended up poking myself in the eye three times. To offset my watery eyes, I bent my head and shook out my hair, going for an air of "don't mess with me." When I peered in the mirror, though, the person staring back strongly resembled Roseanne Roseannadanna. Only way more pitiful.

With a grunt of disgust, I turned away, kissed Otto's wet nose, and lumbered downstairs, entering the kitchen just in time to see Margie exit the parking lot behind the building. She was on her way to the wedding rehearsal. Afterwards, she and John were hosting a private dinner for her family and the wedding party at Hasting's Landing, a restaurant in Drayton, just across the Red River.

As soon as she left, Barbie arrived.

I should have known better. I figured she'd dress down, considering her funk and all. Yet, there she was in full makeup, her lipstick and eye shadow applied with a trowel, the colors perfectly matching her cranberry hair, which was now spiked with gel.

In most instances, the look would have been considered "beyond the pale," but in comparison to what she wore, her hair and makeup were subdued. See, she donned black leggings, knee-high boots, and a black leather bustier with matching jacket, neither covering much of her chest or her rear. Yep, she could have been auditioning for "Betty Boop Does the Hell's Angels."

"Thank God," I gushed. "For a minute, I was worried you'd look outlandish!"

"Hold the sarcasm. I've been to the Maverick. I know what they expect."

She had a point. And it pricked at me. Or maybe it was the studded metal bands around the ankles of her boots.

ဆ   ର

I INSISTED ON DRIVING, and right away Barbie objected, arguing that she had a roomy SUV, while I drove, in her words, "a measly Ford Focus." But I had ridden with her, and it had been a life-threatening experience, though I'd never admit that to her. Rather, I convinced her she had to serve as navigator since I wasn't familiar with the area. Lame, I know, and I suspected she only went along with it because of the aforementioned funk. Well, that and her bustier. Odds were it had cut off much of her oxygen supply, causing her brain to operate at less than optimum capacity. Granted, that raised a host of concerns regarding the evening ahead, but I did my best to tamp them down. It was too late for second guesses.

As soon as we were on our way, Barbie demanded that I switch on the heater, prompting me to remind her that it would take a while for the hot air to blow. In turn, she ragged on about my "worthless, piece-of-junk car." Midway through her tirade, I interrupted to admit I was wrong. The "hot air" was already churning. At that, she stuck out her tongue. I snickered. And we traveled on down the road.

We drove several miles without saying a word. Barbie hugged her scantily clad torso and stared out the passenger window, while I fixed my eyes on the road, the headlights illuminating the patched veins that crisscrossed the asphalt and the dirty snow padding the shoulders. We met very few cars, and I spotted even fewer farmyard lights.

Inside the car, the space between us grew heavy with the conversation we weren't having, and when I couldn't stand it any longer, I said, "Everything all right at home?"

"I don't know if it'll ever be all right." She left that sentence hanging for some time before she added, "He supposedly called his doctor and has an appointment first thing Monday morning in Fargo."

"That's good."

"We'll see."

More silence. Too much silence. I flicked on the radio but got nothing but static. I hit the scan button, and it went all the way around the dial without locating a station. I turned it off, adjusted the rearview mirror, and checked the dashboard gauges. Then, I hesitantly asked, "What about in the meantime?"

Barbie slapped her thighs. "Exactly. A lot of damage can be done before Monday. Yet, he claims he'll be fine. He's going to stay with his AA sponsor. Intends to hit a meeting every day."

I didn't want to be pushy, but I had additional questions, and since I was risking my life on her behalf by going bar hopping in search of a killer, I decided I had the right to ask them. Still, I felt awkward, as if prying, which, I suppose, I was. "Well . . . umm . . . did Tom say any more about . . . you know?" I maintained my concentration on the road, even a glimpse in her direction seemingly too intrusive.

"No," she said, drawing out the "O." "He never even saw your Boo-Boo."

"He wasn't 'mine,'" I muttered, getting mighty sick of making that point.

"Whatever." She fidgeted, and I was pretty sure her unease no longer had anything to do with the temperature in the car. "The problem is, he doesn't have much memory of the last couple days." She hesitated, as if debating whether or not to continue. In the end, she did. "Emme, he has bruises."

My breath caught in my throat, forcing several moments to lapse before I responded. And, when I did, it took the form of another question. "Did you ask him about them?"

"Yeah. He insists he got them falling down."

"What do you think?"

She leaned against the head rest and examined the roof of the car. "I can't accept that he hurt anybody." The words were spoken like a mantra.

℘　℘

WHEN WE WALKED into the Maverick Bar, I had to steal a moment to let my eyes adjust. Afterwards, I wished I hadn't. Margie was right. The place was rough looking. Deer heads lined the wall, some with Christmas lights strung around their antlers, while leather-clad biker types hunched over the bar, none of them decorated for the holidays. The entire space consisted of just a half dozen booths and a dozen bar stools, with a yard-stick worth of room between them. That narrow aisle led to the rear exit, my focus already on it.

Behind us, the door squeaked shut, sounding like it was scoffing at me for having no semblance of a plan. But that wasn't my fault. I had insisted this operation required some "orchestration," but Barbie had argued that she'd "never been mistaken for Paul Schafer or Les Brown or any of those guys." I guess that was her way of telling me she didn't consider our lack of preparation a problem. Then, again, she also considered it a-okay to visit a bar, looking like the love child of Victoria Secret and Sara Lee.

"As I live and breathe!" a monster of a man at the far end of the bar yelled in our direction as he lumbered into the aisle, the wood floor shaking as his boot heels drummed against it. I swear he was eight feet tall and four hundred pounds. Well, that might have been an exaggeration, but he definitely shopped the Big and Tall Store at the outlaw mall. He wore a black tee-shirt, the sleeves ripped out at the shoulder seams, a skull and crossbones emblazoned across the front. His jeans sagged and a silver chain looped from his back pocket to what I presumed was his belt, hidden beneath a slight paunch. As for his hair, it was dark and wavy and practically reached his shoulders.

As he drew near, I felt compelled to scream for help, but my mouth was too dry to get the job done. That's right. Yelling for help was pointless, as was bolting out the back exit. Sasquatch, you see, was blocking my path.

After a nervous review of my options, I concluded I really had none other than easing out the same way we'd come in, and I discreetly tugged on Barbie's jacket, praying she'd understand my intentions. I then shuffled backwards—right into a brick wall—a wall that breathed and smelled of whiskey. *Shit!*

Sasquatch slogged closer, his voice rumbling like thunder. "Well, if it isn't Barbie Bennington."

Huh?

"You know perfectly well I'm Barbie Jenson now." My friend's tone gave nothing away. I couldn't tell if she was scared or enraged, and I was too frightened to twist my head to gauge her reaction.

"What in the hell are ya doin' here?" Sasquatch demanded.

"Me?" Barbie screeched, sending my heart rate into double time. "Why on earth are you here, Tiny?"

Before he could answer, she propelled herself into his arms, but rather than beat him about the head and neck, she wrapped her legs around his waist and kissed him soundly. The whiskey guy behind me— the one built like a brick wall—nudged me aside, where I remained, while "Tiny" twirled Barbie in the air.

"I live here, you big oaf," she teased once he'd set her down. "Well, not right *here*. In Hallock. What about you?"

He studied her with his intense, cobalt-blue eyes. "I'm on a road construction crew. Staying just up the road, at the Motor Inn in Karlstad. Been here a couple weeks." He swept his hair off his forehead. "I can't believe it's you. I haven't seen you in—"

"Forever!" Barbie squealed, a real smile taking shape.

She grabbed my arm and dragged me forward. "Emme, this is a dear friend of mine. We were . . . umm . . . close years ago, when I was single and living in the Twin Cities." The bar's lighting was poor, yet I couldn't miss the flush mottling her neck. "Tiny, this is a new friend of mine, Emme Malloy. She's a newspaper reporter from Minneapolis. She's up here for a wedding."

"Not yours, I hope."

Barbie swatted him on the arm, across his serpent tattoo. "I'm still with Tom."

He eased his massive mitt around the back of her neck and steered her toward him. "Too bad. I was hoping you might have grown tired of him and were ready to give me another chance." He quickly surveyed the room. "He's not here tonight, is he?"

"No." Barbie stepped out of his grasp and swatted him again. "You're incorrigible!"

Tiny offered up a full belly laugh before easing his focus in my direction. "It's nice to meet you, Emme Malloy."

I gripped his hand, temporarily losing most of mine among his fingers. "It's a real pleasure to meet you, too . . . Tiny." And, trust me, I meant every word. With him around, no one would dare bother us.

"What kind of news are you after way up here?" He sounded genuinely interested.

"Nothing exciting. I work for the Food section of the Minneapolis paper."

With those words, his interest naturally vanished, and he refocused on my friend. "You look great, Barbie. Just great!" He once more allowed his eyes to travel from her head to her feet, taking a leisurely respite around her breasts. They were heaving over the top of her bustier.

She pressed her hand against his barrel chest. "Oh, no, I don't, Tiny. I'm getting old and fat."

He growled, the sound coming from deep inside. I didn't care to speculate as to where exactly. "You look just right to me. Now, come on over here and tell me what you've been up to."

⁘   ⁗

WRAPPING HIS ARM AROUND HER, he ushered her to an empty booth, and I followed, the proverbial third wheel. He shouted our drink orders to the bartender before he and Barbie began reliving their glory days, unabashedly flirting with each other the entire time.

I avoided watching them, choosing, instead, to listen to the country music playing on the jukebox while scrutinizing the other men in the room. Remember, we were on a mission. We were in search of a guy with bruises. Someone I expected to be as elusive as the one-armed man.

As I said, the bar was dark to begin with, and now that we were tucked in the back corner, it was nearly impossible to see. Thus, I determined I had no choice but to develop a weak bladder, allowing for repeated trips past everyone seated at the bar as I went to and from the bathroom. But that didn't help, either. I didn't detect anyone with injuries.

I did, however, tick off two biker mamas who looked mean enough to eat their young. They presumed I was traipsing back and forth in an effort to entice "their men." They let me know their opinion of my "plan" after cornering me between the tampon and condom dispensers, opposite the bathroom sink. I assured them they had nothing to worry about. I wasn't at all attracted to the men in the bar, which led them to ask, "Why? You too good for the guys 'round here?

I might have mumbled, "Maybe."

They didn't appreciate that and demonstrated their displeasure by yanking my hair and shoving me against the wall. They also warned me to "get the hell out of Lake Bronson and never come back." I'm not kidding. That's what they said.

As soon as they left the bathroom, I slid to the floor, my legs and bravado too wobbly to support me. I stayed there, on the cracked tile, through a Loretta Lynn song about some floozy who wasn't woman enough to take her man. And, when it was over, I gathered up what was left of my dignity and scurried back to our booth to inform Tiny and Barbie that I was leaving.

Barbie whined that she wasn't ready to go, providing Tiny with the perfect opportunity to propose that he take her home later. Given her current vulnerability and his extreme attentiveness, which included caressing her neck nonstop, I didn't think that was a smart idea. But she averted her eyes, so I was unable to let her know my opinion without voicing it straight out, and I wasn't up to doing that.

At that moment in time, I couldn't have pieced together a coherent argument for why she should leave if I'd been given a two-sentence head start. Of course, my fragile state of mind was wholly due to the bathroom bullies, who now glared at me from their stools at the bar. I'm not ashamed to admit that their scowls sent my mental wherewithal packing, and I hurried to follow it right out the door.

As I started my car, I caught a glimpse of the Legion sign across the street, beckoning folks in for a drink. "You'll have to get by without me," I muttered, "and Barbie, too." I was more than a little disappointed in my friend. But, what could I do?

I backed out of my parking spot in hopes I'd remember my way to Kennedy. Deciding I was in no mood to get lost, I applied the brakes, pulled out my phone, and hit the GPS icon.

As I punched in my destination, I heard a thump against the back window and conjured up images of the bathroom trolls. They had come to finish me off!

Chapter Eleven

*L*ET'S GO," BARBIE SAID as she slid into the passenger seat.

Relieved it was her and nobody else, I pointed my car toward the outskirts of town and hit the accelerator.

We were silent as we made our way down the highway. I watched the road, and Barbie watched for deer, and together we shivered as we listened to the radio. The "borderland station" was now coming in loud and clear, intermixing music with farm news for southern Manitoba and the northern Red River Valley of North Dakota and Minnesota. As Willie Nelson and Sheryl Crow sang, "Today I Started Loving You Again," my breathing eased, partly because the car was warming up and the music was comforting, but mostly because we were putting distance between us and the Maverick Bar.

When the song ended, Barbie punched me in the arm.

"Hey!" I shouted, breaking my concentration on the road long enough to give her a withering look.

"Whose dumb idea was that?"

"Going to the Maverick? I believe it was yours."

She scrunched her eyes shut, as if attempting to hide from what she had done.

"So," I said, deciding to address the elephant in the room or, more accurately, the giant in the bar, "what's the story with you and Tiny?"

Her mouth opened and closed repeatedly, like a fish out of water. Finally, she muttered, "Shit. I can't . . . Well . . . See, with all the trouble Tom and I have been having lately, I haven't felt very . . . you know . . . desirable." She tugged on her bustier. "I'm not making excuses. I'm just saying." Another tug. "As you probably gathered, Tiny and I were hot and heavy years ago. I was shocked to see him in the bar. It's been so long. Yet, it was easy to slip back. It was as if no time had passed." She blew out a weary breath. "I won't lie, Emme. Staying with him tonight would have felt good. And I almost did it. But I would have hated myself tomorrow." She slapped her hands against her knees. "Damn that husband of mine for making such a mess of things!"

"I'm glad you came to your senses. I only wish it had been earlier." With those words, I launched into the story of my adventure in the women's bathroom.

"Are you okay?" She was going for concern, but I detected a hint of laughter.

"I am now! Now that we're out of there!" I stroked my head. "They practically pulled my hair out by the roots."

She coughed to cover up a chuckle.

"It's not funny! The evening was a complete waste of time. You weren't any help, and I didn't spot anyone with fresh bruises. Not that I really thought I would. But, I guess, I was hoping we'd uncover something since we went all the way over there and everything. Yet, we didn't learn a thing. Nothing. Nada."

She twisted in my direction. "I wouldn't say that."

"Why? What did you find out?"

She pulled on the cuffs of her jacket. "Well, first off, I discovered that Janice Ferguson has been frequenting that place. Tiny said that since he's been around, she's come on to him a couple different times in there."

I had lots of questions and was surprised by the first one to pop out of my mouth. "Was she successful?"

"Nah. But, according to him, she didn't seem terribly troubled by it. She persevered and, more often than not, left with someone at the end of the night." She sat back. "Apparently, on one or two occasions, the guy was Owen Bair."

"What?" Being a visual person, I pictured Boo-Boo and Janice doing the horizontal bop. I recoiled at the image, causing me to jerk the steering wheel.

"Whoa!" Barbie shouted as we fishtailed across a patch of black ice.

I held my foot off the brake and steered us out of the spin. "He was at least twenty-five years younger than her!" Those words were on the tip of my tongue when I went into the skid, making them the first to spill out afterwards.

"I guess age wasn't a concern to either of them at the time."

With my car sitting sideways on the highway, I concentrated on measured breaths and waited to speak until my heart rate returned to normal. "Well, it's disgusting."

"You won't get an argument from me. Remember, I'm not Janice's biggest fan anymore."

I couldn't look at Barbie as I confessed, "I feel like an idiot. Once upon a time, I loved that guy. Now I've discovered he'd bed just about anyone."

Barbie snorted. "From what you said earlier, you were well aware of his cheating ways long before tonight."

"But I always hoped he had some standards." I eased the car back down the highway. "I guess he didn't. A pair of human blow-up dolls in a hotel room wasn't bad enough. He also had to take up with a cadaver look alike almost twice his age for last-call hookups in a small-town bar." I found myself blinking back tears. "What does that say about me?"

"Emme, his behavior is no reflection of you."

"Yeah, right."

"That's what I believe. I have to." Her tone inferred she was alluding to her own situation as well as mine. "People need to take responsibility for their own actions." She reached over and squeezed my shoulder. "You're crazy if you think you have any control over them one way or another."

We drove on in semi-silence, the music and the voices on the radio the only sounds inside the car.

As I slowed for the County Road 5 intersection, Barbie piped up. "You know what?" She must have flipped an emotional switch of sorts because her tone was much lighter than it had been only minutes before. "We should go to Hallock."

"Why?"

"To visit Janice."

"What?"

"She'll be at the holiday hockey tournament. Her nephew plays for Kittson Central, and she never misses his games."

"Why would we want to talk to her? It's not as if she has a jealous husband or boyfriend who may have followed Boo-Boo into the park and killed him."

"True, but since she spent time with the guy, she may have learned things. Pillow talk, you know. Otherwise, she might have heard stuff while camped out on her barstool in the Maverick."

I wasn't keen on the idea of reaching out to someone who had slept with Boo-Boo. Not that I was jealous. I wasn't. His liaisons were just so tawdry they now had me judging myself, and I was coming up short. "It's kind of late, isn't it?" Nope, I didn't want to visit Janice. Not that night, at any rate. I needed more time to nurse my wounded Irish pride.

"Since it's a tournament, games are played all afternoon and evening." Barbie checked the time on her cell phone. "Kittson Central was scheduled to play last. They can't be done yet."

She pitched her thumb to the right. "Turn here. Then take a left onto the Two River Turnpike. That'll bring us to Highway 75. From there, we'll go straight into Hallock."

I did as she said and made that first turn, while she mocked me for using turn signals in the middle of nowhere. I didn't respond. I was pre-occupied, racking my brain for a reason to postpone our face-to-face with Janice.

Before coming up with anything, I got distracted by a weather report. During the winter, weather reports trump all else in the Red River Valley. In fact, they usually call for an uptick in the volume on the radio, which Barbie took care of right away. That allowed the announcer to detail, at nearly a shout, how temperatures were expected to fall to twenty below zero overnight and barely climb to five above on New Year's Eve Day. He also described the forecast for the following week as "bleak," nighttime temps dipping as low as thirty below with wind chills hovering around minus forty.

Barbie yanked on the lapels of her jacket in an effort to pull them together. They didn't quite reach. "Where are Margie and John going on their honeymoon?"

"Costa Rica. For a month."

"Think they'd notice if I hid in their suitcase?"

℘　℘

EVEN THOUGH IT WAS NEARLY ten o'clock at night, the hockey arena parking lot was crowded, and it took me a while to find an open spot.

"Ready?" I asked as I switched off the engine.

Barbie gawked at me as if I were nuts. "I'm not going with you."

"What?"

"Janice hates me. She won't reveal anything if I'm there."

"Well, if you're not going, I'm not—"

"You have to, Emme. She might know something that'll help us clear Tom."

"Yeah . . . well . . . I've been thinking about that. Tom hasn't even been charged with anything."

"And we have to keep it that way."

I scooted around in my seat until I faced her head on. "What happened to all that talk about people taking responsibility for their own actions?"

"As I said, Tom's not in any position to do that right now."

"You mean folks get to pick and choose when they're going to be responsible?"

Barbie knew she was on shaky ground. "Please, Emme. I need your help."

I slumped against my seatback. "I don't want to confront her, especially by myself."

"You saw her last night, and you had no problem with that."

"That was before I learned about her and Boo-Boo. Now I'm afraid I'll be picturing the two of them 'together' the whole time I'm talking to her." I flinched. "It'll be way too creepy."

"Wait a minute. You'd let Tom get arrested because interviewing Janice might be awkward?"

She wasn't going to guilt me. Not this time. "Awkward? You mean completely revolting."

"Emme, you're being ridiculous."

"Well, I don't see you—"

"I can't! She won't talk to me."

"And I'm beginning to see why!"

Barbie swallowed hard and blinked over and over again.

When her eyes misted, I relented. "I don't understand why I listen to you."

She exchanged her pout for a grin, all signs of tears miraculously disappearing. "You do it because you're my dear friend, and you believe in justice and—"

"Stop! Don't say another word. I'll talk to her this once. But no more."

"I'm not asking for more."

I unbuckled my seatbelt and reached over the back of my seat to retrieve my down coat. "Tell me something." I laid the coat across my lap. "How did you and Tiny end up discussing Boo-Boo in the first place? Whenever I was in the booth, you were completely engrossed in old times. And each other."

Barbie twisted her face. "I'm not exactly sure. I think Tiny mentioned something about the murder. He seemed fascinated by it."

I shot her a question-mark look, and she replied with, "Well, it's not like someone gets killed around here every day, although whenever you visit, we—"

"Don't go there! You know how I hate getting teased about that."

"Sorry." She didn't look it. "Anyhow, from what I gather, Tiny visited with Owen at the bar during the evenings. Since both of them were from out of town and happened to be staying at the same motel, they gravitated toward each other."

"But Tiny's only been here a couple weeks."

"And, according to him, Owen Bair was around that entire time."

I pulled my scarf from the sleeve of my coat and wrapped it around my neck. "Did Tiny learn anything from him?"

Barbie took a moment, ostensibly to collect her thoughts. "He told him about the wind farm project, but, apparently, he was more talkative early on. Over the past several days, he'd become withdrawn, as if bothered by something. Tiny said he still came into the bar but preferred to keep to himself."

"Except when he went home with Janice."

"I got the impression that relationship ended as quickly as it started. I don't believe he was with her recently."

"And Tiny didn't know what was troubling him?"

"Nope. Although he was eager to hear my ideas."

I felt my eyebrows inch up. "What did you say?"

"Nothing. I don't know why, but, for some reason, I didn't feel I should."

I reached out and patted her arm. "You know, if Janice hasn't been with Boo-Boo recently, she may not have any useful information."

"True. But we won't know until we ask."

"You're throwing that 'we' around pretty loosely for someone who doesn't plan to leave the car."

"Yeah, I suppose I am."

She didn't sound the least bit contrite, leading me to grumble, "Hand me my boots." They were on the floor in front of her. "I've never been in an arena that wasn't freezing cold, and I'm not about to get frost-bite on my toes."

I slipped off my fashion boots and stuffed my feet into my fleece-lined Uggs. "One more question, Barbie."

"What's that?"

"What if Janice is the killer?"

She wrinkled her brows. "Where in the world did that come from?"

"Well, we haven't even talked about the possibility. Yet, you're sending me to meet with her. All by myself."

"Emme, don't be such a drama queen. The arena's full of people. Nothing will happen to you in there. Besides, Janice may be a first-rate pain in the ass, but she's not our killer."

I pulled on my gloves. "How can you be so sure? She was in Lake Bronson yesterday afternoon."

"True, but she's a toothpick. She's not strong enough to shove a man—a former athlete—over the ledge of the observation tower. It's fairly high."

I absently stated, "I'd like to see it for myself."

"We can do that tomorrow morning." Barbie smiled like the Cheshire cat. She was pulling me deeper into the case, and she knew it.

"Besides," she quickly added before I could make a comment along those lines, "she didn't have a motive."

"You don't know that. Maybe she was furious with Boo-Boo for dropping her after . . . 'just a couple rolls in the hay,' as Margie would say."

"Emme, if Janice killed every guy who dumped her after 'just a couple rolls in the hay,' half the men in the county would be dead."

"Well, she did cause at least one guy's death." I was referring to events of a few months back.

"No, Emme, a crazy person was responsible for that. Not Janice."

I raised my gloved hand. "I thought you hated the woman. Why are you sticking up for her all of a sudden?"

"I'm not. She drives me nuts. But we can't cast aspersions on anyone. We need evidence." She swept her hands, motioning for me to leave. "Now, go get some."

"Okay, okay." I opened the car door and sucked in the frigid night air.

"Hey! Turn the engine and the heater back on before you take off. It's getting cold in here."

I did. Then, I stepped outside. "You so owe me."

"When we get back to Kennedy, I'll buy you Cranberry Pudding at the cafe."

"Pudding will not be payment enough."

"Don't be too sure. This is Cynthia Maloney's pudding. It's really good. And I saw where Margie hid it in the fridge."

Chapter Twelve

ENTERED THE ICE ARENA, climbed the stairs, and zigzagged through the crowd to the ticket table. An older woman decked out in a North Face jacket and a dark-green stocking cap with "Bearcats" knitted in red across the front accepted my money and handed me a program.

Smelling freshly made popcorn, I followed my nose to the concession stand, where I waited in line while the three little boys ahead of me debated which Airheads to buy. Their decision finally made, they pushed their money across the counter, gathered fistfuls of the candy, and ran off, two of them using my feet as a springboard.

I paid for my bag of popcorn and limped to the nearest corner to avoid getting trampled any further as folks pushed their way from the warming room to the bleachers along the ice to watch the final period of play. Once it was safe to move, I hobbled to one of the indoor benches overlooking the rink and began my search for Janice. No sense in getting cold if I didn't have to.

I munched on my popcorn and eyeballed the crowd, while the Zamboni finished resurfacing the ice. Not spotting her anywhere, I concluded that Barbie was wrong. Janice didn't make it to every game. I wasn't altogether disappointed, although between exiting the car and entering the arena, I had psyched myself up into visiting with her, so, in a way, I would have preferred to get it over and done with.

A pat on my shoulder and I lurched, sucked in air, and choked on a popcorn hull. I coughed as I twisted around to find the woman in question standing behind me.

"You okay?" Janice asked.

"Yeah," I wheezed. "But, I should quit eating. This is the third time today I've swallowed wrong."

She snorted. "Eating can be tough, with all that chewing and stuff." She glanced from side to side before dipping her voice. "That's why I stick to drinking for the most part." She discreetly pulled a flask from her jacket pocket. "Want some?"

I coughed a couple more times, unable to dislodge the hull. "If you don't mind." I snatched the metal decanter, halfway hidden in a mitten, and took a swig. Peppermint Schnapps. "Thanks." I cleared my throat. The hull was gone.

"What are you doing here?" She shoved the flask back into her coat pocket.

"Well, searching for you, actually. I wanted to ask you about Owen Bair."

She appeared perplexed. "Why?"

Since I couldn't very well admit that my efforts were on Barbie's behalf, I chose another route. "I went out with him a while back. I hadn't seen him in ages. And, well, I heard you two were . . . ahh . . . dating, so I hoped you'd be able to offer some insight about what was going on with him before he died."

She smirked. "Who said we were 'dating'?"

"I'm not sure," I lied. "I just heard it around."

Uncertainty creased her face. "Ed from the sheriff's office already in-terviewed me." Her features softened some. "But, I suppose, it wouldn't hurt to tell you what I told him. It's not a secret or anything. Besides, I owe you."

I had helped her out a couple months back. In truth, I had almost gotten her killed. Still, if she considered herself indebted to me, who was I to say differently?

"Owen and I went out exactly twice," she stated softly, her words clearly meant for my ears alone. "And we didn't do a lot of talking, if you get my drift." I suddenly felt queasy, and it wasn't from the Schnapps. "After that, I refused to see him. He was just too self-absorbed."

While I agreed with her assessment, I chose not to pursue a discus-sion about Boo-Boo's shortcomings. What purpose would it serve? More-over, I was scared what Janice might reveal. When it came to living, she was far more experienced than I was and much more willing to talk about her adventures, such as they were.

"So," I said, instead, "you had no idea what was troubling him?"

"No, and I actually saw him yesterday, shortly before he was killed. Both of us were in the Maverick, but we didn't talk. He was in a bad mood. Real crabby."

"Did he speak to anyone?"

"No. Then, again, there were only five of us there." She went on to offer up the names as she ticked them off on her fingers. "Owen, of course. Me. The bartender. And Burr Nelson." She considered her thumb. "Oh, yeah, a guy everyone calls Tiny, too. He's only been in the area a couple weeks. He supposedly works on a road crew, but he spends an awful lot of time in the Maverick."

"It's been bitterly cold. Hard to do road work in weather like that."

"That may be, but I think there's something fishy about him. He watches everybody real close. And he's not the least bit friendly. I tried to make nice a couple times, but he wouldn't have anything to do with me."

Maybe he wasn't up to date on his shots.

"Well . . . umm . . . why do you go all the way over to the Maverick to do your drinking?" That wasn't what I'd intended to ask, but I was thrown by the nasty remark from the voice in my head.

"I first went there a few months ago with a friend and had a great time. I really like the place. It's laid back. People leave you alone for the most part. And those who do talk are nice enough." Apparently she hadn't been introduced to the bathroom bullies. "Plus, I don't care to drink where I bartend because I always end up working."

"What about Burr Nelson? He lives in Kennedy, doesn't he? Why was he in the Maverick yesterday?"

She whispered, "He hopes to keep the people in Kennedy from finding out he tipples. He figures if he drives to a bar in Lake Bronson, no one he's acquainted with will ever know."

"You know."

"Yeah, but we're friends. See, until recently, he was on the city council, and since I'm the city clerk, we regularly worked together. He's a good guy. Not very bright. But really nice." She palmed both sides of her beehive hairdo. "Anyhow, a month or so ago, when he started coming into the Maverick on a regular basis, I assured him his secret was safe with me." She grunted. "That ended up being a complete waste of breath."

"How so?"

"Well, yesterday afternoon Barbie's husband, Tom, was in the bar. And, a while later, the President stopped in. They both know Burr, which means his secret is out."

I leaned my head back, close to her face, and got dizzy from the smell. It was a mingling of Peppermint Schnapps, floral-scented hairspray, and a perfume I couldn't identify. "But you just said there were only five people in the bar." I bent forward and gulped fresh air.

"Let me explain." She stepped around me and up to the plexi-glass, where she followed the action out on the ice as she spoke. "The people I first mentioned were in the Maverick when Owen was there. But, after a while, he left. He must have had an appointment of some kind because he kept close tabs on the time."

She then yelled, "Come on, Billy, get after it! Yes! Yes! Good job!" She whirled around. "That's my nephew. Number 10. He plays defense."

Her grin lingered as she went back to relaying the activity at the Maverick. "Tom was really drunk. Of course, since he's married to Barbie, I couldn't blame him for getting shit-faced. Truth is, I expected him to start drinking long ago." She weighed what she'd said. "I know you're her friend, but that's how I feel." She bobbed her head for emphasis. "Anyhow, a while later, the President came in. I'd never seen either one in the place before."

"Did they sit together or talk to each other?"

"Oh, no. The President's too arrogant to hang out with a lowly music teacher like Tom."

"Did you speak to either of them?"

"No. From what I could tell, Tom was too hammered to do much visiting. He sat next to Burr and, for the most part, mumbled. As for the President, we don't communicate because of religious differences."

"Really?"

"Yeah, he thinks he's God. I don't."

While I didn't want to like Janice, out of deference to Barbie, I was nonetheless starting to do just that. She was funny, and I enjoyed hearing her bash the President.

"How long did the President and Tom stay?"

"I don't know. I had to get back to Kennedy for Margie's party. I left around five, and they were still there."

"What about Tiny? Was he still there?"

"Oh, no. He took off a long time before that. In fact, he left right after Tom came in. I remember because Tom came in through the front door, and Tiny left by way of the back door, which I considered strange since his truck was parked out front."

I mulled over everything she had said, and something didn't add up. Another minute, and it came to me. "Janice, what were you doing in the Maverick during the middle of a workday?"

She was taking in the action on the ice and spoke without looking at me. "I've accrued so much vacation, I had to take this entire week off. If I didn't, I'd lose the time altogether come the first of the year."

The arena erupted in cheers, and Janice turned my way and jumped up and down. "We scored! We scored!"

I felt a smile shape my mouth. Her enthusiasm was contagious. "You certainly love hockey!"

"Yeah, I do." She made an effort to settle down. "And I'm really ticked off at the city council for moving our regular meeting night. Now I won't make all the home games."

"Why'd they change the schedule?"

Her smile drooped to form a frown. "The President recently replaced Burr, and he wants the council to get together on a different night."

When play resumed on the ice, she stepped forward, pressed her hands against the glass and tracked the puck. "He's a jerk," she muttered. "I swear he forced Burr off the council. I just can't prove it."

"How could he do that?"

"I'm not sure." She slapped the glass and shouted, "Come on, Billy. Check him! Check him!" She glanced at me. "All I know is Burr was fine after he fell into the lake. Hell, it wasn't his first polar plunge. Even so, he resigned, and the President was appointed to complete his term, just like that." She snapped her fingers. "One night at the Maverick I asked Burr about the whole ordeal, but he refused to discuss it. That alone told me something was screwy."

"How can you stand working with the President?"

"I have no choice. I can't retire."

"How do you keep your sanity?"

She tapped the pocket where her flask was stored.

Yep, Janice was a real character, and I got a kick out of her. True, I didn't have to spend a lot of time with her. Nor was I required to attend formal functions with her. And, while in her presence, I constantly had to chase away images of her and Boo-Boo bumping uglies. Still . . .

"Have you heard about that wind farm venture?" She posed the question seemingly out of the blue.

"Yeah, a little. That's what Owen was working on when he died, right?"

"It was his job to court investors up here, although, at our council meetings, the President insists he's the 'point person in the area.'" She mocked the guy by making her voice low and official sounding for those last few words. "He's only been on the council for two meetings, yet he's already pushed through a half-million-dollar economic development loan for the project." She licked her lipstick-stained teeth. "Burr voted against it when it came up a few months back."

"How could the President do that?"

"Jam the loan through?" She immediately answered, "Easy. There are five council members, and two were in favor of the loan and three against. Once Burr resigned and the President came on board, the vote swung to three in favor."

"That's my point. The President shouldn't have voted since he had a financial stake in the project."

Janice gaped at me, her features suggesting I was extremely naive. "Who was going to stop him?"

"You. Other council members. Residents. Take your pick."

She sniffed. "Like I said, I need my job. Besides, the other council members who voted for the loan also had money invested in the project."

"What about the rest of the council? Why didn't they object?"

"That's only two people. And while they always do their best for the city, they can't fight a majority."

"Well, the residents can."

"Emme, most people just want everyone to get along. In these small towns, we see one another all the time. There's not much room for bad feelings." She glanced at the ice, then back at me. "Nobody hardly ever attends council meetings, anyhow. And the minutes aren't published in the paper. So council members can pretty much do as they wish."

"And they get re-elected?"

"Yeah, for the most part."

I didn't know what to say. During one of my graduate school internships, I'd been tasked with reporting on local government. By the time I got through with my assignment, I had a basic understanding of how city councils were supposed to operate. But, from the sound of it, the President and his two council cronies weren't about to let a few laws, rules, or procedures get in their way.

The buzzer sounded, signaling the end of the game. It was met with lots more cheering because Kittson Central had won.

"I have to get going," Janice informed me after high-fiving the fans around her. "It was nice visiting with you. I'll see you at the wedding tomorrow."

"Hey! Before you leave, I have one more—"

"Sorry, but I really need to go." And, with that, she whisked herself toward the door.

As for me, I edged my way through the crowd, dropping my popcorn into the first trash can I saw. Had Janice Ferguson divulged anything useful? Granted, much of what she'd shared was fascinating. But useful? I wasn't sure. Barbie would have to help me determine that. Hopefully, over the Cranberry Pudding she had promised.

Chapter Thirteen

WHEN I GOT BACK TO MY CAR, I found Barbie rocking out to Miranda Lambert on the radio. Together they were singing "Little Red Wagon." I slid in behind the wheel and turned the volume down as Barbie screeched, "You can't ride in my little red wagon. The front seat's broken, and the axle's draggin'."

"You're in a better mood. Your singing's atrocious. But your mood is way better."

She stuck her tongue out and switched off the radio. "I was going crazy just sitting here. Too much time to think . . . about everything. The murder. Tom. Our marriage. My future." She hugged her midsection. "So, come on. What did you find out? Anything good?"

Outside, exhaust mingled with cold air, the resulting odor seeping into the car as I eased forward to wait my turn to exit the parking lot. "Did you know Tom was at the Maverick yesterday afternoon?"

"No, but it's not a shocker. I warned him to get our money back. And since Owen Bair stayed in that area whenever he was up here, it stands to reason Tom would search for him over there."

"Janice was in there, too. According to her, Tom was really drunk."

"Janice was in the Maverick?"

"Yep. I guess she likes to go there so she doesn't get roped into working in the Eagles or the 'V' on her days off."

Barbie paused to ponder something, and I was pretty sure it had nothing to do with how Janice spent her free time. "I suppose it makes sense he was already drunk in the afternoon, considering the wretched shape he was in when I got home from Margie's party."

soゃ ಇ

I FOLLOWED A PARADE of cars to Highway 75 before heading south through town, the scene in the Maverick the previous day, as described by Janice, occupying my mind. Tiny, Janice, Burr, the President, and Barbie's husband, Tom, were in the place right around the time of Boo-Boo's death, and each was linked to him in some way.

Tiny stayed at the same motel and visited with him in the bar during the evenings. Supposedly, the two of them, strangers in the area, enjoyed talking to each other for that reason alone. True, Janice suspected there was more to Tiny, but her take on the man was dubious at best. Since he'd rejected her advances, she may have been bitter and prejudiced against him.

As for Burr Nelson, he was the only one among the five with no direct ties to Boo-Boo, although he did give up his council seat, which went to the President, who used it to garner additional funds for the wind farm project. And that project involved Boo-Boo, so . . .

Then there was Tom Jenson. On the day of the murder, he arrived home late, drunk, and bruised, with little memory of his time in the bar or anywhere else. Yet, according to Barbie, he couldn't have murdered anyone. He wasn't the type. Then, again, who was?

The President. He was definitely the type. And to my way of thinking, he was the most likely suspect. He had a huge financial interest in the wind farm. He knew Boo-Boo. And he disliked him.

And you don't like the President, Emme. Fact is, you pretty much hate his guts. Is that making you biased?

I tapped the steering wheel. Yeah, I suppose I was inclined only to believe the worst about the President. But that didn't mean I was wrong.

ᔆᜭ   ᜪᔆ

THE SKY WAS PITCH BLACK and stretched on forever, millions of stars sparkling against it. Northern night skies never ceased to amaze me. Their vastness always hinted that the answers to all my questions were out there somewhere, if I only knew where to look.

I shuffled in my seat. What if I was wrong, and the President was innocent? Could the murderer really be an irate husband or boyfriend, as the guys at the bachelor party intimated and Barbie hoped? Not likely. Not in light of Boo-Boo's remarks to me on the phone. Although I might have misconstrued them. I sort of was in shock at the time. I hadn't expected to speak to him that day. Or any other day, for that matter.

As my attention veered from the sky to the road, pictures of the five people in the Maverick the previous afternoon passed through my mind once again. Since Boo-Boo was killed shortly after leaving there, I believed one of those five was the culprit. And when two of those faces worked their way to the front of my brain, as if more deserving of my consideration than the others, I muttered their names under my breath. "Tom and Tiny. Tom and Tiny."

Out of respect for Barbie, I immediately skipped over Tom to focus on Tiny. I knew little about the man other than he had a thing for Barbie. And while that may have caused him to be jealous of Tom, I couldn't comprehend how it had any bearing on Boo-Boo or his death. Still, his image, along with that of Barbie's husband, continued to blink in my head like neon signs.

"Tom and Tiny," I repeated on a whisper. "Tom and Tiny."

"Huh?"

As Barbie uttered that sound, a notion struck me, and I blurted out, "Did Tiny and your husband ever meet?"

She made squinty eyes at me. "Yeah, a couple times. Why?"

"Did they like each other?"

"Well, they weren't destined to be buddies, if that's what you mean. But they got along. Why do you ask?"

Uncertain of the importance of my realization, I nevertheless had the strong sense it was worth examining. "Janice said that as soon as Tom came into the Maverick by way of the front door, Tiny left via the back. Now, Tom may have been too drunk to recognize anyone, but Tiny must have seen him. So, why didn't he say hello? And why didn't he mention to you that he'd crossed paths with your husband?"

Barbie appeared to turn that information over in her head. "Maybe he didn't realize who he was. It's been more than two decades. We've all changed."

I didn't buy that. "Tiny recognized you in a split second, Barbie."

"Yes, but he was more intimately acquainted with me."

She had me there. "Even so, I find it hard to believe that Tom looks much different now than he did twenty-five years ago. He still wears his hair in a ponytail, for God's sake. He's a complete throwback."

She squirmed in her seat. "Why are you so concerned about Tiny all of a sudden?"

"I suppose it's because Janice claimed he was 'fishy.'"

"Consider the source, Emme. Consider the source."

"But you, yourself, said there was something about him that kept you from revealing very much."

"Hmm. I did say that, didn't I?"

"Uh-huh."

"Well . . ." She cranked her head my way and tucked her foot under her thigh. "He asked about Tom more than once, which I thought was odd."

"What exactly did he want to know?"

"How he was doing. Stuff like that." Once again she mechanically tugged on her bustier. She really needed pulleys for that thing. "The more I think about it, though, the more logical his questions seem."

"In what way?"

"Well, Tiny was well aware of Tom's past. Lots of people were. I may not have mentioned it to you, but Tom was a drummer in some big-name bands out on the West Coast when he was younger. After he went through treatment at Hazelden, he gave up his rock-and-roll life and settled in the Twin Cities. He signed on with a good therapist, went back to college at the University of Minnesota, and got his teaching degree. That's how I met him. I was a reporter for the college paper and did a profile piece on him. It got a lot of press. I was actually dating Tiny at the time, although things were already falling apart. Once we broke up, I called Tom."

"Really?"

"Yeah. When I interviewed him, he asked me out. I said I couldn't go because I was involved with someone else. He gave me his number and urged me to contact him if my situation changed. And that's what I did."

₧   ⁂

I SLOWED AS I APPROACHED KENNEDY, colorful Christmas lights outlining the buildings and shining brightly against the snow.

"What else did Janice tell you, Emme?"

"Well, she went out with Boo-Boo exactly twice. Then she dumped him."

"Or he dumped her, which is far more likely."

"She also said Burr Nelson and the President were in the Maverick yesterday, around the time of the murder. And while it wasn't unusual for Burr to spend time there, she'd never seen the President in the place before."

She made a noise that indicated interest.

"Barbie, she believes the President somehow coerced Burr into giving up his spot on the council. And as soon as the President got on board, he and two other council members approved a half-million-dollar EDA loan to support the wind farm project, even though they had no business doing that since all three of them had invested their own money in the operation." I hung a left at the Community Garden, where snowdrifts were the only things currently blooming.

"She must have been referring to Booger Bernstrom and his cousin Delmont. They're on the council, and they're the President's minions. Always have been. They're loyal to a fault. In fact, if it came to implicating the President in any type of wrongdoing, they wouldn't say shit if their mouths were full of it."

That was disgusting. Even for Barbie. "Booger's one of the regular hot dish cook-off competitors, right?"

"Yeah, but how did you know about—"

"It's not important."

As I maneuvered the rutted alley behind the VFW and the Hot Dish Heaven Café, I spotted Randy getting into the SUV that served as his squad car. He must have seen me, too, because he got right back out again.

"On second thought, I'm not that hungry for Cranberry Pudding," Barbie announced.

"You don't have to leave just because he's here." I was being magnanimous. In truth, I wanted her to go.

"Nice of you to say, but I don't believe you mean it. If you did, I'd force you to get your head examined."

We pulled in next to the squad car.

"Anyhow, we've talked this investigation to death." She opened the car door. "Maybe Randy has some information that'll help make sense of what we've uncovered thus far. If that's the case, you'll have a better chance of getting it out of him if no one else is around." She shimmied. "If you know how to handle him, that is."

We got out of my car, and I walked straight toward Randy, while Barbie made tracks to her own vehicle, fluttering her fingers in greeting as she passed the good deputy.

A smile cracked the tight line of his mouth. "She never disappoints, does she?"

I punched him in the shoulder.

"Hey!" he yelped, rubbing his arm. "There's nothing wrong with looking."

₮ ‗

I UNLOCKED THE BACK DOOR of the café and flipped on the overhead light in the kitchen. "Margie must still be at the rehearsal dinner. I didn't see her car or John's pickup anywhere."

Randy pointed himself in the direction of the refrigerator. "I'm starved. I didn't have time for dinner or supper. Margie wouldn't mind if I ate, would she? I'll leave cash on the register."

"I doubt she'd care. She insisted I eat whatever I want. According to her, there's way too much food for tomorrow. And, after that, she and John are gone for a month."

He rattled a number of bowls and pans inside the refrigerator.

"While you find what you want, I'll make coffee."

At the front of the café, I brewed a fresh pot. "Hey," I called back to him, "Barbie said there's Cranberry Pudding in there, and it's supposed to be really good."

"Already found it. Along with Upside Down Hot Dish, one of Margie's best. Want some?"

"Do you need to ask?"

Five minutes later, we were seated at the prep table, plates of Upside Down Hot Dish, bowls of Cranberry Pudding, and cups of steaming hot coffee in front of us. The scene captured my imagination, creating a picture in my mind of us as a married couple, eating our supper while catching up on the day's events. Feeling playful, I gave life to the portrait by doing my best June Cleaver impression. "Well, Ward, how was your day?"

Like me, Randy was a devotee of old-time television and fell right into his role. "I missed the Beaver's basketball game because I was in Lake Bronson, investigating Owen Bair's murder."

"Oh? How did that go?"

He set his fork on the table. "I heard the strangest thing." Randy wasn't much of an actor. He couldn't stay in character. Just two lines in, and he no longer sounded anything like the Beaver's dad. Rather, he was back to being a cop. "Several people claimed they saw you and Barbie in the Maverick Bar earlier tonight. Can you believe that?" I snuck a peek at him but couldn't tell if he was upset or merely giving me a bad time. "Of course, they didn't really recognize you. They said Barbie was with a cute redhead. Being a detective, I used my skills to deduce that they were referring to you."

I tried for levity. "You think I'm cute?"

"Emme, do you have something to confess?"

"Are you a priest now, too? Because, if you are, we'll have to re-examine our entire relationship."

He tried to look tough, but since he had to bite his lip to keep from smiling, he didn't come across as very intimidating. "Emme, do you want to tell me anything?"

Hoping to keep him from getting too serious, I stretched my hands out, as if preparing to get cuffed. "Okay, copper, you caught me. Barbie and I were in Lake Bronson."

He took hold of my wrists. "Wanna explain?"

His good humor seemed to be evaporating, prompting me to reply, "No, not particularly."

"Emme." He drew out my name, making it about four syllables long. Never a good sign.

"All right, I'll tell you. But no sermons about how we shouldn't be interfering in police business. And no laughing at our pathetic excuse for undercover work."

"Sorry. I can't guarantee anything."

I sighed in resignation. "Well . . . ahh . . . we went there hunting for bruised men." I might have mumbled those last few words.

He arched his eyebrows.

"See, Barbie figured that since Boo-Boo was bruised, his killer would be, too. She also had a hunch the murderer was some guy who frequented the Maverick since Boo-Boo's body was discovered nearby, and he supposedly hung out there whenever he was in the area." As I stopped to take a breath, I decided that the best way to avoid Randy's lectures or ridicule was to prevent him from speaking altogether, so I hurried on. "She wants to believe the killer is the husband or boyfriend of one of Boo-Boo's recent sexual conquests."

He lowered just one brow, and even while wondering how he did that, I kept talking. "Crazy, I know. And I don't abide by her theory. But I have to give her credit. We learned that Boo-Boo was in the Maverick just before he died." I couldn't keep from adding, "We also discovered that whenever he was up here, he picked up women in there and wasn't particularly choosey."

I then had to steal a couple seconds to try yet again to get past that last aggravating point. And, wouldn't you know, Randy used my momentary lapse into silence to say, "I thought you weren't going to get involved in this investigation. I thought you were leaving it to the professionals. The people actually trained to handle these kinds of things." So much for the evening remaining lecture free.

"I didn't get involved, Randy. I merely rode to the Maverick with Barbie because she didn't want to go by herself. That's it."

"I doubt it."

"What?"

"With you, there's always more."

"Randy, I couldn't turn my back on her. She's afraid for her husband. Afraid he'll be arrested for murder if she doesn't find Boo-Boo's real killer."

"Well, it doesn't look good for him, that's for sure."

He lifted his hand when I would have interrupted. "Emme, you know I can't disclose much about the investigation, but I will tell you this case has the potential to be dangerous. And I don't want you mixed up in it."

Chapter Fourteen

*U*NABLE TO REIN MYSELF IN, I snarled, "You don't want me 'mixed up in it'? When did you earn the right to tell me what to do?"

Randy rubbed his hands down his face. "I'm sorry. I had no business saying that. And, believe me, I realized it as soon as the words were out my mouth." He pushed his hot dish around on his plate before dropping his fork to the table. "I just don't want you to get hurt."

"I can take care of myself."

He flashed me a look that, when translated, read, *Oh, really? Is that why you almost get killed every time you come to town?*

Since it was only a look, I decided it didn't require a direct response and, instead, said, "If I need your help, I'll ask for it." I offered him a conciliatory shrug. "Even then, there's no guarantee. I could still get in trouble or end up hurt."

"If you're trying to make me feel better, you're doing a lousy job of it."

"I'm just saying."

He swiped his napkin across his mouth, stood up, and stepped between my knees. "We need to talk." He paused for what felt like eternity. "I've been . . . been thinking a lot about us lately."

Considering the staid expression on his face, a heaviness settled in my stomach, and my mouth went dry, leaving me barely able to utter, "Are you going to dump me for poking around in Boo-Boo's murder?"

He captured a few wayward strands of my hair and tucked them behind my ear. "No, I'm not going to dump you. In fact, one of the reasons I like you is because you're . . . gutsy."

"Gutsy?" Feeling relieved that our relationship was still intact, I gave him a little shimmy. "And here I was under the impression it was my never-ending curves that captivated you."

He slid his hands around my waist, sending quivers to all my lady parts. "I like the way you look. I like it a lot. But I'm also really attracted to your . . . personality."

"My personality? That's the kiss of death!"

He tightened his hold on me. "Give me a break, Emme. I'm doing my best to be serious here. To tell you how I feel."

"Okay, go ahead. I'm listening."

He captured my fingers—the ones caressing his face—and kissed the tips of them. "Well, it goes without saying that you're pretty and funny and smart."

"No, by all means, say it. I won't stop you."

He groaned. "And, as I've already pointed out, you have a good personality. You're gutsy, fiercely loyal, and very nice. At least most of the time." He dropped my hands to raise his own. "You probably don't want to hear that, but it's true. You're nice. You're kind and considerate and—"

"Stop. You're confusing me with a girl scout."

He chuckled in spite of himself.

"Trust me, Randy, I'm no girl scout." I wiggled my brows. "Though I'd consider wearing the outfit if you'd like. I believe Barbie has one I could borrow."

He briefly lifted his face to heaven, most likely praying for patience. "I simply meant you're always there for your friends."

It was my turn to get serious. "My friends are important to me. Remember, I don't have any family to speak of."

"I guess what I'm trying to say, Emme, is that I'd hate for anything to happen to you. But, you are who you are, and I have to accept that and deal with it."

"Wait a sec. You just got done telling me I was pretty amazing. But now you sound as if I'm someone you regrettably have to put up with."

"See? This 'from the heart' stuff doesn't come easy for me, so let me try again." He once more clasped my hands. "You're going to do whatever's necessary to help your friends. And, on a fairly regular basis, that seems to include butting into police business." He circled the backs of my hands with his thumbs. "I may not always like it. But I understand it. And, on some level, I even admire it."

"Randy, what are you getting at?"

He pressed his finger against my lips to silence me. "Likewise, since you're a journalist and I'm a cop, we'll occasionally be at odds over our work. It's only natural. And, again, I better get used to it."

"I'm just a food reporter."

"Yeah, right. Let's not even go there."

His Adam's apple bobbed up and down as he swallowed several times over. "Bottom line, Emme, I don't want to lose you. And bossing you around is the surest way to do that. So I'll try to stop. But it's tough for me to keep quiet, especially when my work's involved. Besides, you drive me crazy sometimes."

Despite my confusion over what he was saying and why, I managed to utter, "Ditto."

"Good thing we're together then." He gave me a butterfly kiss. "We can drive each other crazy."

I gave up attempting to figure him out, opting, instead, to nibble on his bottom lip. "That sounds kind of fun."

"I agree." He then leaned in for a deep, passionate kiss that truly curled my toes.

℘ ℭ

LATER, AFTER WE WERE done kissing, Randy plopped a Frosted Zucchini Bar in front of me.

"No, thanks," I told him. "I'm not much for vegetables that masquerade as dessert."

"You mean to tell me you don't like carrot cake?"

"Well, yeah, I like carrot cake. That's an exception to the rule."

He gestured toward my Zucchini Bar, while biting into his own. "'rust me. 'ou'll 'ove this bar. Helen Hennen made it, and it's delicious." He motioned toward my mouth. "Go ahead. Taste it."

I wasn't sure I wanted to.

110

"Oh, come on." Another bite and his bar was gone. "Mmm."

Reluctantly, I bit into mine, my bite far smaller than either of his. At least my first one was. After that, I went big. Really big. What can I say? He was right. The bar was scrumptious.

"Told ya," he said as I quickly devoured the rest of it.

"Want another?" I licked cream-cheese frosting from my fingers.

"No, I've had enough." He patted his flat stomach. "But don't let me stop you."

"I won't." I slid off my stool and scooted over to the refrigerator, where I snatched one more from a plastic container.

"Now, let's get back to business." With my mouth full, I asked, "'hat were you 'aying about things not 'ooking very good for Tom?"

"Damn. I was hoping I'd distracted you from that particular subject."

"Nope." I zeroed in on his lips as I swallowed. "But, believe me, I appreciated your effort."

He smiled, although the expression didn't fit his words. "I can't disclose much about the investigation, Emme. You know that."

"Oh, come on, Randy. Reviewing your evidence may actually help you come up with another idea or two."

"I have plenty of ideas about this case. What's more, you aren't genuinely interested in helping me."

"That's not true!"

"Mostly you just want to find out what we've learned so far."

I attempted to look hurt. "You're being quite cynical, and it's not very becoming."

He didn't appear the least bit affected by my words or my pouty lips, leaving me no choice but to beg. "Please, Randy. At least tell me something. Barbie's my friend, and I want to help her, which means I need to have an idea of the kind of trouble her husband's actually in."

He shook his head. "I can't believe I ever thought you'd stay clear of this case."

What could I say? It was a continual battle for me. On one hand, I wanted to live a simple, safe, drama-free life. On the other, I had this weird super-hero-type compulsion to fight for justice. And, if that wasn't bad enough, I also was afflicted by a chronic case of curiosity. A dangerous combination.

Randy absently scraped his empty pudding bowl with his spoon and begrudgingly said, "Well, I suppose it couldn't hurt to go over a few things." He pointed his spoon at me. "But I'm not getting into the nitty gritty."

I gave him a palms up. "Fine. No nitty gritty."

He moved about on his stool until apparently comfortable. "As Barbie no doubt told you, Tom was seen arguing with Owen Bair in the Maverick parking lot yesterday afternoon, just a few hours before Owen was found dead." That was news to me, but I chose to keep that fact to myself. "I guess he demanded his money back. The money he invested in the wind farm venture. But Owen told him it was too late. The money had been deposited, and Tom had his promissory note, so that was that." He appeared to think twice before adding, "From what I understand, Tom got really mad. Furious, in fact."

"How do you know all this?"

"Their argument was overheard."

"By whom?"

"Didn't Barbie tell you?"

"No, she didn't mention any names." Probably because, like me, she wasn't aware the exchange ever occurred. "Go ahead and tell me, Randy. If you don't, I'll just ask her in the morning." Not really a lie since I could always pose the question. Admittedly, she wouldn't have an answer, but that was beside the point.

Randy fidgeted while seemingly arguing with himself over what to divulge and what to keep under wraps. "Ahh, it was the President," he finally supplied. "He was on his way into the bar and saw and heard everything." He briefly pursed his lips. "Well, not everything. He only stuck around long enough to get the gist of the argument. Then, he went inside. An hour or so later, Tom followed him in."

"How convenient that the President saw him." I was being cynical.

"Emme, don't let your personal feelings cloud your judgment."

"Yeah, yeah, whatever."

I finished off my second Zucchini Bar. "You know, even if Tom quarreled with Boo-Boo, it doesn't mean he murdered him."

"True. Although it does make him a prime suspect. And, as for your 'bruised killer' theory, Tom has bruises. He was in a fight."

"Or, he fell down. He was pretty drunk yesterday. Likely too drunk to be a real risk to anyone." Another notion hit me like a whack to the head. An actual defense for Tom. "He certainly couldn't have out-wrestled a former athlete. Not in his condition."

Randy slurped the last of his coffee. "We don't know that Tom was really intoxicated. According to the bartender, he smelled of booze, wasn't particularly steady on his feet, and slurred his speech. But the President says he didn't appear drunk when he was in the parking lot, which leads us to speculate he may have been putting on a show to establish an alibi."

"You truly believe he pretended to be drunk to get people to believe he was incapable of murder?"

"It's possible."

I couldn't keep from rolling my eyes, although I didn't try very hard. "It's also possible he drank himself into oblivion after Boo-Boo refused to return his money."

"No one in the off-sale recalls selling him a bottle."

"Maybe he bought it elsewhere. Or maybe he already had it on him."

Randy fingered the handle of his cup. "I guess we'll find out."

"Are you even looking at anyone else?"

"Like a jilted husband or lover?"

I bobbed my head, astonished I was proffering Barbie's theory.

"We haven't found any evidence along those lines, which leads us to believe it's a dead end. But, we won't completely dismiss the idea."

"Any other possibilities?"

"We're checking to see if Owen had any enemies."

"Any luck?"

"No." He blew out an audible breath. "When you were with him, Emme, do you remember anyone hating him?"

"Other than me . . . at the end?"

"Yeah. Other than you."

"Hmm. No. He was rather well liked."

"That's what we've discovered, too."

"Anything else?" I was afraid for Tom. From a law enforcement perspective, he wasn't faring too well.

"Between Ed and me, we've met with everyone who was in the bar yesterday afternoon. Now, we'll get together and compare notes." He narrowed his eyes. "How about you? Have you learned anything else I should know?"

I wiggled around on my stool. "Well, I . . . I visited with Janice a little while ago at the hockey arena."

That caught him by surprise. "You've been busy. First, the bar in Lake Bronson. Then, the Hallock ice rink."

I picked up my napkin and began tearing it into tiny pieces. When nervous, I normally doodle. But since I didn't have any paper or a pen, I was left to rip my napkin to shreds. "Barbie and I discovered that Janice has spent a fair amount of time in the Maverick over the past several months. She also went home with Boo-Boo on a couple occasions." I shrugged, doing my best to act nonchalant. "Because of that, we figured she might have some useful information."

"Did she?"

I fingered the tiny napkin pieces while considering how much of my conversation with her to share. It didn't take long to decide to skip all references to her feelings about Boo-Boo and stick to what she knew about the other people in the bar. Of course, I began with the President.

"She's pretty sure the President's up to no good. She's of the mind he coerced Burr Nelson into resigning from the Kennedy City Council in an effort to get himself appointed."

"What makes her suspect that Burr was forced out?"

"She doesn't see how a little cold water would send him packing." Randy's lips tipped upwards at the corners. "On top of that, he refused to talk to her about it, which isn't like him. They're friends. They trust each other."

"Anything else?"

"Well . . ." Expectancy captured his face. "There was a monster of a man in the Maverick. He goes by the name of Tiny. He and Barbie used to know each other. In the biblical sense." At that, Randy's countenance changed from interested to stunned and slightly amused. "It was a long time ago. Before Barbie and Tom got married. When she still lived in the Twin Cities."

"And?"

"And, according to Barbie, Tiny asked a lot of questions about Boo-Boo. Enough to make her uncomfortable. I guess the guy's been around for a few weeks. He supposedly works road construction. Janice also knows him, but he swears—and she admits—not intimately, although she's done her utmost to rectify that." Randy shook his head as if having difficulty coming to terms with Janice's behavior. "Anyhow, Janice thinks the guy's 'fishy.' You may want to check him out."

"Thanks. I'll do that."

"Still, I think the President's your best bet, despite what he supposedly saw outside the bar."

I made a pile of my napkin scraps and reflected on the final piece of information I needed to relay. "Randy, there's one last thing." He dropped his head against his chest, feigning exhaustion. "Sheriff Halverson came by the café this morning to 'visit' me."

With those words, he raised his head, and it was plain to see he was back in serious cop mode. "What did he say exactly?"

"Nothing of consequence, though he did warn me to stay out of his investigation."

"We assumed he'd do that." He rubbed his hands together. "I can't wait until the election. Ed's going to whip his ass."

"He also implied any interference on my part could cause you problems at work."

"Let him try."

I rested my hand on his forearm. "Believe it or not, I didn't plan to get mixed up in this case. But Barbie begged me to go with her tonight." I abruptly bit my tongue. I couldn't blame Barbie. I'd wanted to help her. At least to some degree. "Wait. The truth is, I wasn't willing to turn my back on my friend."

"I know."

"What's more, I couldn't let the sheriff bully me. He's a jerk."

"Yeah, you may have mentioned that a time or two."

"And, in spite of myself, my curiosity got the best of me. It does that sometimes."

"I know that, too."

Chapter Fifteen

THE FOLLOWING MORNING, I woke to a quiet room and noisy thoughts. I was still puzzled as to why Randy had gone all Oprah on me the night before. I was also disappointed he went home despite my repeated requests to join me upstairs.

He had insisted our first time together be more than a quickie in a rented room above a café. But, because he was in desperate need of shut-eye, he said he couldn't offer me anything else. Consequently, I let him go, albeit reluctantly. Yeah, that's right. I whimpered just a little. What can I say? Whenever he was around, I was reduced to being a wanton woman in a J. Crew sweater set.

After brushing my teeth, I quickly showered and dressed, then snatched Otto from the bed and made tracks downstairs. Starved, I intended to grab some breakfast before Barbie arrived. We planned to check out the observation tower at Lake Bronson State Park. She also had her mind set on revisiting the Maverick Bar. With the images of the bathroom bullies seared in my brain, I was less than thrilled by that prospect and hoped we'd spend too long at the park and be forced to skip the bar.

Entering the café, I spied Margie at the prep table. Her elbows were propped on the metal surface, her head in her hands. In the background, on the jukebox, Don Henley and Dolly Parton were singing, "When I Stop Dreaming."

I started our conversation by saying, "No one in her right mind is up this early."

"True enough," she muttered without moving.

"Do I sense a hangover?"

She peeked at me through her splayed fingers. "I wish it were that simple."

I detoured from the table to let Otto out. Then, I settled him down with his breakfast near the back door. "Sounds ominous. What's wrong?"

She lowered her hands. "John and I had a colossal fight last night."

"And if the bags under your eyes are any indication, you were upset enough that you didn't sleep a wink."

"Ya got that right."

"Care to talk about it?"

She slurped some coffee. "We've known each other forever, so we've had our share of disagreements, but this was different."

"How so?" I moved to the refrigerator, convincing myself I'd be a better listener if I didn't have to contend with my noisy hunger pangs.

"Well, as ya might imagine, much of the conversation at the groom's dinner centered on Owen Bair's murder."

I pulled out a container of Heavenly Hash. "Makes sense." I scooped a large portion of it into a soup bowl. Since it contained cranberries and nuts, among other things, I decided it made for an acceptable breakfast.

"Everyone had a different theory as to what happened to 'im, but the discussion soon deteriorated into a shoutin' match between John and Burr Nelson. Uff-da, it got so bad I was afraid they might start throwin' punches. Vivian's husband, Vern, must of feared the same thing 'cause he got between 'em, though I don't know how in the world he expected to keep 'em apart bein' he only has that one arm and all."

After pouring myself a glass of orange juice, I returned to the table, my breakfast in hand. "Back up." I settled on my stool. "Burr Nelson was at the groom's dinner?"

"Well, yah, he's John's—or was John's—best man."

"Really?"

"Oh, I guess I forgot to tell ya that John's best friend, Pete, who was supposed to stand up for him, got called to Two Inlets yesterday. His uncle died, and it was up to him to make the funeral arrangements and such."

With both hands, she brought her cup to her lips only to lower it again. "Have ya ever been to Two Inlets? If not, you should go. It's not far from Itasca State Park, so ya can visit the source of the Mississippi River, then scoot on over. Now, there's not much there. Just a Catholic church, a saw mill, an old, one-room schoolhouse, and a little store that serves as a grocery, gas station, bar, and gift shop all in one. Still, it's worth the trip because of the grotto. Father Daley told me about it. And, sure enough, it's beautiful with all the stone work and statues and flowers and such. Even though I'm not Catholic, I liked it a whole lot, just like he said I would."

"Margie, what about Burr Nelson?"

"I'm gettin' to that." She folded her hands and settled them on the table. "Anyways, John asked Burr to fill in for Pete. And he agreed, which was awfully nice of 'im since it was such short notice and all." She grimaced. "But how did John repay 'im? He got into a shootin' match with the guy, that's how." She momentarily pressed her fingertips together. "Made me madder than a pianist forced to play in a marchin' band."

"What happened exactly?"

"I asked Vivian to give me a ride home. I wasn't about to go anywhere with that stubborn old coot, that's for dang sure. Certainly not after he yelled at me right there in the parking lot of Hasting's Landing."

"John yelled at you in public?"

Margie mumbled, "Well, I might of been the one doin' the yellin'." She regarded me sheepishly. "It was real embarrassin'. I'll never dare show my face in Drayton again, which is depressin' since I like the food at that restaurant almost as much as my own cookin'." She stopped for a second. "I can only pray that my bomber hat and the big collar on my parka kept me from bein' recognized."

"Margie, what exactly did John and Burr fight about?"

She swept a strand of fly-away hair away from her eyes. "Well, like a lota folks, Vivian and Vern claimed that Owen Bair was probably killed by some jilted husband or boyfriend. I guess they'd heard stories about him bein' a philanderer and all."

"But what does any of that have to do with John and Burr's argument?"

"Hold your horses. I'm gettin' to that." She slouched over the table. "Ya see, John was of a different opinion. He was convinced the President was somehow connected to the murder."

"I happen to agree."

"Barbie thinks you're basin' your suspicions on nothin' more than your dislike for the man."

"Well, I'm not." I picked up my spoon. "Not entirely, at any rate." I repeatedly turned the spoon over while doing the same with the thoughts in my head. "See, Randy said something last night that's bothered me ever since."

"What was that?"

I set the spoon back on the table. "The President reportedly saw Tom arguing with Boo-Boo in the parking lot of the Maverick Bar on Thursday afternoon, not long before Boo-Boo was found dead."

"And?"

"And, as I said, it bothers me. I can't help but wonder if he's lying."

"Because you don't like 'im."

"No, that's not it." Again, I snatched up my spoon. "I just get the feeling he's attempting to deflect blame from himself by casting aspersions on someone else. Someone too drunk to remember what truly happened."

"Well, John believes Burr might be able to offer some insight regardin' the whole thing."

"Really?"

"Yah. That's why he badgered 'im last night. He said he'd be willin' to bet that the murder, the wind farm project, and the President are somehow linked, and that Burr knows somethin' about it, even if he doesn't realize it."

"Doesn't realize it?"

"Remember, Burr's not real bright. I like the man, but he's so dumb blondes tell jokes about him." Yep, despite the seriousness of our conversation, Margie cracked wise. It was just her way.

"Anyways, to make a long story short, John and Burr ended up yellin' at each other." Margie plucked at her shirt. "And, before the night was over, Burr swore he wouldn't stand up for John if he were the last best man on the face of the earth."

"Oh, no, Margie. What are you going to do?"

"Vern agreed to step in, so that's not a problem." She wrinkled her nose. "Vivian said we should of asked him in the first place."

She continued. "My bigger concern is Burr and John. They've been friends forever. Heck, they both grew up around here and went to school together. I'd hate for some stupid argument to ruin all that."

"Most likely, they'll work it out. Men don't usually hold grudges."

"From your mouth to God's ear."

I reached across the table and patted Margie's hand. "Are you and John going to be okay?"

"Ya mean, is the weddin' still on?" She waved her hand dismissively. "Oh, for sure. But I definitely need to talk some things over with 'im beforehand." She glimpsed at her cell phone. It was lying next to her on the table. "He's called a dozen times already. I suppose I should call 'im back pretty soon." She rose from her stool, the metal legs screeching. "Fact is, I should go upstairs right now and do it. Then I might be able to get some sleep."

"Barbie's picking me up any minute. We're set to view the murder scene. But we can stay here if you—"

"Nah, ya two go on ahead. I'll be fine. Besides, this is between John and me."

"You don't need us here for moral support?"

"No. John and I just hafta get a few things ironed out before the weddin', that's all." She took a moment before adding, "I don't understand what got into him last night. Why'd he get so upset? That murder had nothin' to do with 'im."

           ℰ   ℭ

As Barbie and I drove to Lake Bronson State Park, I filled her in on Margie's problems, assuring her that Margie wanted to be left alone to sort things out with John. I also relayed some of what Randy and I had discussed the previous evening. Specifically, I pointed out that he and the other law enforcement officers didn't put much stock in the theory that Boo-Boo was killed because of his womanizing. The evidence just wasn't there. I also informed her that the President supposedly saw Tom arguing with Boo-Boo in the Maverick parking lot shortly before Boo-Boo's death, and that the police weren't convinced Tom was drunk at the time.

"Well, they're wrong," she stated. "He wasn't faking. He was drunk. I saw him when I got home after Margie's party." She unsnapped her quilted vest and fanned the front of her sweatshirt. Since the car wasn't warm by any means, she must have been struggling through a hot flash. "As for their belief the crime had nothing to do with Owen Bair's womanizing, it's still early in the investigation. They may change their minds."

She wiped her forehead with the sleeve of her sweatshirt. "Did anyone other than the President witness the argument?"

"Not that Randy mentioned, although the deputies were scheduled to meet with the sheriff this morning to brief one another, so he may know more later."

"Are you catching up with him again anytime soon?"

"We're supposed to eat lunch together at the bowling alley in Hallock." I saw my opening and took it. "That's why I doubt we'll have time to drop by the Maverick."

She studied me as if suspecting I had arranged my entire day around thwarting her proposed visit to the bar.

"I guess I can cancel, and we can go to the Maverick, instead. But, then, who knows when we'll learn the latest about the investigation?"

She frowned yet remained mum.

 ❧   ❦

WHEN WE REACHED THE PARK, we eased through the gate and twisted down the road leading to the observation tower and Visitors' Center. "Shoot!" I lifted my foot off the gas pedal. "I totally forgot about checking in at the ranger station to see if anyone there saw anything."

"Don't worry. I spoke to Ed about it yesterday, before I came to the café."

"And?"

"No one saw a thing. Although he did say Owen Bair's car was found parked outside the Visitor's Center. Do you remember seeing it?"

"Hmm. I noticed a car there, though I didn't recognize it. But since Boo-Boo leased new cars on a regular basis, I guess that's not all that odd."

"Well, according to Ed, nothing pertinent was found inside or anywhere around the vehicle."

"No important papers? Nothing like that?"

"Nope. Not on his body, either. The only paper on him was that reminder to meet with you."

As I proceeded down the road, I blew out a lungful of air to relieve the tension building in my chest. "What about other vehicles? Were any spotted around here near the time of the murder?"

"Nope. No one saw a thing beyond a snowmobiler or two, a hiker, and a patrol car from the sheriff's office. They keep tabs on the park."

"Maybe the deputy—"

"The sheriff was driving the patrol car, and he didn't see anything out of the ordinary."

We passed the observation tower, a stone and wood structure built through the WPA during the first half of the twentieth century. Yellow crime-scene tape stretched across the entrance and marked a rectangular area off to one side, where, apparently, Boo-Boo's body had been discovered. My stomach lurched at the sight, leading me to stare straight ahead as I steered the car farther down the road.

At the Visitors' Center, we inspected our surroundings without leaving my vehicle. While Boo-Boo's car was nowhere to be seen, crime-scene tape cordoned off another rectangular area, ostensibly where it had been parked. I wasn't positive, but I thought I recalled a Land Rover there.

I shivered at the notion that only days before Boo-Boo had been lying dead nearby while I had been waiting for him in approximately the same place where I now sat. I swallowed the nervous flutter in my throat. "B-Barbie? There's . . . really nothing to see here, is there?"

She answered with a shake of her head.

"Should we go then?"

Another shake of her head, and I immediately turned the car around and exited the parking lot.

Back at the observation tower, I pulled the car onto the shoulder and shoved the gear stick into park. "Well?"

Rather than responding, my friend twisted her head and gaped out the window. And, before long, I was doing the same thing, while an eerie silence swelled around us.

I wasn't sure what Barbie was focused on, but I was taken by the atmosphere. With the bare bushes and naked trees, the area felt abandoned and more than a little spooky. The howling wind sounded like someone sobbing in the observation tower. And while I knew no one was up there, my neck and arms prickled just the same.

Dropping my gaze, I noticed that the snow around the stone structure was trampled, and Styrofoam cups and pop cans littered the entire area. There wasn't a soul in sight, but we clearly weren't the first looky-loos to visit the scene of the crime. Not all that shocking, I suppose. After all, we were dealing with a murder, and murders were few and far between in these parts. Still, the realization that folks came out here to gawk made me squeamish.

A voice in my head warned against acting too indignant. *Emme, you know perfectly well you're here for far more than evidence. You, too, are curious. Like those other people, you had to see this place for yourself.*

That nagging voice was right, which really irked me. I didn't relish the idea of being lumped in with everyone who considered Boo-Boo's murder nothing more than a novelty. Regardless of how he had treated me, he deserved a little dignity in death, didn't he? "Barbie, now that we're here, I don't see any point in going inside."

Barbie appeared even less eager than I was to explore the tower. In light of the accusations swirling around about her husband and what he may have done up there, I understood her reluctance. "Yeah," she said, her eyes raw with an emotion I couldn't name, "the door's probably locked, anyhow."

"Yeah. Probably."

"And since no one's guarding it, the police obviously have their evidence already."

"Yep. They've even taken the car, so—"

She finished my sentence. "It's unlikely we'll find anything new."

"And I really don't need to see the ledge. You know how high it is."

She nodded, then we both fell silent again.

A full minute or more passed before I asked, "Should we leave?"

She cleared her throat. "Yeah, let's get out of here."

That's all I needed to hear. I shifted the car into gear, pulled back onto the road, and drove toward the gate.

At the same time, Barbie checked the time on her cell phone. "It's still early, but the Maverick should be open. Let's stop there and see what we can find out today."

Chapter Sixteen

I TRAILED BARBIE THROUGH the front door of the bar. She abruptly stopped, and I smacked right into her. "Hey, what gives?" I complained.

She whispered over her shoulder, "We must be living right."

Stepping up to the glossy, wood counter, she greeted the middle-aged man staring into his beer. "Hi, Burr."

She grabbed the stool next to him, while I sagged onto one on the opposite side of her. "We'll have whatever he's drinking." Barbie motioned toward Burr while talking to the bartender. "Give him a refill, too."

The bartender poured three mugs of beer, set them in front of us, and made change from the twenty-dollar bill Barbie handed him before meandering to the far end of the bar, where two old guys shook dice. The bar was otherwise empty. Not all that surprising given it wasn't yet eleven o'clock in the morning.

I sipped my beer, certain I'd never consumed alcohol so early in the day. Not even during my college years. After forcing down a couple more swallows, I returned my mug to the counter and swiveled in Burr's direction.

A cap advertising corn seed was perched on the guy's head, and, like most other men in the area, he wore a Carhartt jacket with a hooded sweatshirt under it. The exposed portion of his face was weathered from years in the sun. His eyes were small and planted in puffy cheeks. And his double chin rolled softly into his neck.

"So," Barbie began, her attention solely on him, "this whole murder thing is unbelievable, isn't it?"

"Yah," he said, glancing at her before looking back at his glass.

"Do you have any thoughts on it?"

I elbowed her. She was coming on too strong. She'd scare him off before we learned a thing.

"Nope," he muttered. "Don't know nothin'."

Barbie tasted her beer while undoubtedly debating her approach. With the police more or less dismissing her "irate husband or boyfriend theory," I was curious if she'd pursue a new tack.

I soon got my answer. "Burr, they think my Tom did it." She set her mug down. "He invested all our savings in that wind-farm project, and the police believe he killed Owen Bair because the guy wouldn't return the money." She inhaled a long, slow breath. "I forced the issue. I threatened to walk out on him if he didn't get the money back. That means, in a way, this mess is all my fault."

Burr fingered the condensation on the side of his mug. "No one really suspects Tom of murderin' anyone."

"The sheriff does."

"Well, he's a fool. And come fall, he'll be out of a job."

"That won't do Tom much good. He'll be in jail long before then."

With those words hanging over us like a dark cloud, we sat silently as the two old-timers at the end of the bar cussed over "unforgiving dice."

"Tom doesn't remember seeing Owen Bair," Barbie uttered after a while. "And even if he did see him, he was too drunk to hurt him."

Burr grunted. "He was pretty hammered when he came in here. That's for sure."

I don't know why, but Barbie chose to play dumb. "You saw him?"

"Oh, yah. He came on over and sat by me. And right off the bat, he asked about Stacy." He blinked at Barbie, his eyes damp with emotion. "I owe your husband a lot. If it weren't for him, my daughter wouldn't of gotten into that fancy music program down in Chicago, there. And it was real important that she did. Important she got outta here."

Barbie smiled. "Tom was more than happy to help. Stacy deserved it. She's a great kid and a fantastic singer and musician. You should be very proud of her."

With a simple nod, he indicated he was.

"I only wish someone would help my Tom like he helped your Stacy."

Burr didn't respond, although he shifted about, which said a lot as far as I was concerned.

"You're sure you didn't see or hear anything?"

Burr's face remained expressionless, but I was willing to bet there was plenty going on behind it. "We only talked about Stacy. That's all. And he was too drunk to say much."

Barbie gnawed on her lips, while presumably considering her next comment. "Well, maybe you remember something that happened else- where that might have a bearing on the murder. Something connected with the city, perhaps?"

One dice player swore at the other, but Burr remained silent until Barbie came right out and asked, "Burr, what's the real reason you left the city council?"

He answered as if offended. "Ya know gall-darn well it was 'cause of my health. Fallin' in the lake ended up bein' real hard on me." He failed to make eye contact.

"But you'd fallen in before." She gave him the once over. "And you seem healthy enough. On top of that, you loved being on the council."

"Well . . ."

"You did a lot of good for the city, Burr." She was relying on Jour- nalism 101—feeding the subject's ego to get him to open up.

"I tried."

"Then how could you give up your seat, knowing the President would take it?"

He glared. Evidently, she'd missed class the day tact was covered. "What makes ya so sure I knew?"

"Oh, come on, Burr. Very little happens in Kennedy without your knowledge."

Burr shoved his empty mug aside. "Even if I did know, that don't mean somethin' out of line was goin' on."

He reached for the beer Barbie had bought him and downed almost half of it, wiping his mouth with the back of his hand when he was done. "I just want everybody to leave me and my daughter be. Understand?" He stood, signaling an end to their conversation.

Barbie, however, wasn't quite ready to say goodbye. "That's all we want, too. Tom and I just want to be left alone to live our lives in peace. But that won't happen if the sheriff has his way."

"I . . . ahh . . . don't know what else I can tell ya."

"How about the truth? Why'd you resign?"

"Like I told the police, I got sick. End of story. As for this past Thursday, I was havin' a beer in here when your Tom came in. I'd never seen him in the place before. Heck, I'd never seen him take a drink before." He waited a beat. "Anyways, a while later, the President showed up. I'd never seen him in here, either. And that's all I know." Then, without so much as a glance in our direction, he left the bar.

"Shit!" Barbie hissed as soon as he was gone. "I was counting on guilting him into divulging something useful. But I went after him too hard."

"No, you did just fine."

"How can you say that? He didn't give us a thing. Not a single piece of information."

"Yes, he did."

Her face exemplified bewilderment. "What do you mean? He didn't reveal anything we didn't already know."

"Oh, I think he did." I pitched her way. "Barbie, ever since Randy shared with me that the President saw Tom confront Boo-Boo in the parking lot, I've had the feeling that some of the pieces to this puzzle just didn't fit. And now I know why."

"What are you talking about?"

"The President's lying!" I tried to keep my voice down. The bartender was only ten feet away, unpacking horns and glittery hats for the evening's festivities.

"I'm not following."

I took another swig of beer. It was starting to taste a whole lot better. "The President said he witnessed Tom and Boo-Boo arguing, although he went into the bar before they were finished. But, according to Burr, Tom came in here ahead of the President. That's what Janice told me, too. I just didn't recall it until Burr said the exact same thing a few minutes ago." I splayed my hands on the counter. "They both can't be mistaken, Barbie, which means the President's lying! And if he's lying, he must be guilty!"

₲   ‑

THE BARTENDER AMBLED OVER. "How about another beer?"

"No," Barbie replied rather curtly, as if upset by the interruption. "We're good."

The guy apparently failed to pick up on her tone because he remained where he was, thumping his hands against the bar to the rhythm of a silent tune. "Weren't you two in here last night?" he asked, his gaze volleying between us.

"Yeah." Barbie seemed miffed by his continued presence.

Nevertheless, he stayed where he was, now eyeballing her from the top of her head to where her breasts came awfully close to napping on the bar. Unlike the night before, though, those breasts were currently stuffed into a Minnesota Gophers sweatshirt. "I didn't recognize you at first," he told the golden gopher stenciled across her bust line. "You were wearing way different clothes."

At that exact moment, a light bulb evidently flashed in Barbie's head because her manner abruptly changed, all signs of irritation instantly disappearing. "Well, I didn't recall you right off the bat, either." With a wry smile and a sparkle in her eyes, she yanked on her sweatshirt until it was stretched tightly across her chest, inviting his full consideration of the gopher logo as well as her other assets.

Obviously, she had decided to go after information to support my theory about the President. And while I appreciated her efforts, as well as her enthusiasm, I didn't care for how she regularly resorted to using her body to get what she wanted, despite the fact that it worked more often than not.

"So, you were the bartender on Thursday afternoon, huh?" Her voice dripped with sweetness.

"Yep." A grin raised the tips of the guy's white mustache. "The police questioned me and everything." He puffed out his skinny chest, while his eyes danced with self-satisfaction. "Yeah," he sniffed as he hitched up his pants, channeling Barney Fife, "I guess they needed my help."

"Were you able to tell them anything they didn't already know?" She was baiting him. Again, Journalism 101.

"Oh, yeah, I had lots of information." He raked his fingers through his straggly white hair. "For instance, I gave them the lowdown on everybody in the bar that day."

"Oh, really? Care to share?"

"Now, why would I do that?"

"Because I'm the editor of the newspaper in Hallock, and I'm writing a story about what happened. I could use a source with lots of knowledge." I believe she winked at him.

"What's in it for me?" He lowered his gaze to her chest, eliciting in me a strong urge to slap him. I only managed to curb the impulse by downing another swig of beer.

"You'd get to see your name in print."

He crossed his arms, tipped against the bar, and sucked on his teeth, reminding me of a weasel, complete with tiny head and drooping shoulders. "The cops warned me not to discuss the case with anyone."

"Well, then," Barbie cooed, "I could refer to you as an anonymous source 'intimate' with the investigation." She actually made the word "intimate" sound dirty.

"I'd expect to be 'intimate' with more than the investigation, if you know what I mean."

I knew exactly what he meant, and it almost made me gag.

"Well, you scratch my back, and I'll scratch yours." Barbie wiggled her fingers, making me want to slap her, too.

"Oh, believe me, I could do far more than scratch."

Yuck! The cocktail of sexual innuendo being served by the two of them slushed around inside of me, mixing with my beer and my breakfast hash until I was pretty sure I'd upchuck the whole works.

Barbie seemed unaffected. "Well, then, reveal something I don't already know, and we'll see what we can do." She inhaled deeply, and I swear the man's eyes almost popped out of their sockets at the sight of her expanding chest.

"I . . . ahh," he stuttered before giving up and starting over. "Did you know that the dead guy was . . . ahh . . . in here just before he was murdered?"

Barbie yawned, as if bored. "Old news. Everyone knows that."

The guy tried harder. "The cops . . . they consider practically everyone in here that afternoon a suspect, including the guy who just left, Burr Nelson."

"Again. Old news. We knew that, too. That's why we were visiting with him."

The bartender squinted until his eyes were nothing but two tiny black specks. "Well, if you already know so much, why do you need me?"

"To make sure I haven't missed anything. So come on. Tell me exactly what happened in here that day."

"I don't think so." He was growing more confident the longer he talked. "Why don't you give up what you know, then I'll tell you if you're wrong. After that, we can negotiate a 'deal' for the right information." He winked, forcing me to swallow the sour taste in my mouth.

"Okay," Barbie replied on a sigh, "if that's how you want to do this. But it seems like we're wasting a lot of time that could be better spent some other way." Barbie tapped her right index finger against the guy's chest, and he shuddered. I did, too, but for a whole other reason, I'm sure.

"Well," Barbie began, "I understand that in addition to the victim and Burr Nelson, Janice Ferguson was in here, as was Tom Jenson, who was sloppy drunk."

The bartender stepped back. "Whoa! No one can blame me for that. Like I told the cops, he seemed loaded when he got here, so I only served him two beers. And he nursed them until I sent him on his way."

"Oh, I'm sure you handled the situation perfectly." Barbie purred the first syllable of that last word. Yep. She *purred*. "You strike me as that kind of guy."

More chest puffing on the part of the weasel. "Well, I do my best."

"I understand John Hanson, a man folks refer to as the President, also came in."

"Yeah, I'd never seen him before."

"And, lastly, there was a guy called Tiny." She angled her head. "How'd I do? I figured I'd start by identifying the people reportedly in here at the time since, as you said, they're all under suspicion."

A laugh burst from the guy's throat. "You got the names right. But I never said all of them were suspects."

"What?"

The weasel drew lazy circles on the back of Barbie's hand. His nails were overgrown, dirty, and utterly disgusting. "Well, well, well, looks as if I might know something you don't. That's gotta be worth a lot." He pursed his lips, and I choked on my beer.

Barbie yanked her hand away from him and slapped me on the back. "You okay?"

I wheezed, "I may never be okay again."

She almost smiled before returning her attention to the man behind the bar. "Who's not a suspect?"

He didn't answer.

"Oh, I get it," she said to his silence. "Burr Nelson had no relationship with the victim, and Janice Ferguson wasn't strong enough to shove him over the ledge of the observation tower, which means—"

"Stop!" He again hitched up his pants. "I don't know about any of that. But I do know Tiny's no suspect."

"Tiny?"

The bartender bent his head forward until his pointy nose was mere inches from my friend's face. "What do you say, girlie? Are you willing to pay to get some answers?" He licked his lips, and I cringed so hard my lungs almost cracked.

"Why isn't Tiny a suspect?" Barbie's voice had lost some of its luster. She must have been getting fed up with this creep, too.

"Because, honey, Tiny's . . . a . . . cop."

At that, Barbie jerked her head back and practically tumbled off her stool. "A cop?"

"Yeah, a cop," the bartender repeated. "He's been working undercover with the police up here for a few weeks now. They're investigating that wind-farm project. Heard of it?"

"Sure, I'm familiar with the wind farm. But, as for an investigation . . ." Her words died on her lips.

"They figure it's a scam," the weasel went on to explain. "A fraud scheme of some kind."

"How do you know?"

He eyed her suggestively. "As I said, I know lots of things. And some of them would make you howl at the moon."

That did it. I couldn't sit there any longer. The President was guilty. And while obtaining corroborating evidence would have been nice, I wasn't about to get sick while Barbie attempted to do it. "We've got to go." I stood up and grabbed one of her arms.

The bartender grabbed the other. "Wait a minute. She promised that if I—"

"She'll have to take care of you another time. Right now we need to leave. We . . . umm . . . have an appointment she forgot about."

"Oh, no, you don't." The weasel let her go but started around the bar. "I had a deal with her."

I hot-footed it toward the exit, dragging Barbie behind me. "And she'll make good on it." I pushed the door open, shielding my eyes from the sunlight reflecting off the snow. "It just won't be now." I propelled her outside in front of me.

"But, if not now, when?"

I didn't answer.

"How about tonight? It's New Year's Eve," he reminded us as the door slammed shut in his face. "I could give her free booze and a night she wouldn't soon forget."

"No matter how hard she tried," I muttered while pushing Barbie along the sidewalk. "Every time she downed a dose of penicillin, she'd be reminded of her time with you."

Chapter Seventeen

As we drove down the road, I yelled, "I'm going to kill him!"

Startled, Barbie bumped her head against the passenger window. "Kill who?"

"Whom."

"Whatever."

"Randy."

"Why would you kill him? I thought you'd be eager to tell him what you figured out about the President."

"That was before I discovered he knew Tiny was a cop, yet he didn't say a darn word about it to me. He just let me go on and on about how he should check him out."

Barbie twisted in my direction. "What?" Her indignation was evident. "You asked Randy to investigate Tiny?"

Oops. "Well . . . I only mentioned that Tiny was new around the bar, and he . . . asked you a lot about Tom."

My explanation didn't appease her. "Emme, I already explained why he likely did that." She pointed her finger at me. I saw it in my peripheral vision. "I don't appreciate you going behind my back. You're supposed to be my friend."

I took my eyes off the road long enough to remind her, "I am your friend. And because I'm your friend, I won't let anyone hurt you if I can help it."

She drilled holes in me until I blinked.

"Barbie, he's a cop, and he didn't tell you. Isn't that a bigger transgression than my asking Randy to ensure your safety?"

"I can hardly believe it."

"That I'd be concerned about your safety?"

"No. That Tiny's a police officer."

"You didn't have a clue?"

"None whatsoever. When I knew him back in the Twin Cities, he was a perpetual student who worked construction."

She went momentarily mute, but I practically heard her mind at work. "Was he only being nice to me last night to get information about Tom?"

"I'm not much of a sleuth, Barbie. But, from what I could tell, he was really into you."

"Now I'm doubly glad I didn't go home with him."

"He probably would have fessed up before anything . . . well, anything of consequence happened."

"Maybe."

At Hawkyards Corner, I turned left and headed west on Highway 175, my anger with Randy still bubbling. "Do you think he lied to me about the President, too?"

"Huh?"

The sun reflected off the snow-covered fields that lined the highway, and I pulled my visor down to guard against the glare. "Did Randy tell me the President heard Boo-Boo and Tom quarreling even though he knew it wasn't true?"

"Why on earth would he do that?"

"To keep me from getting more involved in the investigation."

"Emme, he made a point of promising he'd never keep you from doing what you felt was necessary for your job or your friends."

"Maybe he lied about that, too. Maybe he's lied about everything, including his feelings for me."

Barbie groaned. "He hasn't lied about his feelings, and he didn't lie about the President. He said the President 'told him' he saw Owen Bair and Tom arguing. That's completely different."

"No, it's not. You're just splitting hairs."

She leaned her head against the passenger window. "And you're feeling insecure, and it's putting you in a bad mood."

"I'm not in a bad mood."

"Yes, you are. I know a lousy mood when I see one. I've been in one myself for two months now."

"Well, you're wrong about me."

"Yep, you're in a bad mood, and you're itching for a fight."

"No, I'm not. I don't like fighting. Remember?"

She edged toward me. "You don't like when others fight. But when you get pissed or feel uncertain about things, you don't mind mixing it up."

"That's not true."

"Yes, it is. You also insist on getting in the last word."

"Do not."

"See?"

"What?"

℘   ☙

I LEFT BARBIE AT HER HOUSE. Following lunch with Randy, I'd pick her up, and we'd go back to Kennedy and get dressed for the wedding. Randy couldn't attend the ceremony because of the investigation, which was just fine with me since I was furious with him. As for Barbie's husband, he was with his AA sponsor, which was okay with her since she wasn't even sure she wanted to stay married to the guy. That left the two of us to be each other's dates.

After carefully driving through the rut-filled parking lot at the bowling alley, I found a spot for my car and hurried inside the corrugated metal building.

As soon as I walked through the door, my senses were assaulted by the crash of balls against pins, the smell of sweaty bowling shoes, and the sight of Randy Ryden sitting sideways in a booth, his back against the wall, his eyes trained on me. He was incredibly handsome in his neatly pressed uniform, and the only thing that kept me from jumping his bones right then and there was my intense desire to thrash him.

He stood as I crossed the room, everyone in the place gawking at me, the stranger meeting with the hunky deputy. He gave me a one-arm shoulder hug before ushering me into the bench seat across from him. "You hungry?" he asked.

"Not really." Normally, I was ready to eat at any time. But, at that particular moment, I couldn't get past my ire to locate my appetite.

"The food here is great."

"That may be . . ."

Apparently, my wrath was palpable. "What's wrong, Emme?"

A waitress set a glass of water in front of me. "You ready to order?"

I put on a happy face. "Do you have grilled chicken salad?"

"Yep."

"I'll have that. No dressing. No bread."

She turned to Randy. "Bring me a burger and fries, will ya, Allie?"

"Sure." Allie was clearly tickled that Randy knew her name, and it took all my restraint to keep from doing a major eye roll.

Once she left, he asked, "Why are you eating so light? It's not like you have to worry about your weight. You look great."

Much to the disappointment of my inner feminist, as well as my inner grouch, I smiled to myself. I couldn't help it. I enjoyed compliments. Even so, on the outside, I maintained my ice-cold manner.

"I've got the feeling I've done something wrong. Is that it, Emme?"

"Oh, you're good, Randy. You should be an investigator or something." Yep, I could do sarcasm with the best of them.

"Okay, out with it. What did I do?"

I bent across the table and presented him with a first-class scowl. "You lied to me. You knew Tiny was a cop, and you didn't tell me."

He eased against the back of his seat. "Is that all?"

"Is that all? What are you implying? Lying to me is all right?"

He angled toward me and whispered, "I didn't lie."

I responded in a similar fashion, although my whisper was tinged with a fair amount of hissing. "What would you call it, then?"

"Emme, I met Tiny for the first time this morning. At our meeting in the sheriff's office." I must have looked as if I didn't believe him because he attempted to convince me. "Remember, I've been out of the loop. I've been in North Dakota and the Twin Cities the last several weeks." He flicked his hand. "But that's beside the point. I couldn't have divulged his identity, anyhow."

"Why not? Even the bartender at the Maverick knows he's a cop."

Randy fidgeted, then mumbled, "He's not exactly a cop."

I glowered at him until he confessed, "He's a federal agent."

"A federal agent? Tiny's a federal agent?"

"And he's working undercover."

"What?" My voice was so shrill I was pretty sure it had reached "only dogs can hear this" range.

"Yeah, the feds have been investigating the wind-farm operation for a while now. They suspect it's a sham. Tiny was at our meeting because we're sharing information about the two cases—the murder and what they believe to be financial fraud."

"What's going on, Randy?"

"I'm not at liberty to say."

"Oh, no. Don't you dare brush me off like so much dust. Under the circumstances, I deserve to know—"

"No, you don't, Emme. Not really."

He must have seen my hurt because he began again. "I'm sorry. I realize Owen Bair meant a lot to you at one time, but . . ."

The waitress returned with our food, putting a temporary end to our argument.

As she set the plates in front of us, she asked, "Is there anything else I can get for you?" A glimpse at her and I discovered she was directing her inquiry to Randy alone.

"No, thank you," he replied, and she left, a grin stretched all the way across her face.

"Doesn't that get tiring?" I was more than a tad irritable.

"What?"

"Having women fall all over themselves around you. Doesn't it bug you?" It did me.

He lifted the top of his hamburger bun and squirted catsup across the patty. "They don't 'fall all over themselves.'"

"Yes, they do."

He put the bun back and lifted the burger with both hands. "They merely appreciate that I'm friendly." He managed a huge bite. "You should try it." He considered his sandwich. "Not my burger. Being friendly."

I stabbed some lettuce with my fork. "Oh, shut up."

He chuckled, and I chewed. Really hard. My poor lettuce didn't stand a chance.

After a few minutes of nursing my bruised ego, I set my fork on the corner of my plate. "Fine. I get it. You can't share the details of your investigation. Even though I'm one of the good guys. Even though I'd never blab. Even though that weasel of a bartender knows everything."

"He doesn't know 'everything.' In fact, he wasn't told all that much."

With a stop-sign hand, I kept him from saying anything else. "I get it. It bothers me. But I get it."

"That's mighty big of you." There was a twinkle in his eyes.

He tossed a couple French fries into his mouth and spoke around them. "Now, explain how you 'ound out 'bout the 'artender."

I huffed so hard I felt my nostrils flare. "Really? You expect me to come clean with you when you hardly told me a thing?"

"Yah, Emme, I do. Don't forget, I'm a law enforcement officer, and this is an official criminal investigation."

I glared at him for at least five seconds. "Okay, okay. I'll tell you." Even so, I was determined to take my time just to bug him. I chewed slowly and swallowed carefully. Then, I dabbed my lips with my napkin before returning it to my lap and smoothing out all the wrinkles. "Well," I said with a fair amount of pique after noting that he didn't appear the least bit annoyed by my stalling tactics, "Barbie and I stopped by the Maverick earlier today. It wasn't busy, so we visited with the guy."

"And the murder just happened to come up during the course of your conversation?"

"Yeah, something like that."

"He wasn't supposed to—"

"Oh, don't blame him. You know how persuasive Barbie can be."

Randy mumbled something about the bartender, cocaine, and potential jail time in the guy's future.

I didn't pursue it. I really didn't care. See, I was still stinging because of Randy's refusal to share particulars about Boo-Boo's murder case. What's more, I was nervous about confronting him about the President. And, on top of all that, he hadn't even offered me a single fry.

Chapter Eighteen

ECIDING TO GO AHEAD and rip the bandage off, so to speak, I blurted, "Randy, why weren't you honest with me about the President?"

"Huh?"

"He lied when he told you what he supposedly saw outside the bar the day Boo-Boo was killed."

Randy plated the remainder of his sandwich and wiped his mouth with his napkin. "How did you discover that?"

"It was something Janice said. And Burr mentioned the same thing this morning."

"Where did you see—"

"In the Maverick." I picked at my chicken. "According to him, the President came into the bar well after Tom. And that's when I remembered that Janice had said the same thing."

"Emme, I wasn't dishonest with you. I only discovered the real story myself this morning, at my meeting." He sipped his water, ice chunks clattering against the side of the glass. "I questioned the President at the bachelor party on Thursday night, and he was none too happy about it. He said he saw Tom and Owen Bair arguing in the parking lot next to the bar just before he went inside. But, beyond that, he wouldn't tell me much, although he did warn me he'd make sure the sheriff put me in my place. Said I had no business harassing innocent folks, while Tom Jenson ran around loose." He ran his fingers through his hair, leaving it sticking out here and there. "It wasn't until this morning's meeting that I learned Tom had actually entered the bar an hour or so ahead of the guy."

"Does that mean Tom was in the bar at the time of Boo-Boo's death?"

"It seems that way. Although we're working to get confirmation."

"And the President?"

"Like I said, he came in well after the time of the murder."

"So, as I thought, he's the murderer, and you arrested him, right?"

"No, but I did interview him again."

"And?"

"He stuck to his story. He insisted that anyone who said Tom was there ahead of him was mistaken."

"And you—"

"I'm sure he's lying. One person might get something like that wrong. But we have several people who witnessed Tom enter the place ahead of him."

I recalled that Tiny had left the bar via the back exit right after Tom had made his way through the front door. "Including a federal agent."

Randy bobbed his head. "Including a federal agent."

"Then why didn't you arrest the guy? Like I said, he's obviously the murderer."

"I'm not so sure, Emme. And, even if I were, I'd need—"

"More evidence."

He nodded.

"What are you looking for?" As soon as the words left my mouth, the answer became obvious. "Bruising. Did you check him for bruising?"

Randy exhaled wearily. "He was wearing a sleeveless tee-shirt when I got to his place this forenoon."

"And?"

"Nothing. No sign of a fight."

"Are you sure?"

"Yes, I'm sure. I do know what bruises look like."

"Well, you don't have to get huffy."

He sighed. "Sorry. I'm just frustrated by our lack of progress."

I sagged against the back of my seat. "I'm frustrated, too. I was positive the President was the killer." I raised my fingers, one by one, as I ticked off the points to back up my assertion. "First, he had a lot to lose financially because of the wind farm project. Second, he couldn't stand Boo-Boo. Third, he lied about what he saw outside the bar. Fourth, he lied about when he entered the bar. And, fifth, he's an ass."

"None of which automatically brands him a murderer. That's why it's never good to zero in on one person in the early stages of an investigation."

"I didn't zero . . ." No point in finishing. We both knew better.

"You have to follow the actual trail of evidence, Emme. See where it leads. And, in this instance, it doesn't appear to lead to the President."

Yep, no doubt about it, I was no good at investigative work, despite what Barbie said. "No, Randy, you need to follow the trail of evidence."

"Huh?"

"I'm done."

He scanned my plate. It was piled high with lettuce and slices of grilled chicken. "But you've hardly tasted your food."

"No. I mean I'm done messing around in Boo-Boo's murder. What's the point? This entire time I've been concentrating on the wrong guy. Obviously, I have no clue what I'm doing."

He squeezed my hand. "Don't be so hard on yourself."

I withdrew my hand. "I thought you'd be thrilled I was backing away from police business."

"Not if you're doing it because you think you're incompetent or something."

"Well, I am. I'm a rotten sleuth."

"I don't know about that. Besides, sometimes it's better to be lucky than good. And when it comes to solving murder cases, you're damn lucky."

I was pretty sure I'd just been dissed, but since I had no desire to debate my ineptness, I let it slide. "I'll just tick off people if I continue. I'll probably make the sheriff angry enough to throw me in jail or, quite possibly, cause you trouble on the job."

"Again, don't worry about the sheriff. He's not about to do anything to you, despite his threats. Remember, you have an alibi." He offered a sympathetic smile. "And since he can't let the murder go unresolved, he won't sideline any of his deputies, me included. He can't afford to. He needs all of us hard at work."

"And what about him, Randy? What exactly is he doing other than bugging me?"

"Not a hell of a lot. See, Sheriff Halverson's not much of an investigator. He claims he's more of a 'big picture guy.'"

"Which means?"

"Which means he's all talk. That's why he and the President get along so well. Though, as of right now, the sheriff seems to be avoiding his friend." The corners of his mouth twitched. "I guess the President phoned the office several times this morning, but the sheriff made excuses not to take any of the calls. From what Ed told me, the sheriff's afraid the President might cause him more harm than good this election cycle, so he's decided to keep his distance."

"But how can he cause trouble? According to you, he's innocent."

"Emme, he doesn't appear to be guilty of murder, but I never said he was 'innocent.'"

It took a few moments for me to figure out what he meant. "You're referring to that whole fraud thing, huh?"

"Yep." He fiddled with the edge of his plate. "Given the President's push to get that economic development money, the feds are certain he's involved."

"They don't believe he intended to use those funds on the wind farm project?"

"No. They think he either wanted the money for himself or to split with his co-conspirators."

"But, if that's the case, why would the sheriff avoid the guy? If he hung out with him, he could learn things from him. Things that could help solve the fraud case, if not the murder, too."

Randy twisted about. "Well . . ." He snatched the salt and pepper shakers and played around with them until he accidentally spilled salt all over what was left of his French fries.

"Randy, what aren't you telling me?" *All those fries are ruined!*

He pushed his plate away. "Well, the President's supposedly running around with the sheriff's wife. At least that's what Ed told me this morning."

While Randy wasn't much for gossip, I had no problem with it. Consequently, I edged to the front of my seat. "I didn't realize the sheriff was married."

"No one understands exactly how it happened. But, yeah, he's married."

I flashed him a look meant to encourage him to continue talking, and he did, although he was clearly uncomfortable. "A year ago or so the sheriff brought Mitzie back with him after his two-week vacation on Gull Lake. He introduced her as his bride, and that was that. She's from Brainerd. Her family has money. And, apparently, she covets the finer things in life."

"Then, what's she doing chasing after the President?"

He shook his head. "While you might consider him a pig, the President has lots of money and a fair amount of clout around here."

"Well, he gives me the heebee-jeebies."

Randy flashed a half smile in spite of himself. "Anyhow, from what I gather, Mitzie hasn't been happy since she got here. A couple months back she supposedly informed the sheriff she wouldn't help him finance his upcoming campaign because she wanted out of this 'hellhole.'"

"And, until then, she'd be hooking up with the President?" That made no sense, regardless of how unhappy she was.

"Emme, in spite of his best efforts, the President got nowhere with Margie's sister. Vivian made it clear she wasn't going to leave her husband for him. So, he supposedly moved on . . . to Mitzie."

Randy retrieved his wallet, yanked a five-dollar bill from it, and tucked it under his water glass. "Ready to go?" He grabbed his jacket, and we slid from our seats.

Along the way to the cash register, he stopped at the dessert counter. "Care for anything for the road? The desserts here are really good."

I silently debated buying one or two items to share with Barbie. But, when a voice in my head rightfully claimed I had no intention of sharing and another reminded me of how poorly I'd been eating, I grumbled, "No, I'll pass."

Right away I felt deprived and more than a little depressed. Then I remembered there was pie waiting for me at the café. Margie had insisted I try some, and the thought of doing so inspired a 180-degree change in my disposition. "There's Rhubarb Custard Pie at Hot Dish Heaven. If I have time before the wedding, I'll have a piece of that, instead. Margie claims it's the best."

"Who made it?"

"It's Rosemary Cooney's recipe."

Randy smacked his lips. "Margie's right. She makes great rhubarb pie. Save me a piece."

❧   ☙

Once he paid for lunch, Randy ushered me to my car and gave me a kiss that practically melted the snow at my feet. I accused him of employing fancy lip action for the sole purpose of bribing me into putting aside some pie for him. He didn't deny it. Though he did promise far more "lip action" in the near future. He even whispered a couple of his intentions, and they were so hot they almost started me on fire.

After he left, I had to sit in my car with the windows down in an attempt to cool off. When that didn't help, I resorted to blasting the air conditioner. But, before I got halfway across town, my teeth began to chatter, leading me to flip the air off and power up the windows. In the interest of self-preservation, I also shifted my thinking away from Randy's lip-related talents to my decision to forego probing any further into Boo-Boo's murder.

I assumed I'd have second thoughts, yet I didn't. Sure, uncovering the "who" and "why" behind my former boyfriend's death remained important to me, but I was fine with leaving the job to those trained in such matters. Really I was. See, I was tired of repeatedly running smack dab into my own incompetence. What's more, I didn't want to do anything that might land me in jail since incarceration would put a crimp in my actual plans.

Remember, I'd come to Kennedy for two purposes. One, I was here to attend Margie's wedding. And, two, I wanted to become more intimately familiar with Randy Ryden. Quite frankly, though, his latest kissing demonstration may have propelled that second reason into the number-one spot. Sorry, Margie.

Part III

Set It Out for Everyone to See

Chapter Nineteen

ᴀFTER I PICKED UP BARBIE, we headed back to Kennedy. Along the way, I told her about the shift in police thinking concerning her husband. But, rather than being thrilled, she got upset because no one in law enforcement had communicated with her directly. That, in turn, caused me to agonize over the possibility that I'd spoken prematurely. Yes, it was quite likely the police didn't want that information made known to anyone, Barbie included, until corroboration had been obtained.

I silently berated myself for my big mouth, then pledged to avoid similar missteps in the future, which meant keeping Tiny's true identity to myself. To justify that decision, I convinced myself that because Barbie already knew the guy was law enforcement, withholding his federal status wasn't all that terrible. Besides, skipping that discussion left more time for us to dish about the sheriff's wife and her probable affair with the President. Still, I felt guilty.

When we arrived at the Hot Dish Heaven Cafe, we found the Rhubarb Custard Pie near the back of the fridge, cut two sizeable wedges, and wolfed them down. It was only when we were done eating and drying our dishes that I mentioned I was stepping away from the murder investigation. I didn't dwell on it because I wanted to avoid Barbie's wrath. Nevertheless, she huffed her way upstairs, and I ended up worrying my bottom lip raw as I hid two slices of pie in the refrigerator's crisper, behind a head of lettuce.

"I can't believe you're not going to help me find the killer." That was Barbie's welcome as I entered my room. And she continued to grouse as she painstakingly inched her Spanx over her fleshy legs and wide hips. "The man was your first love for—"

"Don't start with that again. It won't work twice." I donned my dress before sitting on the edge of the bed and slipping into my new high heels. "I simply see no point in the two of us doing any more digging. It's not as if we've uncovered anything new. The police were already aware of everything we found."

"Well, I can't stand by while my husband gets railroaded."

"Like I told you, the police know the President lied. They're pretty sure Tom was in the bar when Owen Bair was murdered. They just have to confirm it. So let's back off and let them do their job." I could hardly believe I was advocating less interference. "We also need to keep quiet about all this for the time being."

I rose and stared into the full-length mirror on the back of the bedroom door, glad for the distraction my image provided.

Starting at my feet, I took in everything. My pumps were silver with a four-inch heel. My slip of a dress was forest-green, short, and silky. And I was accessorizing with silver earrings that nearly brushed my shoulders and a number of chains that draped around my neck and fell across my chest. Like my jewelry, the clip I snapped into my hair was silver and sparkly and held my partial up-do, which left a flood of red curls to spill over my shoulders and cascade down my back.

Normally, my dress would have been considered too racy for a wedding, but since it was also New Year's Eve, it was "perfectly fine" in Barbie's opinion. True, I couldn't trust her judgment alone, so I'd asked Margie about it the day before, and she'd been of the same opinion.

After we finished dressing and were done with our hair, Barbie helped me with my makeup. And, believe it or not, she demonstrated a great deal of restraint, even though she remained irked at me and could have done major cosmetic damage if so inclined. Granted, she heavily painted my lips and shadowed and lined my eyes, but I didn't look ridiculous. To the contrary. She was right. I had my "sexy on."

Speaking of Barbie, she wore a sleeveless, leopard-print number that was two sizes too small and four inches too short. Her hair was spiked, as usual, and she had on the same knee-high boots from the previous night. Now, however, she also sported a studded dog collar. One Otto appeared to regard with envy. I considered asking her to give it to my four-legged buddy or, in the alternative, leave it behind for the evening but ultimately decided I was in no position to make any requests.

With a glimpse at the clock on the nightstand, I noted we were running late. I grabbed the faux rabbit wrap she'd loaned me, while she claimed her black leather jacket. Then, together, we ran downstairs, outside, and across the snow-covered parking lot, to my car. Five minutes later we were at the church, where we snagged seats in the back.

SO   CR

THE CHURCH WAS PACKED and smelled of furniture polish, evergreens, and winter air. The organist softly played an assortment of Christmas music, as the folks around us exchanged their favorite winter-time greeting, "Eh, cold enough for ya?"

While I didn't recognize many of the people gathered for the ceremony, I did spot Margie's niece, Little Val, and her husband, Wally. They were in the front row on the side opposite us. The Precious Moments bridegroom was nowhere to be seen, which I considered a good sign for their marriage, even if Wally was wrangling with another guy—the couple's two-month-old son, Brian. Next to them sat Margie's nutty aunts, Henrietta and Hester, and alongside them were Margie's nephews, Buddy and Buford Johnson.

My heart admittedly fluttered at the sight of Buddy, regardless that my view was limited to the back of his head. Yes, I'd probably always be smitten with the guy. Still, I'd never get involved with him, despite coming awfully close to doing just that a couple months back. Thankfully, I'd stopped myself in the nick of time.

Without question, Buddy Johnson was wickedly handsome and devilishly charming. But, he also was a "player." He enjoyed "flings," and I was in search of something more. Something I sensed I could very well find with Randy Ryden. My instincts told me we had a chance at real happiness together. Maybe long-term happiness. Nonetheless, Buddy was enticing.

The organist began the traditional wedding march, and Reverend Pearson started up the aisle, accompanied by Margie's friend Father Daley. The two of them were followed by Vern and Vivian, Vern in a black suit, white shirt, and gold tie, and Vivian in a long, fitted dress of gold lamé. Adhering to the belief that if a little is good, a lot is way better, Vivian had unwittingly painted her face to resemble a character in a Stephen King novel. Fortunately, Margie and John soon came into view, giving everyone an excuse to redirect their focus.

I had never seen John in anything but a baseball cap, plaid work shirt, and overalls or jeans, and I was astounded at how smart he looked in his high-end black suit, white silk shirt, and lavender tie. I was also amazed by his hair. Because he usually wore a cap, I never even realized he had hair. Yet, he did. It was light in color and buzzed within a quarter inch of his head, but it was there, right above his malleable forehead.

While the skin around the bottom of his face was tan and ruddy, his forehead, which seldom got any sun because of his cap, resembled raw bread dough. The other farmers in the church boasted similar looks. And, collectively, they brought to mind giant pans of brown-and-serve rolls, waiting for the oven.

Speaking of rolls, John still carried one around his middle, though it was far smaller than it had been. "He went on a diet," Barbie whispered, as if reading my mind. "He wasn't about to go to Costa Rica fat."

As for Margie, she wasn't the least bit heavy, regardless of Vivian's inferences during the bridal shower. Her dress fit amazingly well. Her cut-glass jewelry was understated yet elegant. And her lightly streaked hair fell in a soft wave, ending just a couple inches below her chin, perfectly framing her face. Her eyes and lips were done up just right, too. Apparently, she had been far more attentive than I was when Barbie was imparting makeup tips.

"Isn't she pretty?" Barbie asked, her voice filled with emotion.

"Pretty, hell," I whispered, invoking Margie's persona, "she took pretty out back and smacked it around until it cried."

At that, we both covered our mouths to stifle our giggles.

☙　❧

THE WEDDING CEREMONY was short but sweet. Little Val and her husband, Wally, sang "Grow Old with Me," a song made famous by Mary Chapin Carpenter, and Father Daley provided a brief sermon, peppered with his own brand of humor.

"When Margie and John first announced their engagement," he began, his Irish voice booming, "I asked them, 'What in the world took you so long? You've known each other most of your lives. Why'd you wait until now to marry?' And John looked to Margie, who quipped, 'Well, Father, what do ya want? Speed or accuracy?'"

The congregation murmured their amusement before the priest went on to emphasize that the bonds of matrimony were sacred and should never be broken. He warned Margie and John that their marriage, like all marriages, would be difficult on occasion. "You'll have your ups and downs, but don't give up on God or each other." He braced his hands against the sides of the lectern and scanned the folks sitting in the pews in front of him before returning his attention to the bride and groom. "Considering your age, however, you'll likely face far fewer problems than young married couples."

He then grinned as something evidently came to mind. "During our counseling session, I asked John what he thought might be the easiest part about being a middle-aged, first-time bridegroom, and following much thought, he said, 'Very little peer pressure, Father. Very little peer pressure.'"

More tittering as Father Daley took his seat, and Reverend Pearson came forward to lead Margie and John in their vows. The pair pivoted toward each other, clasped their hands together, and, with trembling voices, promised to love one another and be faithful in good times and in bad, for better or worse, for richer or poorer, in sickness and in health, until death.

Out of the corner of my eye, I caught a glimpse of Barbie. She was wiping away tears. Considering all the problems she faced, I doubted they were "tears of joy." And while I felt sorry for her, I had no idea how to help her short of hunting down a killer, and since I had decided against that, I averted my gaze by refocusing on Margie. She was the happiest I'd ever seen her, and I couldn't help but smile, even though my joy was fleeting because of the heartsick friend sitting next to me.

₭   ℞

AT THE WEDDING DINNER, Barbie and I polished off a bottle of wine before we finished our food. It wasn't difficult to do. We were riding a roller coaster of emotions, and our minds were muddled with everything that had occurred over the last several days. Moreover, the wine, You Betcha Blush, was light and fruity and complemented everything on our plates, from the walleye and pork to the Rhubarb Salad and the Cajun Chicken and Rice Hot Dish.

You Betcha Blush was one of three wines served, the other two being Wobegon White and Hot Dish Red. All were award winners produced at the Carlos Creek Winery, near Alexandria, Minnesota, where they knew how to make great wine.

As Barbie opened a second bottle, Buddy's twin brother, Buford, rose from his chair. "Hey, everybody," he shouted over the hum of conversation and the clanging of silverware. "I'd like to start off the night by saluting John Deere, the man my aunt chose to marry. Please join me by raising your glass to John, a great guy, even if he's so old that when he heard he'd get 'a little action' on his honeymoon, he decided he could leave his Metamucil at home."

While folks chuckled, Buddy stood to offer the second toast. "Again," he muttered, plainly less comfortable than his brother at playing the role of jokester, "to John, even if he's so old that to him, 'an all-nighter' means he never had to get up to go to the bathroom." More chuckles from everyone, including John and Margie.

Little Val's husband, Wally, was next to speak. "John, we tease you because we care about you. And we know you and Margie will have a great life together. We're sure of that because you're a kind man. And you're really smart. You graduated from MIT or some such college, right?" He didn't wait for confirmation. "And, as an intelligent guy, you're aware of your limitations, which is a good thing, though Margie may be hankering for a little more effort on your part." He shuffled his feet. "See, the other day she complained to Little Val and me that when she recently asked you to carry her upstairs and make love to her, you answered, 'Now, Honey, you know I can't do both.'" That earned both gasps and giggles, with Margie's up-tight sister, Vivian, beginning and ending with the former.

As the best man, Vivian's husband, Vern, was the last to offer a toast. "It's not a true toast," he clarified as he scraped back his chair and took to his feet. "And it's not about marriage per se." With his one hand, he rubbed the stub of his missing arm, something he routinely did when nervous. "It's more of a joke. An Ole and Lena joke to be exact."

Right away the crowd hooted. These folks loved their Ole and Lena jokes.

"Anyways," Vern began as Vivian watched him with a critical eye, "da day after Ole passed away, Lena realized she couldn't go on without 'im. Yah, dat's right. She wanted to die, too, but she hated pain and knew if she was gonna kill herself, she had to do it fast. So she called da doctor and asked him exactly where her heart was located, and he informed her dat it was directly beneath her left breast. Well, den, Lena hung up da phone, grabbed a butcher knife, and stabbed herself in dat very spot. But, wouldn't ya know, a few minutes later Sven found her and rushed her to da hospital, where she was admitted for a knife wound—to her left knee."

Everyone howled, partly because the joke was funny, but mostly, I believe, because Vivian appeared ready to kill her husband, then die of humiliation herself. For his part, the usually docile Vern ignored his wife and soaked up all the attention, which eased only after folks began tapping their silverware against their wine glasses. As customary, John and Margie then rose and kissed, prompting a hearty round of applause and more than a little blushing by the bride and groom.

Once the applause died down, John cleared his throat in a discernible attempt to regain his composure. And, after accomplishing that, he addressed his guests in a Scandinavian accent so strong I had to listen carefully to understand him. "Tank ya all for comin'," he said. "Dis is da happiest day of my life, and havin' all of ya here means an awful lot to da both of us, don't ya know." He put his arm around Margie's waist.

"Anyways . . ." He self-consciously pulled his arm back and stuffed his hands into the pockets of his trousers. "Da other day, when Margie and I visited with Father Daley, he wanted to know why it had taken me so long to settle down. 'Didn't ya ever find any girls ya wanted to marry before now?' he asked. And I answered, 'Well, for sure, I did, Father. But whenever I took one of dem home to meet my parents, my mother disliked her.' With his brow furrowed, Father Daley den asked, 'Why didn't ya search for girls just like your ma, den?' And I had to tell 'im, "I did that, too, Father. But whenever I took one of dem home, my dad hated her guts.'"

Everyone guffawed until John hushed them by tamping down his hands. "Well, I'm . . . I'm glad I waited 'til now. I'm glad," he repeated, his voice a raspy whisper, his gleaming eyes steady on his new wife, "because I just married da best woman around."

As you might expect, that led to a collective "awww" from the guests, as well as another kiss from Margie.

℘ ℘

A WHILE LATER THE VFW's middle room was transformed into a dance hall that smelled of stale beer and fried fish and sounded like a carnival, with children screeching and musicians tuning their instruments.

The band was unknown to me, but Barbie was acquainted with a few of the members and informed me they hailed from Lancaster. "Several have won Kick'n Up Kountry karaoke awards," she explained. "And a couple have even been featured on national television."

Before I had a chance to ask what Kick'n Up Kountry was, the leader of the band introduced its first song, "I Don't Dance," and Margie and John took the floor amid cheers and whistles.

Barbie whispered to me, "Are you truly done?"

"Done?" My eyes were glued on Margie and John. Happiness radiated from them. It was a sight to behold, and I wished that Randy was there to share it with me.

"Done with the case."

I vacillated between feeling shame and frustration. Barbie was my dear friend, and I didn't want to let her down. But, at the same time, she refused to accept that I was weary of being threatened, second-guessed, or just plain wrong at virtually every juncture of this investigation. "I don't see what good it would do, that's all. Now that I know the President didn't kill Boo-Boo, I'm clueless about how to move forward."

With a ticked-off look on her face, she swung her attention away from me and toward the bar, then uttered, "Well, speak of the devil."

From our table along the west wall of the middle room, I could see most of the bar area, and even though the space was illuminated by nothing more than neon beer advertisements and the light above the pool table,

I had no trouble picking out the object of her interest. It was the President. He was bellied up at the far end of the bar, basking in the sickly yellow glow of a Miller Beer sign.

The last time I'd seen him, he was much thinner. But that was then. Now he was extremely heavy, reminding me of Porky Pig, only way uglier and sleazier. Come to think of it, the comparison was totally unfair to the pig.

The guy slurped a mixed drink as he conversed with a couple men, one bald and scrawny, the other big with facial features so squished together there was barely room for his bulbous nose between his mouth and beady eyes. Bald-and-Scrawny didn't contribute to the conversation, but Mr. Beady Eyes spoke whenever he wasn't picking that big, red nose of his.

"Is that Booger Carlson?" I asked. What were the chances there'd be more than one public nose picker in a town this small?

"Yeah, that's Booger. But how did you—" She stopped. There was no need to go on. The scene spoke for itself.

"Is that his cousin with him?"

"Yep. That's Delmont. Those two usually travel in tandem."

"So, what do you make of them?"

She peered at me. "I thought you didn't care."

Chapter Twenty

$\mathcal{I}$ EXPELLED A BIG PUFF OF AIR, letting it hiss as it passed between my lips. "I never said I didn't care, Barbie." With the reception and dinner over, I had switched to beer and took a long pull from my bottle. "But we can take up another topic of conversation if you want. It doesn't really matter."

My tone suggested indifference, and Barbie took notice. "No, that's fine. Let's talk about them."

I intended to stall to prove I really didn't care one way or another, but since that wasn't true, only a second or two lapsed before I asked, "Do you think they're aware of the fraud investigation?"

Barbie stared at the three men, as if she'd learn more by boring holes in them and peeking around inside. "If they are, I'm sure the President's convinced it won't lead anywhere. I expect he's confident he can outsmart everyone."

When the bride and groom's dance ended, Vern and Vivian joined them on the floor, and the band started playing, "When I'm Sixty-Four." Being a huge dance fan, not to mention a devotee of the Beatles, I soon found myself dividing my attention between the President and his minions and the two couples undulating to the unusual wedding song.

I was impressed by John and Margie's moves. Granted, they wouldn't be featured on *Dancing with the Stars* anytime soon, but they clearly knew what they were doing, making me speculate they had taken dance lessons recently. Yet, despite their possible training, they were no match for Vivian and Vern, whose rhythm and agility truly amazed me.

Vern only had one arm. Still, he deftly guided his wife through a variety of spins and turns. He demonstrated great control and authority, causing me to wonder if the happiness he exuded was from his love for dancing alone, or if it had something to do with being in charge when out on the dance floor. From what I knew of the couple, that normally wasn't the case.

"Don't look now," Barbie muttered, triggering my eyes to snap right back to her. She bobbed her head toward the bar.

"Well, I'll be." It was one of Margie's favorite phrases, and it seemed appropriate for the occasion. Burr Nelson, you see, now stood alongside the President.

"You still don't care what those guys are up to?"

Using my thumbnail, I absentmindedly scraped at the label on my beer bottle. "I already admitted to being curious. But, based on what Randy told me at lunch, the President isn't a suspect in Boo-Boo's murder. And, as for the others—"

Barbie didn't let me finish. "You said the police suspect the President's mixed up in that fraud scheme, which means Booger and Delmont are probably involved, too." She paused. "Not Burr, though. He has no connection to the wind-farm project. None whatsoever."

"How can you be positive of that?"

She continued to concentrate on the quartette at the bar. "When you were at lunch, I phoned deputies Dumb and Dumber. They told me Burr didn't invest a dime in that venture. They also shared a number of other noteworthy tidbits."

I waited, and when she didn't elaborate, I prodded, "Such as?"

My words jarred her from her apparent reverie. "Sorry. Guess I was preoccupied." She tapped her index finger against her lips. "What in the world is Burr doing with those three rejects?"

଼ୠ ଔ

"HEY!" SHOUTED A MAN in very close proximity to us. "Come on, you two. It's time to dance!"

With a start, I whipped around to find Margie's nephew Buford grinning at me.

After catching my breath, I hollered over the music, "It's great to see you, Buford!"

"Right back at ya, Red." He chucked me under my chin. "Looking mighty festive in that outfit of yours." He waggled his eyebrows.

I felt my grin stretch coat-hanger wide. "You're quite the looker yourself." It was something I never imagined saying to the guy. When I'd seen him previously, his face was scarred, and his brows and lashes were all but missing due to an alcohol-related grilling accident. His face had healed nicely. Now, he even sported thick, dark eyebrows.

"Come on, ladies, let's shake a leg." He lifted his leg, shimmied, and fell backwards, right into his twin brother.

I did a double take at the sight of Buddy. As I mentioned earlier, he was incredibly handsome. On that particular night, he wore form-fitting jeans, a tweed sport coat, and a white, open-collar, button-down shirt that played nicely against his tan skin. His coloring was thanks to his mother, a Latina known locally as Lena. The twinkle in his whiskey-colored eyes, signaling his relaxed attitude toward life in general and his brother in particular, was of his own making.

He planted Buford back on his own two feet and extended his hand, while his gaze wandered over me in an assessing manner. "How about it, Emme? Will you dance with me?"

I measured my response. The music was upbeat. I loved to dance. And I knew the twins, like me, were extremely light on their feet, in spite of Buford's present demonstration to the contrary. Furthermore, any heterosexual woman who'd pass up a few minutes in Buddy Johnson's arms was a fool. Did I mention he was sexy?

My own gaze traveled from his soulful eyes to his full, sensual lips. They were slanted in a half smile that oozed confidence, triggering my mouth to go dry and my pulse to pound wantonly in my throat. That's when I decided it was imperative I remain more than an arm's length away. "No . . . umm . . . thank you, Buddy. I'm not up to dancing tonight."

Buford clasped Barbie's hand. "You don't care if the two of us give it a whirl, do you?" I guess it was a rhetorical question because, without waiting for an answer, he towed her in the direction of the dance floor, leaving Buddy and me behind to stare at each other awkwardly. At least, I felt awkward.

"Why won't you dance with me, Emme?"

Unprepared for any verbal jousting, I stuck to my story. "I'm just not up to it."

He pulled out a chair and sat down, motioning to a waitress to bring him a beer. "Did Dudley Do-Right order you to stay away from me?"

I shot him dagger eyes. "I don't take orders from anyone except my editor at the paper, and, according to him, I'm not particularly good at that."

"Well, then?"

I plopped down on my chair after ensuring there was at least one empty seat between us. "Don't be a jerk, Buddy. I wouldn't appreciate Randy dancing with someone he had been . . . drawn to, and—"

He broke in. "You were 'drawn' to me?"

"Well . . ."

He left me to struggle, a smug expression overtaking his features.

His manner infuriated me, and that anger loosened the stranglehold on my tongue and jacked up my attitude. "Yes, Buddy, I'll admit I was drawn to you. But, thankfully, I came to my senses before anything serious happened between us. That would have been a monumental mistake! An utter disaster! An epic calamity!"

He reared back and laughed. "I suppose I deserved that."

The waitress returned with his beer. Buddy handed her a few bills, urged her to keep the change, then savored a long drink. "Should I leave? Or can I stay and visit for a while?"

"Umm," I hummed while the voices in my head argued over how best to respond. Because the music was too loud to hear what they decided, I was forced to make a unilateral decision. "You can stay. But only if you're nice."

He winked. "I can be nice, Emme. You just never gave me the opportunity to show you how—"

"See! There you go."

He chuckled. "Sorry. I couldn't help myself. You set me up perfectly. But that's it. I'm done. No more suggestive remarks."

I passed him a disbelieving glance before challenging him further. "No more cracks about Randy, either."

He flashed me the Boy Scout sign. "I promise."

"I like him, Buddy."

"I understand."

"A lot."

He combed his fingers through his dark, wavy hair. "Okay, Okay. Enough said, Emme."

With a sense of satisfaction, I sipped my beer. I had established ground rules! My therapist would be impressed.

"How are you?" he then asked to restart our conversation.

I followed my index finger as it traced a line of moisture down the side of my bottle. Buddy was easy to talk to, but I quickly determined it would be best to keep our visit on a superficial level. "I'm fine. Just fine."

He leaned forward. "No point in pretending, Emme. I know the guy who got murdered at the park was your old boyfriend."

My jaw dropped. "Does everyone—"

"It's a small town. Everyone knows everyone else's business, yours included."

"I could never get used to that."

A smile slowly split his face. "Sometimes it's a good thing."

I offered a noncommittal shrug. "Then, I suppose you also know that Barbie's husband's been questioned?"

"Yep."

"Barbie's positive he's innocent, and—"

"Of course she is. And I hope she's right. I've always liked Tom. Even if he's a bit different." The twinkle in his eyes began working overtime. "He's not from around here, you know." He added without skipping a beat, "He grew up in California, of all places."

I positioned my hands over my heart and feigned shock. "Oh, no!"

A chuckle slid from his throat.

I sipped my beer and listened to the band's take on a country classic. "Anyhow," I said following the song's refrain about a good-hearted woman loving a good-timing man, "Barbie's of the mind that he was too drunk to do anyone true harm, especially an athlete like Boo-Boo. And the police—"

"Whoa! Back up. Boo-Boo?"

I cringed. "That was Owen's nickname. His last name was Bair. He was rather small. And when he played professional ball, he hung around with a guy known as Yogi, as in the old Jellystone Park cartoons." My words struck me. "Hey! You must have heard of him. He played for the Twins several seasons and—"

"I've never followed baseball. I'm more of a—"

It was my turn to interrupt. "Hockey fan. I know. But there are other sports."

"They pale by comparison. And based on what the folks around here told me today, your Boo-Boo wasn't really all that good, so it's not that surprising I'm not familiar with him."

"He wasn't mine," I mumbled.

"What?"

"Nothing." What was the point?

"So, Emme, if Tom didn't kill the guy, who did?"

I knitted my brow.

"Oh, come on. I'm sure you and Barbie have done some reconnaissance. What did you discover? What's the real story?"

"How should I know?" I practically had to shout to be heard over the noise currently emanating from the dance floor. I didn't spot Buford or Barbie out there, but almost everyone else in the place was stomping and clapping their way through the chicken dance. "Remember, I work for the newspaper's Food section. So I'd only be included in the investigation if the crime had been committed with a bundt cake."

"Yeah, right. Like you and Barbie wait to be invited into police business."

"Believe it or not, I'm staying away from murder investigations. Far, far away."

"That doesn't sound like you."

"It's the new me."

"In that case, I'm glad I got in trouble before you turned over this new leaf."

He was referring to events of a few months back, when I'd inadvertently helped him out of a jam. "I'm happy everything worked out for you."

He reached across the table and molded his hand over mine. "Mostly because of you, Emme. And, for that, I'm forever in your debt."

Embarrassed by what sounded like genuine gratitude, I reclaimed my hand and twisted my torso to watch the action on the dance floor. I had a hard time maintaining indifference toward Buddy Johnson when he was cocky. It was darn near impossible when he was sincere.

As soon as the chicken dance ended, the band eased into a song perfect for a country swing, and Buford and Barbie resumed their places in the middle of the floor and at the center of attention. But, rather than performing a traditional swing dance, they proceeded to do some moves that, at a minimum, were three steps beyond risqué.

"Oh, my God," I muttered at the sight.

While pleased that Barbie had finally left her worries behind, I was more than a little taken aback by her approach for getting into the festive spirit. You see, she was twerking against Buford's crotch, while he was tugging on her dog collar and thrusting his pelvis in her direction.

Glancing around the room, I saw mothers shield their children's eyes, while fathers openly gawked. As for me, I turned back to Buddy, assuring myself that, in spite of my convoluted feelings for the guy, dealing with him was far less dangerous than watching Buford and Barbie.

I drank my beer and tried not to swallow my tongue. "So what were we discussing?" My face was burning.

"Murder." He flashed me a smile full of awareness but didn't otherwise acknowledge my flustered state. He truly was attempting to be kind. "I asked for your thoughts about your Boo-Boo's death."

In an effort to cool down, I finished off my beer. "Well . . . at first, some folks figured he was murdered by a jealous husband or boyfriend." Because my cheeks remained hot enough to fry eggs, I pressed the cool bottle against each of them, one after the other. "See, Boo-Boo was a womanizer."

Buddy mugged. "If that's why he got killed, maybe I better watch my own back. Until the culprit's caught, in any case." To a nearby waitress, he signaled for two more beers.

"Now, though," I continued, determined to re-establish my equilibrium, "there's speculation that the crime may be connected to Boo-Boo's job with that wind farm venture. Are you familiar with it?"

Fiddling with his empty bottle, he merely replied, "Yeah, I am."

"Well, that particular scenario makes the most sense to me."

More fiddling. "Why is that?"

I glanced over my shoulder. The band had abruptly ended the swing dance, opting, instead, for the Macarena, which prompted people of all ages to flood the dance floor, thankfully putting a stop to Barbie and Buford's exhibition.

I expelled a pent-up breath. And when I turned back to Buddy, I felt more relaxed, and my words flowed with ease. "Initially, it was only because of something Boo-Boo said to me on the phone. But this afternoon I learned the wind farm operation is being investigated by the feds. They suspect it's a fraud scheme of some kind." I inclined my head in the direction of the bar, where Burr Nelson was sidled up alongside the President, Booger Carlson, and Delmont. "From what I gather, the President's presumed to be a part of it."

As soon as I put a period on that last sentence, I wished all my words back. Once again I'd divulged information that Randy may have intended for my ears only. "That's just between you and me," I added in an effort to do some damage control. "I don't believe that whole fed thing is common knowledge."

He nodded, and I wondered if the glint in his eyes signaled his recognition of my blunder.

"As for those other three guys," I quickly said before he could comment one way or another, "I have no ideas."

"That sounds about right."

"That I have no ideas?"

"No. That if there's a scam underway, the President's in the thick of it."

"Oh." I picked imaginary lint off the bodice of my dress. "What about the murder, Buddy? Do you think the President was involved in that?" Admittedly, I was like a dog with a bone. I couldn't let go of the notion that the President was somehow responsible for Boo-Boo's death, notwithstanding the fact that he failed to sport any tale-tell bruises.

"I have no thoughts about the murder, Emme."

"But surely—"

"Nope. No thoughts whatsoever. And don't call me Shirley."

"Very funny."

I slouched in my chair. "For what it's worth, the police don't believe he was responsible. The President, that is."

Buddy tipped his head from left to right, as if weighing what to say. "Fraud is serious business. But murder? That's something else entirely. It's huge. I can't imagine . . ." He stared past me, his expression indicating he was concentrating on something.

"Buddy? What is it?"

His eyes slowly found their way back to mine. "Nothing, Emme. Nothing at all."

I didn't believe him.

Chapter Twenty-One

*Y*OU'RE HOLDING OUT ON ME, BUDDY."

"No, Emme, I've told you everything." He picked up his bottle, then set it right back down. "What does it matter, anyhow? I thought you were staying out of police business."

"I am."

"Then why all the questions?"

I slapped the table. "Can't anyone understand? I'm simply curious. It's my nature." I took a second to inhale a calming breath. "Besides, if we didn't talk about the murder, what would we talk about?"

Buddy eyes grew a shade or two darker. "I'm sure we'd come up with something."

"That's what I'm afraid of."

He laughed, and I couldn't help but smile at the sound of it, although I quickly got serious again. "Now, since you insisted you were indebted to me for helping you out, you need to tell me everything you know about the fraud case as well as the murder." I let him consider that for a second. "Unless that was all talk."

He locked eyes with me, faux indignation on parade. "Why Emerald Malloy, if I hadn't heard it for myself, I never would have believed that you'd stoop so low as to attempt to extort information."

I stiffened my back. "You're the one who said I only had to ask."

"And here I was under the impression you were meek and innocent and—"

"Well, I guess I'm not the pushover you took me for. Now, shelve your bogus righteousness and spill what you know."

"But I don't—"

"Buddy!"

He rocked onto the back legs of his chair. "And if I don't give you what you want, what are you going to do? Use a rubber hose on me?"

"Wishful thinking on your part." I examined my hands. "I'm immune to you and your wicked ways, so—"

"Wait a minute! I thought you were 'drawn' to me."

"That was before." I forced myself to meet his gaze. "I'm completely unaffected by you now."

"Really?"

I had to move on before I embarrassed myself. "I promise I won't repeat anything you tell me."

"Right." Clearly he meant the opposite.

"If you think I can't keep a secret, you're wrong."

He snorted, most likely reflecting on my earlier slip of the tongue.

"Please, Buddy. I won't even tell Barbie or Margie." I stalled before deciding to go all in. "I won't say anything to Randy, either."

He considered my proposition for a long minute before grumbling, "Oh, hell. All right. I'll tell you. But you better not breathe a word to anyone."

I flashed him the Boy Scout sign. "I promise."

He momentarily closed his eyes as if suddenly struck by a headache.

"What? You can be a Scout, but I can't?"

He dismissed my remark and checked over both his shoulders. Apparently spotting no eavesdroppers, he leaned forward and said in a husky whisper, "Buford and I invested $50,000 in that wind farm deal about a year and a half ago."

Stunned, I only managed to utter, "And?"

"And we were supposed to receive dividend checks right from the start."

"Even though the wind farm hasn't been built yet?"

"The local wind farm is part of a bigger operation made up of wind farms across the state, some of which are already up and running and earning profits. At least that's what we were led to believe." He rubbed the back of his neck. "The investors in this wind farm were to share in those profits, too. And the first year we received regular payments, but over the past six months, we haven't received a dime."

"Did you ask about it?"

"Oh, yeah. We called Greg Rogers lots of times. We've dealt with him directly from the beginning. From what I gather, your 'Boo-Boo' didn't get involved until recently."

I ignored the "your Boo-Boo" reference. In truth, I was getting used to it. "What did Rogers tell you?"

"We never got through to him. We left messages, but he never called us back." He went from rubbing his neck to scratching his head. "Then, about a month ago, the President dropped by the house to let us know he'd spoken with Rogers personally. Supposedly, Rogers assured him that none of us had anything to worry about. We'd make our money back and then some. The President claimed we just needed to be patient. According to him, operations like this often 'hit snags.'"

"How'd he know you guys were investors? Wouldn't that information be confidential?"

"We figured as much. That's why we assumed he had an in with Rogers. Was a partner or something."

"Or maybe Rogers was stiffing him, too." I felt conflicted. I loved imagining the President losing his shirt, financially speaking, but I also had a strong desire to see him mixed up in the fraud scheme so I could watch him get taken down by the law.

"Emme!" Buddy jiggled my forearm, and the Etcha-Sketch image of the President being cuffed and hauled away by federal agents was shaken away. "Did you hear me?"

"Umm . . . no. Guess not."

Buddy raised his voice, obviously believing the noise around us, and not my musing, was to blame for my distraction. "I said anything's possible. Although I doubt the President wanted to commiserate with my brother and me over lost funds. See, while he was at our place, he encouraged us to put up even more money."

I leaned across the table. "What?"

"Yeah. He called it, 'priming the pump.' He said that whenever a deal showed signs of struggling, investors had to 'prime the pump.'"

"How did you and Buford react to that?"

"We said if we ever discovered he was involved in scamming us, we'd prime his pump."

"Huh?"

Buddy tilted his head to the side. "Yeah, I don't know exactly what we meant, either." A grin cracked the tight line of his mouth. "It sounded good at the time, though."

The waitress cozied up to Buddy while handing him two fresh bottles of beer. After she left, a hefty tip in her pocket, I asked if he knew anything about the other investors.

"Nothing I'll share." He handed me one of the bottles. "Other than to say that over the past six months, a number of them have been griping about the lack of return on their investments."

"Really? I've only heard about the push for more investors."

He twirled his beer bottle. "That's because the folks who are afraid they've lost their shirts aren't talking."

"Why not?"

"They're embarrassed. No one, myself included, wants it known that they were taken." He narrowed his eyes. "That's why you aren't going to utter a word. Got it?"

"But it wasn't your fault."

"Maybe not. Or maybe Buford and I should have done a better job of due diligence before handing over our cash."

"You were investing with Greg Rogers, for God's sake. What more did you need to know?"

"If it turns out he was scamming us, we should have learned a hell of a lot more."

I looped some hair around my index finger and twisted it while mulling things over. "By keeping quiet, Buddy, you're allowing the fraud to continue."

"No, Emme. It's not up to me. Federal investigators are calling the shots now."

His tone gave me the impression he had known about the investigation long before I'd mentioned it. And when I asked if that was the case, he said, "Yeah, I've been aware of it for a while."

"Why didn't you say anything earlier?"

He only shrugged, but I didn't belabor the point since I was far more interested in learning about the investigation itself. "So, what have the investigators discovered?"

"They don't keep me in the loop, Emme. Like everyone else, I'll just have to wait and see."

Unwilling to let go, I peppered him with a few other questions. "Have you actually met with any of them? Any of the federal agents, I mean? What did they tell you?" I specifically wanted to learn if he had talked with Tiny, but I didn't dare go so far as to reference him by name.

"Yeah. I've met with the feds a couple times. But I'm not at liberty to discuss those meetings, so don't bother to ask me about them."

"But—"

"Emme, I'm not going to risk word getting back to the folks involved in the scam. It could ruin everything."

"But I won't—"

"Emme!"

"Why doesn't anyone trust me?" I mumbled.

"What was that?"

I grabbed my bottle, desperately wanting to wring its neck. "Nothing."

Given Buddy's forbidding manner, I concluded that additional brow-beating would do no good. He was determined to keep quiet, and there wasn't a damn thing I could do to change his mind. It sucked. But . . .

"So," he said, "the police really think the murder and the fraud are linked, huh?"

He tilted his head, indicating at least some interest, so I immediately stated, "Well, if the crimes aren't connected, Boo-Boo, a member of the wind-farm group, just 'happened' to get killed while up here on wind-farm business, and his murder just 'happened' to be committed at the same time authorities were investigating the wind-farm operation." I waited a couple beats. "It'd be quite a coincidence. And the police don't believe in coincidences."

☙   ❧

"WHAT A BLAST!" BARBIE EXCLAIMED as she skidded to our table. "I needed that."

She bent down and whispered to me, "There's talk I shouldn't be here since my husband's a 'person of interest' in a murder case." Again, she added air quotes.

"Where'd you hear that?"

"In the bathroom. We took a potty break during the chicken dance. It's just not my thing."

Well, that explained a lot. Not about the chicken dance. There was no explanation for that. But it did help me understand Barbie's outrageous behavior on the dance floor. She was reacting to careless remarks about her husband. Of course that didn't excuse her x-rated show. Still . . .

I urged her to dismiss their comments and she, in turn, dusted off her shoulders as if wiping away the criticism. "It doesn't bother me. Not a lot, anyhow." She put on a brave face. "My husband didn't kill anyone. And I'm where I'm supposed to be, celebrating my best friend's wedding."

"That's right."

She examined her boots. "Even so, will you come with me?"

"Come with you?"

She lifted her head. "I could use something to snack on, and I don't want to go get it by myself."

"Barbie, you've never needed a friend to tag along before."

"Well, things feel different tonight."

Without question, Barbie was the personification of contradiction. Totally shameless one minute and utterly vulnerable the next. I had never met anyone quite like her.

"Okay," I said. "I'll go."

"Good. The food's set out in the café. Alice Smith made some bars I've got to try. They're called Telephone Bars because the recipe was passed along via the phone. Kind of funny, huh?"

As Buford sat down next to his brother, Barbie and I gave them a wave and made tracks for the café.

Chapter Twenty-Two

HE COUNTER IN THE CAFÉ was packed with platters and bowls full of food, free for the taking. Dozens of hot dishes, a variety of salads, and plenty of bars, cookies, and pies fought for our attention. It was plain to see, Margie didn't want anyone to go home hungry.

I pulled a paper plate from the pile at the end of the counter, snatched a set of plastic silverware, and served myself a small amount of Queso Mac and Cheese along with some Cauliflower and Sausage Rigatoni Hot Dish. Barbie picked up a couple Peppers Italiano, explaining they were made from a recipe provided by Ray Ecklund, someone Janice knew through the League of Minnesota Cities. "Unlike Janice," she added, "Ray's nice, and he's a good cook."

Setting our plates down, we poured ourselves coffee, then slid into a booth. For a while, neither of us spoke. We were fixated on our food. I wasn't sure how we could eat again so soon after our fish and pork dinner, but we managed. And we weren't the only ones. A man and a woman I didn't recognize sat in a booth across from us, their plates nearly overflowing. And four little boys in wrinkled shirts and dress pants divided their time between twirling around on the counter stools and taste testing various desserts.

"You guys better watch it," Barbie shouted in their direction. "You keep eating and spinning those stools, and you'll throw up."

One of the kids burped, and the other three gazed at him in admiration. "No, we won't," the burper argued. "Besides, we don't hafta listen to you. You ain't the boss of us."

Barbie bent her head and whispered to me, "God, I hate that kid. I know it's wrong to hate anyone, especially a child, but I can't help it. That kid's a jerk. And if there's any justice in the world, he'll be up all night, puking his guts out."

"Barbie?" I aimed to change the subject. "I'm sorry people made snide comments about you and Tom. I can't believe they did that." Using my fork, I shoved some Mac and Cheese around on my plate. "I'm also sorry I gave up on you."

"What do you mean?"

I laid my fork down as images of Barbie tearing up during the wedding ceremony played through my mind. "I've been thinking about the murder case. And while I don't want to get tangled up in—"

"You've already made that perfectly clear."

She sounded snippy, and even though I felt bad for her, I was miffed by her tone. After all, I was about to propose a compromise.

I sucked in a long breath and exhaled slowly while silently counting to ten. It was something Randy often resorted to when dealing with me. He said it calmed him. But it did nothing for me. Reaching double digits, I still was chafing and couldn't stop myself from exclaiming, "Staying clear of the investigation makes even more sense now that federal agents are involved." *Oops!* What was wrong with me? Why couldn't I keep anything to myself?

"Federal agents? How do you—"

"I shouldn't say. Just trust me, okay?"

She nodded, knowing full well the source of my information. "Do you think Tiny's one of those federal agents?"

I couldn't outright lie to her, so I hedged. "That would be my guess."

"Well, I'll be . . ."

"Barbie, my point is that while it wouldn't be smart for us to keep nosing around, we can discuss the case. And, if we come up with any good ideas, we can pass them on to Randy or Ed or even Tiny."

She lifted her chin. "You'd do that?"

"Don't act so shocked. I'm not a complete ass."

"But you were adamant about—"

"I know. I know. And, I'm still not going to sneak around or ask questions of people I don't trust. This case is getting way too complex for us amateurs. On top of that, I have no interest in going to jail, which is exactly where Sheriff Halverson would prefer to put me. Yet, I'm willing to review things with you. If you want, that is."

Her eyes swam with emotion. "Thanks, Emme. Even though Randy believes Tom may be home free, I'm not naïve enough to think we can sit back and assume everything will work out."

"But, from here on out, we won't interfere with the investigation. Deal?"

"Deal."

I wiped my mouth with my napkin. "So, what have you heard tonight? Anything new?"

She chewed on her pepper while apparently filing through a catalog of thoughts. "Well, as I told you earlier, I phoned Dumb and Dumber when you were at lunch with Randy. The two of them were on duty at the sheriff's office."

"Why do you even bother talking to those guys? You can't possibly believe anything they say, can you?"

She hitched her shoulders. "I don't know. I'm usually able to smell when they're blowing smoke, and this time around they seemed smoke free." She offered a sly smile. "What's more, I had them read directly from a document. That way I was certain the information they provided was accurate."

"A document? What kind of document?"

"A list of all the wind-farm investors, how much money each put up, and when those investments were made."

"Where did they get the list?"

"Off Ed's desk."

"Couldn't they get in trouble for that?"

She dismissed my concern with a grunt. "They're deputies, too. They have the right to know what's going on. Besides, no one's ever going to find out, are they, Emme?" Her tough countenance hammered home the intent of her remark.

"Okay, okay, I won't say anything to anybody. Not even Randy." At the rate I was going, I'd soon be unable to talk to the man about anything except the weather.

"So, Barbie, where did the police get this 'document'?"

"From a search of Greg Rogers' office down in the Cities."

"And how'd you convince Dumb and Dumber to divulge the information on it?"

"Blackmail," she retorted, her voice even, not the slightest sign of guilt.

I had nothing to say to that.

"Emme, like I told you before, Burr wasn't on the list. He didn't invest in the project. And other than my husband and the President, there were only a few big-dollar contributors."

I almost uttered Buddy and Buford's names before remembering I'd promised to keep quiet.

"Buddy and Buford were on there," she stated, making that promise moot. "They handed over $50,000 apiece early on."

I schooled my features, hoping they wouldn't betray me. "Oh, really?"

"Yeah. And about a year ago Booger and Delmont each invested $50,000."

"Well, we expected that."

"True, but I don't believe either of us expected to see John Deere's name pop up. Yet, it did. He invested $100,000."

"No way."

"Yep. He was one of the first investors in the local project. He invested directly with Greg Rogers a couple years ago." She fiddled with the handle of her cup. "From what Dumb and Dumber said, John told Randy all about it at the bachelor party."

"But, when he spoke with Margie, he claimed he never invested."

"Well, he was one of the first. And, from what I understand, the President only got involved late last year. So, perhaps, he didn't realize John had already given money when he made his pitch for investors at the bachelor party."

"That's possible, I guess." I dissected a noodle with my fork. "Now what? Do we tell Margie?"

"Tell me what?"

Oh, no! I'd been too caught up in our discussion to hear the new bride approach. "Oh . . . umm . . . hello, Margie," I stuttered.

"What do ya need to tell me?" While directing the question at me, she slid in next to Barbie.

At the same time, I gaped at Barbie, hoping she'd help me out. But, rather than doing that, she became mesmerized by her food, as if she'd never seen a stuffed pepper before.

That left me with no choice but to answer, "It wasn't anything important." I raised my coffee cup in a half-assed attempt to hide behind it.

Margie snorted. "Emme, you're a terrible liar. Worse than her." She pitched her thumb at her seatmate. "Now, out with it."

"It was nothing. We were just gabbing about the murder case."

"And?"

"And . . . I found out there's a fraud investigation underway, too."

"A 'federal' fraud investigation," Margie emphasized. "And Ed just phoned John to tell 'im federal agents arrested Greg Rogers in Minneapolis about an hour ago. Supposedly, he was at the center of it, and he was gettin' ready to skip the country."

That didn't make sense. "Why did Ed call John?"

"Because it turns out my new husband was not only one of the first local wind farm investors, he also was the first person to go to the authorities with suspicions that the state-wide wind-farm network was nothin' but a gall-darn Ponzi scheme."

I tapped the table to get Margie's full attention. "I thought he told you he never got involved in that deal."

"He did. Though he confessed otherwise this mornin', when we were workin' through the fallout from our fight last night."

Barbie twisted her torso to face Margie directly. "Why'd he lie, Margie? Did he have a good reason?"

Recalling what Buddy had said, I responded on Margie's behalf. "My guess? He assumed he'd lost his money and was too embarrassed to admit it to anyone, especially Margie."

"You're right. But that's only half the story." Margie checked over her left shoulder before proceeding in a hushed tone. "See, in the beginnin', he reckoned the wind farm would be a real money maker, so he told Buddy and Buford about it and even mentioned it to Little Val and Wally. And, wouldn't ya know, the twins invested right away, and about a year ago, Little Val and Wally did the same. Now it appears the whole lot of 'em has lost everythin'. No one's seen a dividend check in months."

She tsked. "As you can imagine, John feels responsible. That's why he went after Burr the way he did at the groom's dinner. Ya see, shortly before the rehearsal, Ed phoned from the sheriff's office with an update." She took a much-needed breath. "Since John was the first to contact authorities about the scam, they keep him posted. Well, the local cops do, at any rate. Unofficially, of course." A pinch of pride dusted her features.

"Anyways, Ed told John he had interviewed Burr and would do so again real soon. Ed was certain Burr knew more than he was admittin'. And while it was awfully nice of 'im to fill John in, it wasn't particularly smart because, right away, John decided he'd have a better shot at gettin' the truth out of Burr, bein' they're friends and all. But, uff-da, we all know how that worked out."

Barbie pushed her plate away and leaned an elbow on the table. "You mean to tell me that John kept quiet all this time because he was humiliated?"

"Not to mention a tad scared." Margie smirked. "See, Vern and Vivian don't believe in takin' chances with money. I guess Vivian and I are a lot alike in that way. So John and the others didn't mention the deal to me or either of them." She knocked her knuckles against the table, but I got the impression she would have preferred to knock her new husband's head a few time. "If Vivian ever discovers what happened, she'll be fit to be tied. Especially if she learns it was at John's urgin'." She paused. "In that case, we won't dare come back from Costa Rica. Ever!"

"Still," I stated, "the fundamental questions remains, if Boo-Boo's death was related to that fraud scheme, who with ties to it wanted him dead? And why?"

Barbie was quick to answer. "I can't help you with the 'why,' Emme, but I'll remind you that Tom's been more or less scratched off the 'who' list."

"And John certainly didn't have anythin' to do with it," Margie assured me. "Nor the twins. Remember, since they were early investors, they never even met your Boo-Boo and had no reason to do 'im any harm. Wally and Little Val can't be serious suspects, either. Though this does explain why

Wally started gamblin' this past October. Obviously, he was tryin' to recoup the money they'd lost." She shook her head. "And here we thought the pressure of havin' a baby simply got to 'im." She smiled. "He's doin' just fine now, though. Goes to meetin's and everythin'. He realizes how close he came to losin' his family. He'd never risk them again. That's for darn sure."

I eyeballed Barbie. "Okay, let's consider the other investors. You know who they are and the amounts they put up, as well as—"

"Wait a minute!" Margie appeared perplexed. "How do ya know—"

"Don't ask." Barbie pulled her plate back in front of her, picked up her fork, and poked at her stuffed pepper. "There were dozens of other local investors. But their outlays were $25,000 or less, not enough to lead to murder in my estimation. And Ed agrees with me on that."

I wagged my finger. "Even so, tell us who they were."

Barbie pursed her lips, determined commas forming in the corners of her mouth as she clearly worked to recall some names. "Father Daley and Reverend Pearson. If I remember correctly, they each invested $5,000. One of the Sorensons and two of the Petersons were also on the list. But I can't remember the amounts they contributed. It was either $15,000 or $20,000." She grinned. "Mitzie Halverson, the sheriff's wife, put up $25,000."

Margie butted in, her hand cupping her mouth. "I just heard she's diddlin' the President, if ya can imagine that."

Barbie dropped her fork. "I'd already been made aware of that but had managed to banish the images from my mind. Now, thanks to you, those pictures are back—some in vivid color—which means I'm all done eating." She tossed her napkin on her plate.

"Doggonit, Barbie, don't kill the messenger." Margie smoothed the front of her wedding dress, her features suggesting her feelings were hurt. In the blink of an eye, however, her desire to gossip must have won out over any sore feelings because, with a nod in my direction, she added as if she couldn't help herself, "I was also told she's been runnin' around with lots of men, includin' your Boo-Boo."

Deciding a discussion of Mitzie Halverson's dalliances wouldn't get us any closer to solving the matter at hand, and could possibly lead to nightmares on my part, I directed our conversation back to the investors. "Barbie, did any of the investors give you pause?"

She pulled on her bottom lip. "Since Owen Bair was only after financial backers here in the Red River Valley, investors in the Twin Cities and elsewhere had no interaction with him and no reason to do him in."

"So . . ."

"So, if we drop them from our list of suspects, along with all the small investors, as well as Tom and John, Buddy and Buford, and Little Val and Wally, we're left with just the President, Booger, and Delmont."

I groaned. "Remember, the police don't believe the President's guilty."

"Okay. Then we're down to Booger and Delmont."

"I don't know." While I had no evidence one way or another, my gut told me that neither of them was responsible for Boo-Boo's death. Then, again, my gut hadn't been performing all that well as of late.

"Just two suspects." Margie inclined her head. "That's not much. But, I guess, it's better than nothin'." She caught Barbie's eye. "Now what?"

"We visit with Booger and Delmont. Hear them out."

I raised a finger. "Hold on. You swore we'd take our ideas to the police."

"Emme, I know these guys. It won't be like I'm interrogating them. I'll just visit with them, so to speak."

"But—"

"You don't have to go with me. I'll do it on my own."

I narrowed my eyes. "You've got that right."

Margie scooted from the booth. "Well, you two figure it out. I can't be lollygaggin' back here all night. I need to get back to the party."

She leaned her fists against the table. "I mostly came in here to get away from Myrtle Benson. She's in the other room, yapping about Bingo again." Her pale blue eyes crinkled in amusement. "See, Lori Swanson's cousin from out of town was visitin' last week and won the Bingo jackpot at the Eagles. But since the cousin had unknowingly sat in Myrtle's chair, Myrtle decided the jackpot was rightfully hers and demanded that it be handed over." Margie tsked. "Of course, that didn't happen, so Myrtle's on a rampage. She's actually petitioning for new Bingo rules. She wants to assign seats and limit play to local residents." She clicked her tongue a couple more times. "If ya see her comin', clipboard in hand, high tail it as fast as ya can."

Margie stepped toward the door before hollering at the boys play-ing on the stools along the counter. "Come on, it's time ya kids got back in there, too."

The smart alec responded, "We don't hafta."

Margie settled her hands on her hips, her expression fierce enough that I almost hurried from the room myself. "What did you say?"

The boy opened his mouth, but no words came out.

"Yah, that's what I thought." She crooked her finger at all four kids. "Now, get goin'."

With barely a sound, the boys got to their feet, then ran from the room, giving Margie a wide berth as they passed. She followed them out, muttering something about "all four of 'em goin' to hell in a handbasket."

"If she could bottle that, she'd make a mint," Barbie remarked.

"No wonder John was afraid to confess he'd lost all that money. She can be scary."

Barbie wiped her hands on her napkin. "The two of them intend to keep their finances separate, so Margie probably doesn't really care what he does with his money. But, as you said, he doesn't want to look foolish in her eyes."

"Now, let's talk about Booger and Delmont. Would losing $50,000 be a problem for either of them, Barbie? Would they kill over it?"

"Well, no one likes losing that kind of money. But doing so wouldn't put either of them in the poor house. Don't forget, most of the farmers around here are well off." She hesitated. "The truth is, with the exception of my husband, all the big investors had the financial where-withal to speculate the way they did. That's why I'm still not convinced the murder's tied to the wind-farm operation."

"But the police—"

"I don't care what the police say. A part of me continues to believe your Boo-Boo was killed because of his philandering."

"But—"

"Emme, it's how I feel. And, as reporters, we can't discount our feelings."

"I used to believe that. Now, I'm not so sure."

She waved my comment away.

"Well," I began with no small amount of hesitation, "what exactly are you proposing?"

"We need to create another list of suspects. One based on my theory."

I held back a sigh. "I doubt—"

"Emme, what harm could it do?"

"But Booger and Delmont?"

"I'll talk to them. I just want to compile this other list, too."

"And how are we supposed to do that? Aside from Janice, I have no clue as to the identities of Boo-Boo's so-called lovers."

"I have some ideas."

"Oh, goodie."

Barbie glowered.

"Sorry. It just feels like a waste of time. Not to mention, terribly humiliating for me."

Her eyes turned sad, and, of course, they tugged at my heartstrings.

"Oh, all right," I grumbled, mostly irritated with myself. Why did I always give into my friends? It was something I'd have to work on in counseling. My therapist would be delighted since she planned to remodel her kitchen and would then have the means to pay for it. "Okay, if you want to make a list, we'll make a list."

I didn't sound the least bit enthusiastic. Nonetheless, Barbie said, "Thanks, Emme. But, before we do that, I need a bathroom break. Then, I'd like to go outside and get some fresh air."

"Okay." I wiggled my way out of the booth. "I'll meet you out front."

Chapter Twenty-Three

I WRAPPED MYSELF IN MY borrowed jacket and stepped into the night. The sky was black. Dense clouds hid the stars. And cool air danced with the hem of my dress.

I watched as people milled about near the highway and the side street that bordered the cafe. Janice was among them. Poised under the spotlight of a street lamp, she smoked a cigarette and visited with Burr Nelson.

Noticing me, Burr shuffled away, but Janice remained.

I tiptoed in her direction, moving carefully to avoid slipping on the icy sidewalk. "Hi, there," I murmured upon my approach, my breath frosting the cold air white.

"Don't fall." She took a long drag from her cigarette. "I did that a couple years ago. Slipped on the ice, fell backwards, and fractured my ankle. Damn thing still aches whenever it gets real cold."

"The weather's not all that bad tonight."

"No. The clouds are keeping the temperature from falling as far as originally predicted."

With her free hand, she retrieved a pack of cigarettes from the pocket of her Polaris snowmobile jacket. "Want one?"

"No, thanks. I just came out for some air." I wasn't about to mention that Barbie was joining me.

I looked across the road and watched Burr climb into his pickup. It was parked alongside the elevator, its nose against a giant pile of snow. "I didn't realize you and Burr were friends."

"Huh? I told you we were, remember? When he was on the city council, we did a bunch of work together."

"Oh, yeah, I forgot." I hadn't really. I just couldn't conjure up another way to bring his name into the conversation. But I shouldn't have worried because Janice went right on talking about him.

181

"Yeah." She flicked ashes from her cigarette. "Just so you know, I . . . I told him you asked about him."

"Is that why you left the hockey arena in such a hurry? To report back to him?"

"It wasn't like that. We're friends, and I figured he deserved to know."

"Barbie and I spoke with him earlier today."

"That's what I understand." She sucked on her cigarette one last time before dropping it on the sidewalk and grinding it out with the toe of her boot. "I don't want to see him or his daughter get hurt, Emme. They've been through enough."

"How so?"

She wrapped her arms around her midsection, her bare hands bunching up the sides of her open jacket. "Well, it's really not my place to say." She eyed her crushed cigarette. "But . . ." She kicked at the butt before raising her head. "Burr's wife died years ago, leaving him to raise their daughter all alone." She stopped, as if reconsidering her decision to talk about her friend. Believing it was best to bide my time and wait her out, I said nothing.

"He's not the brightest person around," she finally uttered into the void, "and he's made some bad farming decisions, which have cost him dearly. Like a lot of men, he's got a big ego and doesn't always ask for advice when he should." She peeked over her shoulder. Burr's truck was headed out of town. "Anyhow, money got tight. Real tight. And Stacy, his daughter, wanted to help out, but he wouldn't let her get a job. He insisted she concentrate on her studies and her music. She was in high school, and college scholarships were becoming a real possibility."

She again claimed her cigarettes, tapped one out of the pack, and raised it to her lips. Returning the pack to her coat pocket, she exchanged it for a Bic lighter, flicking it until a flame caught and held. She breathed in deeply. On the exhale, she coughed. "Excuse me." She cleared her throat. "Long story short, Stacy stole $1,000 from her 4-H club. As soon as Burr found out, he paid the money back and pulled her from the club. But the President was involved in some way. On the board or some such thing. Anyhow, he became privy to what happened. And he used that information to get Burr to resign from the city council. Said if he didn't—or if he said anything about it—he'd notify the administrators at Stacy's college, and she'd lose her scholarships." She coughed again. "That would spell the end of college for her."

"Not necessarily."

"Well, Burr wasn't willing to take that chance. You can understand that, can't you?"

I said the only thing that came to mind. "The President's an ass."

"I knew you felt that way. That's why I trusted you with their story." She stole another drag from her cigarette. "I only heard it for the first time last night. Burr finally confided in me." A white plume of smoke held its shape around her face.

"Why didn't the President simply make Burr vote his way? Why force him off the council?"

"I asked that very thing. And he said the President didn't trust him. Not even under the threat of blackmail."

"Hmm."

"The President also figured being on the council would prove useful in other ways as time went on."

The crowd outside grew, along with the noise. I heard someone mention something about the band being on break.

Janice appeared to be getting antsy, as if the cold air was becoming an issue, even though she was dressed in tall boots, thick black tights, a sweater dress, and a parka. She'd also donned a bulky fashion scarf around her neck.

None of it looked quite right on her. Probably because Janice normally enjoyed showing off her body. It was the one trait she and Barbie had in common. Yet, while Barbie was dressed in barely-there leopard skin, she was covered from head to toe. It didn't make sense. Particularly on New Year's Eve.

I immediately called to mind the hockey game. There, Janice wore a turtleneck, parka, jeans, and another scarf. I didn't think much of it at the time. It was far from warm in the arena. Most people were bundled up, myself included. But now . . .

I then flashed back to Margie's party, where Janice sported a long-sleeve turtleneck and slacks. But, again, the weather was lousy, so there really wasn't anything odd about her outfit. Nevertheless . . .

Is she hiding something?

"That's what I want to know," I muttered in response to the voice in my head.

"Huh? What did you say?"

"Ahh ... nothing, Janice. I mean ..." Luckily, I didn't have to finish that sentence because we got interrupted. Unluckily, the person who interrupted us was Barbie.

"What's going on?"

"Just passing the time," Janice replied. "Not that we have to answer to you."

Barbie snared my arm. "Come on, Emme, let's go back inside. The last thing I need right now is to listen to her smart mouth." She shivered, complete with sound effects. "Besides, it's so cold out here the hot flash I just had actually felt kind of good. And I'm pretty sure that's bad."

"Why didn't you wear your jacket?" I wanted to know.

She hugged herself until her breasts practically squeezed out of the top of her dress like toothpaste from a tube. "I didn't plan on staying outside very long." She edged in my direction and lowered her voice. "Truth is, I didn't even think about a jacket. I guess being cold's the last thing on my mind."

"Yeah," Janice chimed in, obviously overhearing, "from what I understand, you've got a whole lot of bigger problems to be concerned with."

"What's that supposed to mean?" Barbie dropped her arms to her sides, where her hands formed tight fists.

"I'm just surprised you're here, that's all. With all the trouble your husband's in."

Barbie stepped forward, her body coiled with tension. "My husband's not in any trouble."

"Well, I hear different." Janice flicked ash from her cigarette as she sing-sang, "Oh, how the mighty have fallen."

Before she ended her last note, Barbie grabbed the front of her parka and shook her like she was nothing but skin and bones. Which she was. But still ...

"Take that back!" Barbie hollered.

"Who's going to make me?" Janice's arms and legs were wheeling.

Of course, my initial impulse was to step between them, but it didn't take long to change my mind. After all, Barbie and her determination outweighed me by more than seventy pounds, and even though Janice was scrawny, she had a whole lot of temper going on. What's more, I was wearing spiked heels, and the sidewalk was glare ice in spots.

Cursing a blue streak, Janice staggered backwards, and her cigarette fell to the ground. With both hands free, she then charged forward and slapped Barbie across the face. First, from one direction. Then, the other.

"Ouch!" Barbie shrieked. "You scratched me with those damn claws of yours!" She swung an outstretched arm of her own, Janice ducked, and Barbie missed her head yet connected with the beehive on top of it. If the thing had been alive, she would have knocked it out cold. As it was, it toppled over, coming to rest on Janice's right shoulder.

"Oh, no," Janice howled, "see what you've done?" After attempting, but failing, to reset her hair by blindly stabbing bobby pins every which way, she dipped her head and charged. "You're nothing but a bitch, you know that?"

For another second or two, I again considered separating them but concluded there was no way I could do it on my own, and while a mob had formed around us, no one in it seemed particularly interested in assisting me. In fact, I spotted a few women from the bridal shower, and I was pretty sure they were once more taking bets. "Knock her senseless, Barbie," one of them yelled, while another shouted, "Janice, don't let her get you on the ground. If you do, she'll squash you."

"Break it up! Break it up!" At the sound of that thunderous voice, I jumped back, as did everyone else in the vicinity, which left Tiny with plenty of room to reach in and clamp Barbie's arms with his meaty hooks. Then, with a growl, he lifted her off the ground like a construction crane, maneuvered her away from Janice, and not so gently set her back on the sidewalk, retaining a firm grip the whole while.

"Let her go," Janice hollered. "I can take her. She's no threat to anything but the buffet table in the café."

"Why you . . ." Barbie wiggled, but Tiny held on tight.

"That's all folks," he shouted to the crowd. "On your way. The show's over." He glared at Janice. "You, too. Get goin'."

"But she started . . ." The man's dark and dangerous demeanor must have convinced her to forego completing that sentence because she clamped her mouth shut and wisely scurried off with the others.

I remained rooted in place, even though a big part of me wanted to follow everyone else. Tiny scared me when he was nice, and at that moment, there was nothing about him that seemed "nice." He growled like a bear and was dressed like a member of a biker gang. He wore all black, silver chains hanging from his pockets, and a red do-rag covering the top of his head.

He spun Barbie around. "Now, what in the hell was that about?"

"She's just a big—"

He cut her off. "Oh, the hell with it. I don't have time for this."

Barbie pulled on the bottom of her leopard-skin dress. During the melee, it had hiked up well beyond the point of decency. "Well, no one asked for your assistance in the first place, now did they?"

"What?" Tiny was incredulous. "Was I supposed to let you get beat up?"

Barbie's chin jutted out, and her eyes sparked. "I was handling her just fine."

Tiny expelled an exasperated breath. "Whatever."

"Why are you even here?" When he didn't reply quickly enough, she added in an equally flippant manner, "Don't you have some work to do elsewhere, Mr. Federal Agent Man?"

He retreated a couple paces. "Take it easy. Randy told me you two found out I'm working undercover." He dropped his voice until those last couple words were barely audible.

Barbie stepped forward, into his personal space. "Something you should have told me."

"But if I'd done that," he said, "I wouldn't have been undercover anymore."

Barbie poked her finger against his chest. "You confided in that bartender!"

He grabbed her finger. "I had to! I needed his cooperation."

"And you decided you could get my cooperation through other means, huh?" Her inference was disturbingly obvious.

"I wasn't using you, Barbie." He softened his voice as well as his stance. "Sure, I was interested in what you knew. I saw Tom come into the Maverick drunk the day Owen Bair got murdered. And, the next day, when I learned he was a suspect, I wanted to find out everything I could about what was going on with him." She pulled her finger from his grasp as he confessed, "But that doesn't mean I was feeding you a line of bull. It was great to see you." He reached out and caressed her cheek with the back of his massive mitt. "I've always had a thing for you. You know that. If you recall, I wasn't the one to end things between us."

Barbie eased away from him. "My husband could very well be arrested for murder, yet no one tells me anything." She quivered with emotion. "You supposedly care about me, and you're right in the middle of the investigation, but you won't even confide in me. Emme and I have been forced to poke around on our own."

"Which is totally unsafe," he reminded her.

"Which is 'totally understandable,'" she replied, "since it's the only way we'll find out anything."

At that, they took time to scowl at each other, neither willing to budge.

I edged back a few feet, determined to slink away and give them a chance to work things out on their own. Another step, though, and I slipped on the ice, my legs shooting out from under me. I shrieked, and Tiny caught me before I landed on my butt. "So much for sneaking off," I muttered.

"Please, don't go," Barbie pleaded.

"But you two need . . ."

Tiny looked at me, then Barbie. "I need to get inside."

"Why?" While only a single word, the question was huge. Barbie wanted to know if Tiny trusted her enough to let her in on what he was doing.

He rubbed his hand over his face, unmistakably at odds regarding how to proceed. His job required prudence. At the same time, he had a dear friend—someone he admittedly cared for deeply—teetering on an emotional cliff.

He huffed, puffs of white air exiting his nostrils. "Oh, come on, you two." He hooked his arms through ours. "You better go with me before you both end up hurt."

He lowered his voice. "Now, as far as anyone in the 'V' is concerned, I work road construction. I knew you years ago in the Twin Cities, Barbie. We unexpectedly ran into each other up here. You introduced me to your friend. And now the three of us are sharing drinks. Got it?"

Chapter Twenty-Four

By THE TIME WE GOT OUR DRINKS and located an empty table, Barbie appeared far less perturbed with Tiny. When I began to talk about Janice, however, she seemed more than a little upset with me.

"Unlike you," I said, "I like the woman. She's funny. And while she's outrageous, I believe, deep down, she's a loyal friend." Barbie made some kind of guttural noise, indicating either disagreement or heartburn. "Even so," I continued, "the change in her wardrobe makes me suspicious."

Tiny lifted his glass and spoke around it. "Emme, you're way off base. It's winter. Lots of people wear scarves and turtlenecks. But, more importantly, Janice is neither strong enough nor tall enough to heave a former pro athlete over the ledge of the observation tower. It's too high."

Barbie was quick to add, "And, as I said before, if she were to push to their deaths all the guys who've dumped her, it truly would be raining men."

I ignored her remark and asked Tiny about Janice's alibi. "Was she really in the Maverick at the time of Boo-Boo's death? She claims she was."

He hiked a shoulder. "The bartender's not positive what time she left. Still, we don't think—"

"Okay, okay." I threw my hands up and surrendered. "You're probably right. Most likely, she had nothing to do with the murder." I allowed myself to slouch down in my chair. "Yet, I find it weird that she's dressing . . ."

I let the rest of the sentence go unsaid, choosing, instead, to concentrate on my beer. It was cold and strong, while my theory about Janice was . . . Well, evidently, it wasn't the least bit strong.

After consuming my fill and listening to a "women of country" medley by the band, I decided to share Janice's story about Burr and his daughter. Despite Janice's request, I had no qualms about confiding in Tiny since he was in law enforcement. And Barbie? Well, she was my friend, and I still felt guilty about withholding information from her earlier. Plus, as a journalist, she, like Tiny, routinely dealt with situations that required discretion. True, she didn't always practice it, but she was familiar with the concept. I was pretty sure of that. Besides, who was I to judge? I'd discovered that I, too, was way chattier than I ever imagined myself to be.

After I finished my story, Tiny pointed a finger at me. "Did you get a sense from Janice whether or not Burr knew about the fraud scheme?"

I felt my eyebrows jump. "You think I'm capable of capturing nuances like that?"

"Oh, the way I hear it, Emme, you have a pretty keen nose."

I crossed my eyes in an effort to examine it. "It's really not that good."

He chuckled. "Seriously, I'd like your take on Burr."

Desperately wanting to impress him, a federal law enforcement agent, I pondered everything I'd learned about Burr. Unfortunately, it wasn't much. "Sorry. I've got nothing. Nothing beyond what I already told you."

He waved me off. "That's okay."

"I didn't even think to ask her about the fraud scheme."

"Don't worry about it. It's no big deal."

It was to me. Every time I attempted to demonstrate even the most fundamental fact-finding skills, I came up short. So why did I keep trying? Why did I continually set myself up for failure?

"Tiny, what's your theory?" Barbie asked, while I continued to sulk.

He was watching the President, Booger, and Delmont. The three of them remained at the short end of the bar.

"My theory?" he repeated without diverting his focus. "About the murder? Or the fraud?"

"Either," Barbie answered. "Or both."

Tiny blindly lifted his glass and gulped more of his drink. Plain Coke on ice, served in a mixed-drink glass. "I shouldn't say." He set the glass down and turned toward us. "But, it may not matter. From here on out, I'll probably be assigned to desk duty. Permanently."

"What?" Barbie was dumbfounded. "Why would you—"

"I screwed up, Barbie. Really screwed up."

"How so?"

He stretched his neck from side to side, as if working to rid himself of a heavy load of stress. "Well . . ." He stopped, clearly vacillating about what, if anything, to reveal.

Barbie leaned closer. "Come on, Tiny. What happened?"

He squirmed. "Well, you see, we were on to Greg Rogers."

I leaned in, too. Between the music and the din of laughter and chatter, the bar was really noisy, making it difficult to hear.

"After John Deere and a few other investors came forward about their experiences, we knew we were dealing with a Ponzi scheme. But we needed someone on the inside to help us out." His gaze jumped between us. "It didn't take long to decide that Owen Bair was our best bet, and I was assigned to bring him on board."

He continued. "I rented a room at the same motel as him in Karl-stad and frequently 'ran' into him at the Maverick Bar. I struck up con-versations and even bought him a few drinks, relying heavily on the line that I was from out of town, just like him, and didn't know anyone else." He scrubbed his upper lip with his knuckle. "I was gaining his trust. Yet, before I had a chance to come clean and ask for his assistance, he got skit-tish, so I backed off. Then, before I could get close again, he got killed."

Barbie caressed his thick forearm. "That wasn't your fault."

"I didn't read the situation very well, that's for damn sure."

"What spooked' him?" I asked.

"We don't rightly know. We can only assume he got threatened and wasn't sure where to turn."

"And that's why he asked to meet with me?"

"Probably," Tiny replied. "While you two weren't together any-more, he must have figured he could count on you to help him."

A sharp pain pierced my heart. "But I arrived too late." I pressed my hand against the ache. "If I'd gotten there on time, he might still be alive."

Tiny grunted. "Or you might be dead, too."

His words left me speechless. They also cast a pall over our table that lifted only after a waitress delivered us another round of drinks.

With her refill in hand, Barbie asked if Tiny believed the murder and fraud were connected.

Tiny stroked his jaw. "We really shouldn't be discussing any of this."

"I'm not insisting you unveil any big secrets or strategies. I just want to know if you believe the two crimes are linked."

Regardless of what she said, Barbie was seeking full disclosure, and Tiny knew it. Twin lines creased the space between his furrowed brows, while his eyes held a challenge. For her part, Barbie refused to wither as she returned his stare.

"Fine," Tiny grumbled, giving in way sooner than I had expected. "I'll tell you what I know. But what I say can't go beyond this table. I'd like to save my job if there's any chance and yapping about this case isn't likely to help."

Barbie switched her attention from Tiny to me before pledging on behalf of both of us, "We won't utter a word."

Tiny hunkered over his beer bottle and spoke very quietly for a big man. "We're almost one-hundred-percent positive the cases are related."

Barbie protested. "What about the idea that the murder was due to the victim's philandering?"

"We don't see it."

She glared, as if that might more effectively convey her message. One that suggested she didn't agree with his assessment.

"Barbie, you asked for my thoughts."

"I know but—"

"Well, then, this is the way we see it." He shifted slightly. "To start, Greg Rogers heard there were investment opportunities up here. He also assumed the people around here weren't very sophisticated and could easily be duped."

I raised my finger. "His first mistake."

"True. Yet, that's what he believed when he started peddling the whole wind-farm idea around Kittson County a couple years ago." He stopped, ostensibly to put his thoughts in order. "There never was to be an actual wind farm, you know. At least not much of one. The guy was simply in search of money to spend on himself and his wife. And once the money dried up, he planned to announce that the operation had encountered 'unforeseen' problems and needed to be scrubbed. In the meantime, to keep investors from becoming suspicious, he used some of the funds obtained from folks in this area, as well as some of the money from investors in his other wind farms, to pay out dividends."

"The other wind farms were scams, too?"

"Yep. At each site, he only developed as much as necessary to entice people to part with their cash. The first one, down in southwestern Minnesota, was actually near 'completion' when it began 'encountering problems.' By then, though, he had what he wanted, namely, a few dozen windmills dotting the landscape for potential investors to get excited about. Consequently, he didn't have to do much at the second site. Talk alone generated enough buzz to prompt folks to hand over their hard-earned dollars." He rested for a beat. "And, as you know, the third site—the one here in Kittson County—wasn't even scheduled for ground breaking until this coming spring."

With her brows cranked into a "V," Barbie appeared to struggle with what he'd said. "The investors up here were able to receive dividends even though this wind farm wasn't operational?"

"Yep. Rogers marketed each wind farm as part of a major campaign comprised of several wind farms. When people invested in one, they supposedly invested in the whole works and were to receive returns from the get-go."

"But since no farm was truly making money, those dividends were paid from investment funds, which meant new investors were continually needed." Barbie appeared pleased with herself.

And Tiny grinned. "Thus, a pyramid scheme was born."

He took a sip of his drink and wiped his lips with the back of his hand. "Anyhow, Rogers and his trophy wife spent way faster than the investment money came in. That's why the so-called dividend payments started getting delayed. That's also why Owen Bair was hired. Rogers reasoned that someone with his sports background and easy-going personality could persuade folks around here to invest their money. But Owen soon discovered doing so was much harder than Rogers anticipated."

He canted his head in Barbie's direction. "As you are no doubt aware, even though a fair number of farmers in the Red River Valley have significant assets and cash, they're careful with both. They don't easily give them up, which Owen Bair tried to explain to Rogers. But Rogers wouldn't listen. He assumed Owen was simply a poor salesman. So, after he got the President to invest in the operation, he encouraged him to make some sales, too, offering him a generous cut of any money he obtained."

"How did Rogers coax the President on board in the first place?" Barbie asked.

"He stroked his ego," Tiny answered. "Before long, the President was telling everyone within earshot that he was 'partners' and 'friends' with billionaire businessman Greg Rogers."

I did a mental eye roll, while Barbie made another point. "That's when the President began going after folks, insisting they weren't 'civic minded' unless they financially supported the wind farm project."

"Yep," Tiny supplied. "After Rogers's arrest, he was more than willing to explain the President's role in the scam."

"Then, why don't you arrest him?" I looked in the direction of the man in question. I tried to take him all in, but without a wide-angle lens, it was tough. Remember, he was a big guy.

"Rogers isn't a reliable source. He's got his own agenda. He'll say whatever he has to in order to lessen the prison time he's facing. So we need other evidence. And that's what our guys are after, both here and in the Twin Cities. We'd also like to help local law enforcement connect the President or his buddies to the murder, if at all possible. And that's easier done if they're out and about, where they're likely to get cocky and make mistakes."

I cleared my throat. "Well, at least, we now know a few things for sure." I wiggled two fingers. "Why the President pushed Burr off the city council as well as why Burr was reluctant to talk about it with anyone, including the police."

"Yep," Tiny agreed. "You did good work there, Emme."

"Thanks."

Barbie spoke up. "We also have an explanation for why the President moved to Kennedy in the first place."

At that, Tiny and I leveled her with matching looks of puzzlement, prompting her to explain. "See, the President grew up in Hallock. And Hallock and Kennedy are fierce rivals. Have been for decades. So it struck me as odd that the man would move here. It's just not done. Of course, Margie insisted he simply wanted to be closer to Vivian. But he could have chased her from wherever he lived. Plus, Vivian had given him the brush-off. And, from what we've learned, he had taken up with someone new." She gulped air. "But he had to be a resident of Kennedy to get a spot on its city council. And he had to hold a seat on the council to get access to large sums of money with very little oversight."

"He couldn't do that in Hallock?" Tiny wondered aloud.

"No. Even with fewer than a thousand residents, Hallock's too big. The minutes of city council meetings are printed in the newspaper, and lots of people read them. I know because I'm the one who usually attends the meetings and does the reporting. But, in tiny towns like Kennedy, council meetings aren't covered by reporters, and the minutes aren't published, which affords crooked council members lots of opportunities."

"Well," Tiny said, adjusting his do-rag, "I better call all this in." He glanced between Barbie and me. "Yep, you two did real good."

Chapter Twenty-Five

U PON TINY'S RETURN TO THE TABLE, I reminded him that while he had shared his thoughts regarding the fraud case, he hadn't revealed his theory about the murder. "I don't want you to get in trouble by divulging too much but—"

"Oh, I think it's a little late to worry about that." He lifted his glass, tipped it to his mouth, and finished off his Coke.

"My best guess," he went on to say while chomping ice, "is that Owen Bair got killed because he uncovered the fraud scheme but refused to go along with it."

While I wasn't looking for an argument, I felt compelled to respond. "Tiny, I knew Boo-Boo pretty well. And, believe me, he wasn't one to lug around a bunch of scruples. So I doubt he'd avoid a scam if he thought it might make him rich."

Tiny closed one eye and carefully considered me with the other. "What if he was scared the scam might come crashing down courtesy of law enforcement?"

I ran that possibility through my mind. "Well, under those circumstances, he'd be torn. See, he had an unnatural fear of the police and jail." I pulled a shrug. "I don't know why. Perhaps he was afraid of what an arrest would do to his reputation or his legacy. Whatever the case, he was terrified by the prospect of getting tangled up with the law."

"Maybe he had reason to be," Barbie observed. "Maybe he was up to no good all along, and you just didn't know it, Emme."

Tiny answered for me. "I don't think so. His record was clean. Not even a speeding ticket." He glanced my way. "Nevertheless, a fear of law enforcement may have contributed to his nervousness in the days leading up to his death. Think about it. He uncovered a scam and confronted some of the participants. They threatened him into keeping quiet, which, naturally, frightened him." He angled his head thoughtfully. "Or, he may have heard we were already investigating the project and was afraid he'd get tangled up in the dragnet."

Barbie waved her hand as if she could hardly wait for her turn to speak. "Perhaps, after he learned of the fraud scheme, he blackmailed the wrong people, and they killed him."

"Not everyone blackmails people," I muttered, referring to Barbie's earlier comments about doing just that to Dumb and Dumber.

She flipped me the bird.

And Tiny? Well, he ignored our exchange and simply said, "Owen Bair didn't blackmail anyone. He wanted nothing to do with the scam. Otherwise, he wouldn't have asked Emme for help."

"Hmm," I uttered. "That makes sense. It's also nice to think he had a few morals." I then stopped to consider the consequences of his actions. "However, that means someone involved in the scam got worried because he wasn't willing to play along and decided to . . ." I couldn't finish. I'd been dealing with Boo-Boo's death for days, yet, at that moment, I was overcome by the thought of it.

"Decided to kill him!" Barbie had no trouble finishing for me, her volume several decibels louder than normal.

"Geez, quiet down," Tiny scolded.

She lowered her voice. "The murderer could be anyone connected to the fraud, you know." She scrunched up her nose. "Or, Greg Rogers may have hired someone from outside to do the job. Maybe an actual hit man."

Tiny snorted. "A professional didn't commit the murder. It was way too messy."

"Messy?" Recalling what he had said about me getting killed right along with Boo-Boo, I felt the blood drain from my head. "What do you mean, 'messy'?"

"Not in a gruesome way," he hurried to assure me, my ghost-like appearance apparently freaking him out. "I didn't mean it like that. It's just that a professional would have been more inconspicuous. He would have dragged the guy into the woods, for instance, and buried him where his body wouldn't be discovered for years."

Barbie wrung her hands. "Well, my husband certainly wasn't part of a murder plot or a major fraud scheme. Yet, since no one's any closer to finding the real killer, he could very well end up being the scapegoat."

Tiny reached out and squeezed her hand reassuringly. "Don't worry."

She yanked her hand away. "I have to. One way or another, the sheriff will 'solve' this case. And he's going to do it soon. He has to with the election coming up."

Exhaustion settled on Tiny's large frame. It was plain to see the investigation—and Barbie—were tiring him out. "We're doing the best we can, Bar—"

"And what exactly does your 'best' entail, Tiny?" Her words had an angry bite to them. It happened whenever she got scared.

"I'm assisting the local cops. And right now I'm watching those halfwits at the bar. If they're in any way responsible for Owen Bair's death, they'll slip up."

"What if the killer's someone else?" She had jumped from grouchy to whiny, something else she routinely did when scared. "Someone who's already back down in Minneapolis. Then what?"

"From what I'm told, people are covering the most likely suspects down there, too."

"Are there a lot of them?" I asked. "Other suspects, I mean."

"No," he answered. "You're looking at the prime targets."

I peeked at the men from behind my raised beer bottle. "But, according to Randy, the President can't be the killer."

"He's right."

"Well, if that's true, why are you concentrating on—"

"Because those two idiots alongside him will do damn near anything he asks."

"Even kill someone?"

He shrugged.

"Has anyone interviewed them?"

"Ed has. Twice."

"And?"

"They claim they were together, working on some piece of farm machinery at the time of Bair's death."

Barbie asked, "Can anyone corroborate that?"

"They stopped by the local John Deere dealership late in the day, requesting a part."

"Convenient," Barbie uttered.

"What about bruises?" I asked. "Do either of them happen to have unexplained bruises?"

"Both do."

Barbie and I jerked our heads around in tandem and spoke in unison. "Really?"

"Yep, although they aren't 'unexplained.' They supposedly got in a fight the night before John's bachelor party. Allegedly, they were drunk and ended up going at each other over a girl."

"And?"

Tiny inhaled deeply. "Well, they were here in the 'V.' Both were drunk. And, there was a fight."

"Still, pretty flimsy alibis," I muttered.

"Yeah," he agreed. "Nevertheless, they have 'em."

"Tiny, do you think Tom's alibi will hold up?" Barbie sounded terribly worried.

Tiny reached over and, once again, covered her hand with his, the man's tough appearance at odds with the tenderness he obviously felt for my friend. "Honestly? I don't know. Janice and Burr confirmed my statement that Tom entered the bar ahead of the President. But neither is sure of the time. I believe it was around 3:30, though no one—"

"What about the bartender?" she interrupted to ask. "Can't he—"

Tom snorted. "That man couldn't find his ass with both hands."

He leaned back and folded his arms over his broad chest. "Barbie, we can't have Tom's freedom dependent upon me alone. Some folks might argue I'd say whatever was necessary to help your husband because . . . Well, you know."

The two of them locked eyes, seemingly communicating an awful lot without actually saying a thing.

"Sooo," I hummed as I stood, feeling as if I was intruding on an intimate conversation, "since it doesn't appear as if we'll solve the murder in the next five minutes, I'm going to the bathroom."

Barbie wavered before also taking to her feet. "And I'm . . . umm . . . off to the café to get a small plate of . . . umm . . . something or other."

"What?" I was surprised by how eager she appeared to get away from Tiny.

"Mostly I'm after a piece of frosted chocolate cake covered in watermelon chunks," she rambled. "It's a great taste combination. Margaret Dukowitz told me about it. According to her, Bill Cooney, her dad, always ate the two together."

She glanced at me, the tips of her ears flushed. "I'll bring him some, too." She bit her lip as she pointed a finger in Tiny's general direction but, evidently, couldn't bring herself to make eye contact with the man.

As for Tiny, he hid his amusement behind his closed fist. He obviously knew the effect he had on my friend and was quite pleased by it.

Chapter Twenty-Six

*D*ONE WITH MY BUSINESS in the bathroom, I aimed myself back toward our table, my progress halted first by a group of kids running unchecked, and next by a hand snaring my arm. With a sharp intake of air, I spun around, not at all sure whom I expected to find. My brain shuffled through a deck of names and faces, Randy Ryden's not among them. He was working, after all. That's why I was stunned to see him. Right there in front of me. In street clothes.

"Hi." A smile lit his face.

"What? What are you . . ."

He chuckled. "Nice to see you, too."

I stroked his clean-shaven cheek. "I'm just surprised you're here. You're supposed to be working."

"I am working." He bent forward and whispered, "I'm providing Tiny with backup. We decided I'd be less obvious if I dressed like I was simply enjoying myself at the wedding dance."

I pitched myself onto the tips of my toes and whispered in return, "You think people will actually believe that? Remember, you're supposed to be hunting down a murderer."

He gripped my bare shoulders and pulled me close. Shivers radiated from my very core to the tips of my fingers and all the way down to my toes. "We're spreading the word that Greg Rogers got arrested for fraud a few hours ago." His breath tickled my ear. "We also let it leak that he's being interrogated in connection to Owen Bair's murder."

"That's not true, is it?"

"Well, he did get arrested for fraud. But we're pretty sure he had nothing to do with the murder. Still, we're hoping if Rogers is viewed as a suspect, those three dolts will feel more at ease." He tipped his head toward the President, Booger, and Delmont. "Which should make them careless."

I was intrigued. "So, what should we do in the meantime?

He choked back a chuckle. "'We' shouldn't do anything."

"You mean we're just going to sit around and stare at them? Tiny's already been doing—"

He cut me off. "No. We're going to dance." He brushed the back of his fingers down the side of my face. "We've never danced together, have we?"

"Nope."

"And it's New Year's Eve. So we definitely should dance." He tucked a wayward strand of hair behind my ear. "Now, I may not be as good as some of your partners." Undoubtedly, he was referring to Buddy and Buford. "But I'm confident I can hold my own."

I brushed my lips against his and uttered, "Okay, deputy, show me what you've got."

₨   ℛ

As RANDY LED ME to the dance floor, I reminded myself just how lucky I was. He was a wonderful man and handsome, too. He was dressed in black jeans, a light-weight sweater, and a tweed sport jacket. And while he was clean shaven, his hair was in need of a trim. The ends curled just above the collar of his jacket, and when he circled toward me, a wavy band of it fell across his forehead. From what I gathered, the sheriff routinely ordered him to get it cut, but I had the sneaking suspicion he put it off just to irritate the man.

After finding an opening on the crowded floor, he pressed his hand against my lower back and silently urged me to tuck myself against him. I happily obliged. He felt good. And he smelled good, too. A combination of soap and musk and a scent all his own.

He lifted my chin with his finger. "Are you sniffing me?"

I cringed. "Umm . . . no?"

He dropped his head back and laughed before starting me across the floor.

The band was playing the old jazz classic, "What Are You Doing New Year's Eve?" The song was made famous by Ella Fitzgerald, and while the woman who sang it for us obviously wasn't on par with that legend, she definitely was first-rate.

As was Randy. He was a marvelous dancer. True, he didn't incorporate the creative footwork regularly put to use by Buddy and Buford. But he was smooth and sure of himself, which meant he was easy to follow. Exactly what I'd hoped for since it allowed me to concentrate on him rather than my feet.

"Randy," I murmured as we two-stepped around the edge of the dance floor, "are we okay?" Normally I avoided serious discussions, but I felt compelled to find out why he had acted so strangely the previous evening. It had weighed on me all day long.

"Of course we're okay. Why do you ask?"

"Well, I guess I'm still confused about last night."

"Emme, I told you I had to get some rest. I hadn't slept in almost two days. I couldn't have performed—"

A giggle got past me, stopping him mid-sentence. "I didn't mean that. I understand why you didn't stay over. But I don't get the point of all that talk about never interfering with my work or my friendships."

We shuffled around another couple.

"I probably shouldn't have said anything."

"But you did. So explain."

He nestled me against his chest and spoke in my ear. "It was nothing."

"Randy, please tell me."

He sighed. "Oh, all right." He then whistled along to the music but otherwise remained mum.

"Now, Randy. Tell me now."

"Okay. Okay." He sighed again as he put some distance between us. "Well, you see, when I got home from Minneapolis after Christmas, Margie asked how our time together went, and I told her it was great. I also told her how much I . . . cared about you. And that I didn't want to screw things up this time."

"Wait a minute. I was the one to cause us problems." With a spin, he led me past several other dancers. "I was the one who kissed Buddy."

He pulled me closer. "Don't remind me. But that wasn't what I meant." He swallowed hard. "Ahh, you see, Rosa dumped me because she said I bossed her around. And I didn't want that to happen again."

Every muscle in my body went rigid. I actually felt it happen.

Randy must have felt it, too, because I heard him mutter, "Shit."

That pretty much summed up my feelings, as well. I dreaded being compared to his old girlfriend. It was a no-win for me. I'd seen her. I couldn't stack up against her, and not just because she was really stacked. She was gorgeous, too, and she came across as sophisticated and self-assured. All the things I wasn't. But how could I tell Randy how I felt without sounding insecure?

"Emme? I wasn't making a comparison." Maybe I wouldn't have to. Apparently, the guy was clairvoyant. "I just didn't want to wreck what we had going. When we were apart, I realized just how much I wanted you in my life."

"Then why'd it take you so long to accept my apology?"

His laugh bounced off the ceiling as he twirled me under his arm at the end of the song.

ஐ   ௧

"I ASKED MARGIE FOR ADVICE," Randy explained as we waited for the band to begin its next tune. He had tugged me against him, my back to his chest, his arms around my waist. "See, I never even realized I was doing it. Being bossy, I mean. Or putting what I wanted ahead of what she wanted. But that's what Rosa claimed." He kissed the top of my head. "Anyhow, Margie told me to make sure you knew I respected your job and your friendships."

I was glad he was behind me because I didn't want him to see the tears pricking my eyes. "Too bad you didn't ask Margie for advice earlier." I made an effort to sound detached. "If you had, you still might be with Rosa."

He swung me around. "I don't want to be with her." He clasped my shoulders and peered into my eyes, his own eyes resonating sincerity and, in turn, putting me at ease. "I want you, Emme. Only you. I'm just not very good at expressing myself."

I offered him what I'm sure looked like a cockeyed smile. "And what I just said? Well, that was my insecurity getting the better of me." I shrugged. "It happens sometimes."

"Don't be insecure about us."

"I'll try."

He caressed my cheek. "And let me know what I can do to help."

"Well, you can start by kissing me."

He did. It was soft and warm and wonderful.

"And, Randy? Don't worry about bossing me around. You can say whatever you think needs saying. But, in the end, I'll pretty much do what I want."

"Believe me, I've figured that out."

I chucked. "So, are we okay?"

"I don't know."

"What?"

"Dance with me some more, and I'll see."

I smiled. "Okay, boss."

℘   ℭ

WHEN WE REJOINED BARBIE and Tiny at the table, they were looking especially somber, notwithstanding the funny cardboard New Year's Eve crown on Barbie's head.

As I sat down, she handed me a crown of my own, and I worked it into my hair.

"Now Vivian's not the only queen around here." Despite her cheerful tenor, she was clearly on edge.

Wanting to ease the tension in the air and put a genuine smile on my friend's face, I decided to tease Tiny. It was a daring move, but I did it just the same. "So, Tiny, where's your crown?" I bit the inside of my cheek to keep from smiling. "Don't you want to be a queen, too?"

He snarled, which would have been scary if Barbie hadn't laughed. "Tiny, you have to admit that was funny."

He glowered. "I don't have to admit anything."

That made her laugh all the more, and I tentatively joined in as I snatched a piece of watermelon from the small plate in the middle of our table.

Randy also grabbed one, popping it into his mouth before whispering something to Tiny.

204

Right away, Barbie and I hunched forward to listen in, prompting them to fall silent.

"What?" Barbie asked incredulously. "It's rude to whisper in front of others. In fact, you should be ashamed of yourselves." She squared her shoulders. "Now, what were you discussing?"

Tiny must have figured sandbagging her would be impossible because he instantly answered, "Burr Nelson. We were talking about Burr Nelson."

"And? What did you say about him?"

Tiny scowled, but his quirked lips belied his otherwise stern expression. "Randy just told me it sounds like the guy didn't know anything about the fraud scheme. At least not initially."

The waitress approached the table, and Randy paid her for our drinks. "Thanks, Kate," he said with a wink. Kate's cheeks turned red, and my eyes rolled all the way back in my head.

"'At least not initially?'" Barbie repeated. "What does that mean?"

With his voice uneven from laughing over my reaction to his exchange with the waitress, Randy answered, "He probably caught on at some point. It'd be tough for anyone, even someone as clueless as him, to be oblivious forever." He passed out our drinks. "But we've been unable to find evidence along those lines. And he wasn't involved in the scam himself."

"How about the other two council members?" Barbie asked. "The two who didn't invest in the wind farm?"

"They've been cleared," Randy noted. "They may have become suspicious, but that's it."

"Let's return to Burr for a minute," I said.

"Yeah," Barbie agreed. "Why was he in here earlier, yakking it up with the President and those other two yahoos?"

"That's what I was about to explain to this guy." Randy nudged Tiny's arm. "Ed called just before I got here. He caught Burr on his way out of town and interviewed him for a second time. I guess Burr caved and told him the President had blackmailed him into resigning his council seat after his daughter—"

I waved my hand to stop him. "We know all about that, Randy."

Visibly baffled, he opened his mouth but closed it right away again.

"We just can't figure out why he was in here." Barbie subtly pointed her finger in the direction of the bar. "With them."

Randy shook his head in an obvious attempt to clear his confusion. "He wanted to make sure the President wouldn't cause any trouble for him or his daughter. Supposedly, he was afraid the guy might do something drastic."

"Drastic?"

"Yeah. You see, Burr messed up. He was supposed to confirm the President's story. The one about him entering the Maverick ahead of Tom. But he didn't do it. Either on purpose or—"

"Because he's so dumb he got confused," Barbie finished for him.

"This is all very interesting." Tiny pushed back his chair. "But, I have to go see a man about a horse." He flicked Randy's shoulder. "The President's on the move. Headed for the john." Tiny hoisted himself up, then did the same with his pants.

"If you aren't back in five minutes," Randy said in a hushed tone, "I'm coming in after you."

"Oh, God, now I'm so excited I won't be able to do my job."

Randy showed him his middle finger, and Tiny chuckled as he lumbered away.

"Well, I'm going back to the café for a minute." Barbie got up. "When I was in there before, I noticed Sherri Bjorklund's 'Broccoli, Cheddar, Chicken, Tater Tot Hot Dish' on the counter."

"What?"

"It's a mouthful. And it's incredible. She won this year's Pelican Pontoon Pussycat's annual cook-off at the Breeze Barn down in Tracy, Minnesota."

"Tracy, Minnesota? That's a long way from here, isn't it?"

"Yeah. But that doesn't stop folks from entering the competition. They just hook batteries and converters to their cars to keep their electric skillets warm, and off they go."

I gently pulled on her arm. "Barbie, I know you're worried, but you simply can't keep eating like this."

She swept my hand away. "You wouldn't say that if you saw that hot dish." She patted the front of her spandex dress. "So, are you coming along or not?"

I looked at Randy. "I better go with her. If I don't, she might do something extreme, like devour an entire pie."

"I only did that once!"

I looped her arm. "Come on. Let's go." I glimpsed over my shoulder. "We should be back in a minute. If we aren't, call—"

"An ambulance?" Randy suggested.

"No. Overeaters Anonymous."

Chapter Twenty-Seven

E STARTED ACROSS THE MIDDLE ROOM, Barbie two steps ahead of me. "I have to make a pit stop," she said over her shoulder while gesturing toward the bathroom.

At the same time, I spotted Booger and Delmont moving in the direction of the back door. Randy saw them, too, his demeanor clearly communicating his dilemma. He wanted to keep tabs on the pair, but, as Tiny's backup, he had to stay put.

I pivoted, fully intending to inform Barbie that this was her chance to visit with Booger and Delmont without the President interfering. Just one problem. She was no longer in front of me. In fact, I only caught a flash of her leopard print as the bathroom door closed.

Damn! I snuck another peek. Booger and Delmont were definitely on their way outside. If they were headed home, we'd lose our opportunity to learn what they knew about Boo-Boo's death. After all, striking up a conversation in a bar was one thing. Following them to their houses to discuss murder was something else entirely. Even Barbie would have misgivings about doing that.

Muttering an entire string of colorful curses, I weaved my way through the crowd, toward the pair. While I hadn't planned on involving myself any further in the investigation, I couldn't wait for Barbie. Who knew how long she'd be? Just pulling her Spanx over her thighs and hips would take a while. I'd seen that firsthand.

As I neared the back door, Randy caught my eye, and it was obvious from his expression he was aware of my intentions and didn't approve of them. He glowered while shaking his head.

In response, I merely looked at him quizzically, as if I had no idea what he was trying to convey. Then, I gave him a little finger wave while assuring myself that later—perhaps, much later—he'd be pleased that I'd trailed after the idiots for him.

℘ ☙

ONCE OUTSIDE, I BECAME Nancy Drew in four-inch heels and a mini dress.

Right away I noted that my "subjects" had rounded the corner of the "V" and were dogtrotting across the back parking lot. I followed at a distance. They stopped at a red, extended-cab pickup, complete with topper, and, there, under the glow of a streetlight, lit cigarettes while loitering near the driver's door.

As for me, I sauntered past their vehicle, as well as the next three, before strategically meandering back to the rear of their truck. Assured I was hidden from view, I then folded my arms and rebuked myself for not grabbing my jacket from the back of my chair. Of course, that would have meant getting close to Randy. And he would have handcuffed me to the table to keep me from following these clowns. So . . .

"Can we trust him to keep quiet?" That was one of the men.

"Oh, yah," answered the other. "He wouldn't dare say a word about us because we can incriminate him."

The first guy then mumbled something I couldn't make out before the second man scoffed, "To my way of thinkin', he got himself killed. It was his own damn fault."

More mumbling, leading me to edge along the back of the truck in an effort to hear better. I even considered sitting on the fender and tilting an ear farther in their direction but decided against it when I noticed all the highway salt that coated the truck.

I pushed forward another step, though, and that's when my foot slipped, and a shriek escaped my mouth. I reached for the bumper, hoping to save myself from falling on the icy asphalt, but I grabbed nothing but air and landed on my butt.

Booger and Delmont rushed around the back of the truck to discover me sprawled out on the ground, my dress barely covering my lap. "Whatcha doin' back here?" Distrust filled Booger's beady eyes.

"I slipped." I stated the obvious to buy time to come up with a plausible story. "I . . . umm . . . you see, I put my purse in my car so I wouldn't have to lug it around, and I fell while walking back to the bar." As stories went, it wasn't bad. "Guess my heels are just too high to wear outside during the winter." I lifted my hand, and Delmont dragged me to my feet.

"Where's your car?" Rubbing the end of his nose with his fist, Booger considered the long line of vehicles that packed the parking lot and cluttered the alley.

"Ahh, back over there." I gestured vaguely before wiping the rear of my dress.

I wasn't sure of my original intention. Had I merely intended to watch where these two went? Or, had I actually planned to question them? I suppose it didn't matter. With them glaring at me, I now only had one goal in mind. To get back inside, among lots of people, as quickly as possible. "Well . . . I better go. My friends are waiting for me. If I don't return soon, they'll hunt me down." Booger didn't budge. "Yeah, well, thanks again for helping me." I volleyed a glance between the two. "Now, I really need to leave."

Booger scowled at me for what seemed like forever but, most likely, was only five or ten seconds. Even so, it was downright frightening. Then, finally, he shuffled to the side, allowing me to scoot between him and the truck and scurry away.

₮&#9) &#9) ℞

As I APPROACHED OUR TABLE in the bar, I saw that Barbie was back. A plate of what I assumed was "Broccoli, Cheddar, Chicken, Tater-Tot Hot Dish" was in the middle of the table, a small stack of Styrofoam bowls and plastic forks next to it.

Reaching my chair, I snatched my jacket and slid it over my arms before sitting down. "Ohhh, it's cold out there."

Randy frowned, the wrinkles along his forehead so deep he could have planted corn in them. "Really? And it's only winter. Who would have thunk?" Apparently, he was serving sarcasm with his hot dish.

Not having an appetite for the former, I turned to Barbie. "These two won't even try it," she said, gesturing toward the plate, "but I know you will because you appreciate good food."

I honed in on the hot dish. Occupying myself with good eats just might help me avoid Randy and his wrath, so I lifted a bowl from the stack and filled it up.

"What did you learn out there?" Tiny asked as I claimed a fork.

Unwilling to come right out and admit I'd messed up, I shoveled food into my mouth and mumbled, "Not much. How 'bout you? Learn anything in the 'athroom?"

Tiny adjusted the do-rag on his head. "Not a damn thing. The President used the john and went back to the bar without a word to anyone." He shuttered. "He didn't even wash his hands."

Randy's eyes tugged at me like magnets, and when I gave in and peeked at him, I noticed that curiosity had apparently chased away most of his annoyance. "Did you talk to them?" he asked.

"A little." For some stupid reason, I then added, "After they found me spying on them."

"What?" He practically jumped out of his chair. "See, Tiny? I told you I should have gone after her."

"It's okay," I assured him with a pat on the hand. "I fast-talked my way out of it."

He didn't seem placated. "What happened exactly?" He looked from me to Tiny and back again. "Tell us everything."

So I repeated Booger and Delmont's exchange verbatim, including what they said after discovering me behind their truck.

Once I was finished, Randy hunched closer. "Are you sure they believed you were just passing by?"

"I think so, although Booger did seem kind of wary. I may have imagined that, though. See, I was . . ." I cleared my throat. "Okay, I'll admit it. I was a little scared."

Tiny spoke next. "You didn't hear them refer to the President by name?"

"No. I just assumed they were talking about him."

"And they didn't mention anyone in particular when they discussed Owen Bair's murder?"

"No, they didn't even reference Owen specifically."

Tiny turned to Randy. "We need more."

With a sigh, Randy pushed back his chair. "I'll find them."

"Then what?" I asked.

"I'll keep watch over them."

"While I keep tabs on Mr. Big." Tiny bobbed his head at the President.

"What about backing each other up?"

Randy stood. "Change of plans."

The back door squeaked open. Booger and Delmont strolled in. And Randy dropped back down on his chair. "Looks like I won't be going any-where, after all."

The two men snaked their way through the crowd, even passing by our table, where only a glimpse was necessary to determine that Booger was glowering in my direction. When they approached the President at the bar and began talking, another glimpse was all I needed to conclude that I was the subject of their conversation.

"No doubt about it," Tiny said, "those guys are definitely worried about you, Emme."

Randy clasped my hand and groaned. "Remember how I told you I'd never keep you from doing what you wanted, although, at times, I wouldn't necessarily like it?" He didn't wait for me to respond. "Well, this is one of those times."

℘ ☙

WHEN THE BAND STARTED PLAYING "Crying Time," Randy invited me to take another spin around the dance floor. Granted, he may have issued the invitation in an effort to alter his surveillance, but I suspected it had more to do with keeping me from taking the song literally and crying my eyes outs. You see, once Tiny's words sunk in, I started to shake. And since I was wearing my jacket and the place was nearly stifling from all the people milling about, Randy, the detective, deduced that, most likely, my shivers were from debilitating fear rather than plain, old, cold air.

"It's going to be okay." That's what he whispered to me over and over again as we waltzed across the floor.

"I wish I never would have stepped outside." I was lightheaded from the realization that the people quite possibly responsible for Boo-Boo's death now had me in their sights.

"Don't worry. I think Tiny was mainly trying to scare you. Pay you back for that 'queen' comment."

I glanced up at him. His jaw was set. His lips were pressed into a tight line. And his eyes were hard.

"Yeah, right," I uttered. "For a minute, I almost believed you."

He kissed my temple. "I won't let anything happen to you, Emme. I promise."

"You may not be able to stop it."

∾   ℞

When our dance ended, Randy and I literally bumped into Margie and John. It was closing in on eleven o'clock, and the two of them, along with a number of their friends, were practicing bringing in the New Year by blowing horns and shaking those cheap metal rattles.

"Are you having a good time?" Randy asked, determined to put on a good front.

"More fun than a gopher in soft dirt." Margie answered.

She then pointed at my jacket with one hand while fanning her rosy face with the other. "Aren't ya hot in that thing?"

"I'm actually kind of cold. I may be coming down with something."

"Oh, that wouldn't be good." She winked. "It would definitely put a damper on your evenin'."

John chimed in. "And right now da only thing puttin' a damper on da night is all dat nonsense 'bout da wind farm and murder and such."

"Yeah," Randy agreed. "But, hopefully, we'll get it all straightened out real soon."

"Well, if I beat ya to it and get my hands on da son-of-a-gun who hoodwinked me and my loved ones, dere won't be much left of 'im by da time ya show up."

"Now, John, don't do anything rash," Randy cautioned. "Especially tonight."

"I won't. But I enjoy thinkin' about it."

A woman I didn't recognize drew near and, after a few words in Margie's ear, steered her toward a small group of ladies on the opposite side of the room, saying something about needing a picture of the bride with her bowling team. As for Randy and John, they continued to huddle over the investigation, while I allowed myself to eavesdrop on two women nearby. I didn't want to think about murder for a while, and their conversation sounded as if it might be the perfect escape.

"Oh, yah," one of them said in response to a comment about her nephew's recent wedding in Lancaster, "I couldn't believe it. Da dance wasn't even over yet, and da bride took off with one of da groomsmen."

"Took off?" the other women repeated. "What do ya mean 'took off'?"

"She went home with him. Left her new husband, my nephew Earl, right there on da dance floor, all by himself."

"Oh, for land sake," the second woman exclaimed. "If that don't beat all."

"Oh, yah, it was da darndest thing I ever seen. Earl's beside himself. He don't know what to do."

"Well, I suppose, he just has to put it behind him and get on with his life. There's no point in beatin' a dead horse."

"No, but it can't hurt, either."

§   ⟡

RANDY AND I WERE ON OUR WAY back to our table when we heard the band leader announce a dance-off. Naturally, I abruptly applied my brakes.

"Oh, no," Randy objected. "I realize you're anxious, and you want to distract yourself, but I won't be a part of any dance contest."

"You won't be dancing by yourself. I'll be right there with you."

He looked at me as if peering over the top of eye glasses. "No, Emme." I offered up a pouty bottom lip, but it did no good. "You aren't going to guilt me into it."

My shoulders drooped. "This is turning out to be a shitty night." I nodded toward the jerks at the bar.

"You knew better than to go after them." He pulled me into a hug before leaning his head back far enough to see into my eyes. They must have provided evidence of how troubled I felt because he said, "Okay. Tell you what. I won't dance, but I will watch these other fools with you, if you want to do that."

Not exactly what I had in mind, but better than nothing. "Fine. But let's get a little closer."

He glanced down. Our bodies were pressed together, not a speck of light between them. "To get any closer, we'd have to get naked. And while that's an appealing idea, and I thank you for the offer, I'm technically on duty, so I'll have to take a rain check."

I slapped his chest. "Very funny." He was obviously trying to make me laugh, and he'd almost succeeded. "Come on." I grabbed his hand and towed him to the edge of the dance floor, where a crowd had gathered.

₨ ‒ ‚

BEFORE WE HAD A CHANCE to watch the first contestants, Randy leaned over and said, "Sorry, Emme, but I have to go." With long, no-nonsense strides, he then made his way back to our table, me following in his wake.

Tiny was already standing when we got there. "The President and his buddies just headed out the back door."

"Okay." Randy kissed me on the cheek. "I'll phone you when I can. But don't wait up. It could be an all-nighter." He followed up with a brief hug. "Don't worry, Emme. You'll be perfectly safe. Between Tiny and me, we'll keep tabs on them until word comes down to make an arrest."

At that, both men took off, while I slumped into the chair next to Barbie.

"Happy New Year to us," she deadpanned before downing the remainder of her drink.

"I suppose you didn't have a chance to talk to Booger and Delmont before they left."

She set her empty glass on the table and picked up the swizzle stick. "Tiny said it was too risky. He said he didn't like the way they were looking at you, so I needed to keep my distance." She paused. "Since he was deadly serious, I didn't try to argue with him."

I shivered. "Thanks for sharing."

"Well, you asked."

I scanned the room, not noticing much of anything. "Now what?"

"I guess we see what tomorrow brings." She snapped her swizzle stick in half. "As for tonight, I'm going home. While I like you well enough, Emme, I don't want to be kissing you at midnight."

ॐ   ॐ

AFTER BARBIE TOOK OFF, I stopped by the café for a "poor me" plate of desserts. Midnight was approaching, and I was all alone. My plan was to have a private pity party, fall into a sugar coma before the stroke of midnight, and, with any luck, wake to news that all the bad guys had been apprehended, and Randy was free for a few days.

Returning to my room, I picked up Otto and carried him downstairs and outside for a quick potty break. On our way back, I heard arguing around the corner of the building. I stopped in my tracks, not at all sure what to do. I didn't want to intrude, but, at the same time, I had no desire to trek all the way around to the other entrance. Not in my ridiculous heels. So, I bided my time, hoping the tense-sounding back and forth would soon end.

To ensure I wouldn't be discovered while waiting—something that could prove embarrassing—I used one hand to muzzle Otto and the other to balance myself against the wall and prevent another noisy fall. Then, because I'm me, I put both my ears to work deciphering what was being said. And, by whom.

"You dipshits," one of the men halfway shouted. "I still can't believe you let her hear you."

"Wait just a gall-darn minute. Like I already explained, we don't know for sure she heard anything."

"Right," the first guy replied in a mocking tone. "She wasn't following you. She just happened to be wandering around outside on a winter night, wearing not so much as a jacket."

A third man, his voice far more timid than the other two, entered the conversation. "She told us she was—"

"Yeah, yeah, I know what she told you."

I inhaled a deep breath of cold air, praying it would somehow freeze my nerves so they'd quit rattling. See, it wasn't necessary to glimpse around the corner to make any identifications. The guy doing the yelling was the President, and the other two were Booger and Delmont.

I looked at the darkness that surrounded me. Tiny and Randy were out there somewhere, watching. But whether or not they were close enough to hear what was being said was another matter. It would have been nice to help them out by remaining where I was and listening in and reporting back to them, but I was too scared. These guys were talking about me. And they weren't debating my finer points. Given that, I simply wanted to scram.

First, though, I had to come up with a plan for getting from Point A to Point B without being detected. I glanced ahead and behind, the breeze catching my hair, and a tangle of it drifting across my face. As I swept it back, Otto wiggled from my grasp, jumped to the ground, and scampered in the direction of the men, barking as he went.

"Damn!" I had no choice but to give chase, slipping and sliding and practically smacking into the President as I took the corner.

I propped up my hands to keep from slamming into his chest. "Oh, I'm s-sorry," I stuttered.

"What the hell?" He gripped my upper arms

I flinched. "I was . . . umm . . . walking my dog before bed, and he got away from me." I wiggled out of his grasp, reached down, and snatched up Otto.

"Don't people usually have their dogs on leashes when they walk 'em?" He glared, and I cowered under his scrutiny.

"Well . . . I . . . I just took him out so he could go potty. I guess I wasn't really w-walking him."

While I could hardly believe it was possible, the man's glare actually intensified. "How long have you been listening to us?"

"I . . . I w-wasn't listening. I was chasing my dog."

The President stepped closer. Otto growled. And the President reached for him, or so I thought.

Instinctively, I jumped back. "Don't touch my dog!" I was shocked by the force of my words.

The President laughed, the creepy sound of it making my breath hitch. "I wasn't going to touch your dog." He teased a twig from my hair.

"I was just reaching for this." He tossed it on the ground. "We wouldn't want you to get scratched or hurt in any way, now, would we?"

His threat made my heart thud against my ribcage.

Skimming the parking lot, I searched for signs of Randy and Tiny. I figured it was a good time for them to make an appearance.

The President followed my gaze. "You expecting someone?" He chuckled, his tone colored a very dark shade, probably "menacing black."

Randy and Tiny were nowhere to be seen. Neither was anyone else. An hour earlier scads of people were outside. But, now, everyone was inside. Evidently, they were waiting for the ball to drop.

I guess, in a way, I was, too. Waiting for the ball to drop, that is.

Chapter Twenty-Eight

STREAM OF PEOPLE HUSTLED from the bar. The band was taking a short break before ringing in the New Year. And the crowd was providing me with the perfect opportunity to flee. The President and his groupies wouldn't dare hold me against my will in front of all these witnesses.

I edged away as the three men glared. Another step backwards and I twirled around and rushed inside and up to my room.

There, I locked the door, set Otto on the bed, and called Randy. I got his voicemail and left an incoherent message, realizing halfway through it that neither the President nor his minions had said anything truly incriminating. But the man had issued a threat of sorts, which was enough for me to beg Randy to call as soon as possible.

Hanging up, I donned my pink flannel pajamas and climbed into bed, slipping under the covers and propping up the pillows. Then, with Otto beside me, I started in on my dessert plate, determined to replace all scary thoughts with nice, sugary ones.

My first selection was a Fabulous Fudge Bar, made famous by Bread and Chocolate, a small eatery in St. Paul. But, despite its gooey goodness and the cacophony of festive music and high-spirited voices from the party below, a sense of dread filled me until there was no room for anything else. Not even incredible chocolate.

Returning the half-uneaten bar to my plate and my plate to the nightstand, I flicked off the lamp and snuggled under the blankets. I willed Randy to phone, if for no other reason than to talk me out of the fear that had me in its grip. The clock on the nightstand read 11:45 p.m. Otto wiggled against my back. And I must have nodded off.

$\wp$ $\wp$

I AWOKE TO THE WIND howling and the stairs creaking. It was 3:00 a.m. The party was over. No more music. No more laughter.

The wind didn't bother me, but the noise coming from the stairwell caused goosebumps to sprout along my arms and legs. I told myself the sounds were nothing but the aching of any old building, the result of wood shifting against the cold. And I almost had myself convinced until the creaking grew louder, as if moving closer.

I shook my head to clear the sleep that dimmed my senses and listened more intently. No, it wasn't simply the groan of stairs. It was something else. I leaned forward, sticking an ear out front. It sounded an awful lot like . . . footsteps. Yes, footsteps. And they had topped the landing and were crossing the hallway.

I picked up my phone, and punched in Randy's number. Again, the call went to voicemail. My muscles tightened before a thought worked its way through my sluggish mind. Maybe the boots drumming against the floor outside my door belonged to Randy. Maybe he was in the hallway. I dropped my phone and hollered his name, suddenly feeling foolish for allowing my nerves to get the best of me. "Randy, is that you?"

Nothing. No answer. And, just like that, feelings of foolishness were replaced by the weight of impending doom.

I grabbed the phone again. I'd call 911 and reach Randy that way. Or, if not him, Tiny or Ed. I pressed a button. The screen lit up. And that's when I caught a whiff of smoke.

My call forgotten, I fumbled for the bedside lamp, almost knocking it over before locating the switch. Twisting it on, a pool of light illuminated the room enough for me to see smoke seeping in under the door.

I threw off my blankets and discovered Otto behind my knees. I swept him into my arms, swung my legs over the edge of the bed, and stuffed my feet into my tennies.

I needed to call for help. But where had I set my phone? I'd just had it. I tossed the covers about. Checked the floor as well as between the bed and the wall. But it wasn't anywhere to be found.

Unwilling to waste more time searching, I grabbed my purse from the bureau, hitched it over my shoulder, and rushed toward the door, Otto snug against my chest. Once there, I hesitated. Was someone on the other side? Had I really heard footsteps? Or was it only the crackling of a fire?

I shook off those questions. The answers didn't matter. Regardless of what was going on in the hallway, I had to pass. I had to get out. And I had to do it now.

Cautiously, I extended my free hand and patted the door, surprised to feel no heat. I touched the knob, first tentatively, then more insistently. No, the knob wasn't hot, either. Still, smoke persisted in filtering into the room and curling through the air. How could that be?

Totally confused, I leaned my ear close to the door but heard nothing. No more sounds of fire. No creaking or crackling. Yet, smoke continued to wind its way in.

I unlocked the deadbolt and slowly turned the knob. I inched the door toward me until I was able to peek into the hall. And once I had, I blinked as my brain worked to make sense of the scene before me.

There was no fire. Not a house fire, at any rate. Rather, Sheriff Halverson was crouched in front of me, a stack of Styrofoam, café, to-go boxes on the floor next to him. In his hands, he held one of those boxes and a lighter. Much of the box was burning, creating a lot of smoke and a terrible stench.

He stood when he saw me, a sneer tipping the corners of his mouth. "Great for making smoke," he explained, waving the box in the air.

"What are you doing?"

He snorted. "Getting you to open the door. I didn't think you'd do it if I knocked."

"But . . . why?" I had trouble finding the words needed under the circumstances because the circumstances made absolutely no sense. "Why are you here? Why are you doing this?"

"Why? Because you're causing me problems." His eyebrows twitched. "I warned you there'd be trouble if you stuck your nose in my business, but you just couldn't help yourself, could you?"

My heart picked up its pace, the pounding reverberating in my ears. "But I didn't—"

"Stop! Don't lie to me. I'm well aware that you and that nosy bitch of a newspaper lady were asking questions. Snooping around."

"No, not anymore." With fear squeezing my chest, my breathing grew shallow, making it difficult to speak more than a few words at a time. "I'll admit it. We poked around. But we stopped."

"That's not true. You were caught eavesdropping twice tonight." He dropped the Styrofoam box and lighter and raised both arms, bracing them against the door frame.

"But . . ." I stepped back. "I didn't hear anything. I just happened to be—"

"Save it! I know you're on to me. And I wanted those idiots, Booger and Delmont, to do something about it, but they can't do anything right." His eyes were almost fully dilated. "They couldn't even shake off your boyfriend and that federal agent, so I guess I'll have to take care of you myself."

"Take care of me?" As I repeated the words, the reality of the situation hit me. The sheriff intended to kill me!

I jumped forward and pushed against the door, desperate to get away. But the crazy man in front of me shoved his foot across the threshold and used his shoulder to bang against the partially closed door, sending Otto and me stumbling backwards onto the bed. I grabbed Otto, sprang to my feet, and slapped the man, while Otto growled, barked, and nipped.

The sheriff pushed me back onto the bed. "Don't even think about leaving." He rubbed the cheek I'd hit. "You had your chance. You should have left town when I told you to. But you didn't. Now, it's too late."

"I don't . . . I don't understand. Why are you doing this?" Terror engulfed me. I was being held captive in a bedroom above an empty café, in a tiny town that was fast asleep.

"You really aren't very bright, are you? Everyone considers you some sort of whiz kid because you've 'solved' a couple murders. But you just tripped over the truth both times, didn't you?"

"T-That's r-right."

"You aren't a better investigator than me, are you?"

"N-No, I'm not. Not at all."

"Neither is Ed." His eyes glazed over, as if watching something at another time and place. "He's never solved squat. Yet, he has some cocka-mamie idea that he'd make a better sheriff than me."

I slowly scooted to the edge of the bed. He appeared distracted by his thoughts, and I was hellbent on taking advantage of that.

Before I could press my feet to the floor, however, he slapped my face and yelled, "Stay put!"

My head jerked back, my right cheek stinging, and the metallic taste of blood trickling down my throat. My eyes filled with tears. Even so, I glared at him defiantly, refusing to let them spill down my face.

"I figured that cow who runs the newspaper would be my biggest problem." Spittle sprayed from his mouth as he spoke. "But I came up with a damn good plan to take her out of the picture." He had the face of an insane person. I knew the look. I'd seen it a couple times before. Right here in Kennedy. "I'd make her nut-job husband take the fall for the murder." He tilted his head. "Get it? Take the fall? I didn't even try to be funny, but I was." He shrugged. "Comes natural. I'm smart like that. Too smart for the likes of you or my no-account deputies or even the feds."

I couldn't think straight. Since I was too scared to plan an escape, I had no choice but to buy time by keeping him talking. "How did you make Tom the main suspect?" I did my utmost to sound intrigued instead of scared out of my gourd. "How did you know he couldn't get his investment money back?"

"The President heard him and Owen Bair arguing in the parking lot next to the Maverick."

"But I thought . . ."

"Yeah, I know what you and my deputies thought. Remember, I was at the law enforcement meeting this morning. Hell, I was the one who scheduled it." He smirked. "How else was I to keep tabs on what my men were discovering? How else was I supposed to direct their moves?"

Staring at me, he uttered, "Not very bright at all." He crossed his arms and propped the door frame with his shoulder. "Yeah, the President stopped in Lake Bronson to buy a bottle of whiskey at the off-sale. He heard them arguing, just like he said. But, instead of going into the Maverick, he called me. See, I wanted to talk to Owen Bair, but I couldn't find him."

"Then, you followed him to the park?"

"No, the President did. On his snowmobile." He stopped me from interrupting by saying, "He supposedly likes to ride in bad weather. Gives him some kind of thrill or something." His disgust for the man was evident by his tone.

"Anyhow, I was on duty, but I was grabbing lunch at John's Bar, in Halma." He smirked again. "Even a dedicated cop has to eat." He chuckled at that. "I told the President to tail him until I got there. So, that's what he did. I only found out later you were supposed to meet the guy at the Visitors' Center."

"I was late." The words were barely audible.

"Yep," he nonetheless replied. "Makes all of this your fault in a way, doesn't it?"

I attempted to swallow the surge of guilt that rose against the panic lodged in my throat.

"Anyhow, the President parked his snowmobile in the woods and kept to the tree line, so Owen Bair never even noticed him. Then, when I got there, I had me a chat with him. Mr. Bair, that is."

"That doesn't explain what happened in . . . the observation tower."

He lifted his brows. "That was a mistake. I only intended to talk to the guy. But I saw someone in the woods. It ended up being the President, though I didn't know that at the time. I didn't recognize him. He had his snowmobile suit on. Helmet, too." He altered his stance. "Anyhow, I was afraid we were going to be interrupted, and since I wasn't done speaking my piece, I asked Mr. Bair to go with me to the tower."

"And he went willingly?"

"Well, I'll admit I had to 'encourage' him a little."

"'Encourage him?'"

He shrugged. "I'm a cop. I carry a gun."

"So you planned on killing him all along?"

He gawked at me, as if I were a simpleton. "No! I already told you I only wanted to talk to him. I needed to persuade him to leave my wife alone." He shook his head. "You really have to keep up."

Despite his snide remark, I couldn't stop myself from seeking clarification. "You wanted to talk about your wife?"

"Yeah. She's a good woman, but she's easily swayed. And he'd convinced her to . . . spend time with him." He dragged his hand over his face. "It's partly my fault. I work too much. And she gets lonely. Still, he had no business leading her on."

"And what happened when you confronted him?"

"He got cocky. Started going on about how she had initiated the whole thing. Claimed he wasn't the only one, either. Said she'd hooked up with lots of guys, including the President." He shifted from one foot to the other. "Naturally, I called him a liar. Told him I'd heard that rumor. That I'd even asked the President about it."

"And?"

"And the President said that folks got the story mixed up. That Mitzie was really running around with Owen Bair, not him." His eyes flashed with hatred.

"What happened then?"

"Bair made fun of me. Called me gullible. Said it was no wonder my wife couldn't stand me. I wasn't even man enough to face what was happening in my own marriage." He stared past me and spoke in a modulated tone, as if merely narrating what he was watching. "That's when I hit him. And he hit me back. We struggled over my gun, though it got away from both of us. He was strong, but I'm strong, too, and I'm a whole lot bigger. So, before I knew it, I had him bent backwards over the ledge. He jerked, and I pushed, and he fell." He stopped for the count of two. "I knew he was dead as soon as he hit the ground. His neck was broke. I could tell by the angle."

With a deep breath, I attempted to ease my pounding pulse. It was hard to listen to the details surrounding Boo-Boo's death. Granted, I'd wanted to know them. But, now that I did, I wished them away.

"Anyhow, here we are," the sheriff muttered.

His words tugged me back into the moment. "You're saying it was an accident?" My tongue was sticking to the roof of my mouth. "People will understand an accident. In fact, I'll help you explain what really happened." Not really. But he didn't need to know that.

"I don't think so, Miss Malloy. Contrary to what some folks think, I'm not a sucker. At least, not anymore. Besides, I have an election coming up. I can't be implicated in any wrongdoing, accident or otherwise."

With those words, I pictured all my hope circling the drain. "People will figure it out, you know." I rambled on, not expecting any good to come of it but unable to stop. "Especially if you kill me, too. You have good deputies and—"

"Shut up! They won't figure out a thing. They only do what I tell them." He rested for a second. "Plus, I have a plan."

"A plan? What kind of plan?"

He snorted. "It doesn't matter. You won't be around to see it play out."

That remark made my knees wobble. "Well, then," I uttered, my voice equally shaky, "the least you can do is tell me what it is." *Appeal to his ego*, a little voice in my head reminded me. *Appeal to his ego.* "I imagine it's pretty clever," I quickly added.

His face lit up, and his crazy eyes danced. "Oh, it is." And, after that, he laid it all out for me, the words tumbling from his mouth. "Right after the incident in the tower, I called my wife and got her to admit the President had seduced her. Then, because of that, along with the fact that he had lied to me about it, I wanted to pin Owen Bair's death on him. But it would have been too risky because he'd seen the whole thing. That's why I decided to blame Tom Jenson. Steer my deputies in his direction."

"And the President?"

"He liked the idea. Particularly after I told him it would keep Tom's nosy wife occupied. Keep her from snooping around in the murder investigation or the fraud."

"The fraud?"

He measured me with his gaze. "A few weeks back, the President and Booger and Delmont made the mistake of drinking too much when we were playing poker. Before the night was over, I knew all about that wind-farm scheme." He pointed his finger at me. "Never drink. You need to be in control at all times." He wagged a finger at me in warning.

"Anyhow, I promised not to say or do anything about the scam as long as they gave me the $25,000 Mitzie had invested. See, I have a campaign to finance, and my wife's not being very supportive about helping out. But they agreed. Then, when Owen Bair died, his death just became a part of . . . our agreement, too."

"Is that why the President claimed to enter the Maverick ahead of Tom Jenson?"

"Yep. We didn't want anyone questioning the timing of things. If they did, they'd realize Tom couldn't have done the deed because he was in the bar." His expression turned stormy. "Besides, the President's never had any qualms about lying about anything."

It was evident there was much more to that statement.

"Yeah, the President thought he'd get away with corrupting my wife and lying to me about it." There was a maniacal bend to his smile. "Took me for a fool. But I'm nobody's fool." He puffed himself up. "He got real nervous when he learned the feds were investigating the wind-farm project. We were sure we could manipulate the murder investigation since I was overseeing it. But the fraud investigation was another matter. Even the mighty President had little chance of finagling that, and deep down, he knew it. Plus, I fed the feds information that led them straight to the man." He stopped. "Get it? I fed the feds." He chuckled some more.

"So, how was the President involved in the fraud exactly?"

He squinted at me. "Why do you care?"

"Just curious." I absently petted Otto. I couldn't keep him talking much longer. I had to come up with a plan for escape. Thus far, though, I was drawing a blank. "Think of it as a . . . last request."

He snickered. "Fair enough." He wiped perspiration from his upper lip. "The President invested lots of money in that project, and when Greg Rogers started missing payouts, he confronted him, and the truth came out. But since the President was so enamored with the guy, it was easy for Rogers to convince him to become part of the conspiracy."

"Wait! If you plan to implicate Tom Jenson in Owen Bair's death and the President in the fraud, why hurt me? It'll serve no purpose."

"I can't trust you to keep your mouth shut. And you have to admit, I gave you a chance, but you wouldn't leave town. That means you pretty much brought this on yourself."

He contemplated me for a long minute. "You know, when I visited you at the café, I considered incriminating you. I knew you and your old boyfriend had a rocky past, which would prove useful in creating a motive." He mopped his brow with his forearm. "But your lack of bruises posed a problem. On top of that, you had that damn gas receipt. Given all that, I had to keep to my original plan. Still, I worried about you poking around in my business, and—"

"I didn't uncover anything."

"You listened in on the President and those other two dopes. And you would have figured out things soon enough. Especially about the murder, which was my main concern."

"It wouldn't have happened. Like you said earlier, I'm not that bright. In fact, if you let me go, we can forget this whole thing." Not a chance in hell. But, again, he didn't need to know that.

"I don't think so, Miss Malloy." He straightened and stepped forward, giving me the feeling my time was just about up.

"What about the President?" I was grasping at straws. "If he's arrested for fraud, won't he or Booger or Delmont confess your role in Boo-Boo's death?"

He offered me a droll smile. "I took care of that. Remember, I'm a pretty smart guy." He tapped his right temple. "My wife's prepared to swear she refused the President's advances, which infuriated him. She'll say he swore he'd get back at her. So, if he insinuates anything, we'll contend he simply has an ax to grind."

"Why? Why would she go along with that?"

"She doesn't want her daddy upset with her. And he would be upset if he learned she'd been involved in a series of . . . inappropriate liaisons. Even if she was coerced."

"What about Booger and Delmont? What will stop them from talking?"

He waved his hand dismissively. "Everyone knows they do whatever the President says. Given that, their statements would never hold much credence."

He stepped directly in front of me, and my mind went blank, as if it knew the end was near. As if it knew there was no point in further fighting the inevitable.

Tears clouded my vision, and I was just about to ask if he'd let Otto go before he did whatever he was going to do to me, when I heard what sounded like a car door slam in the alley.

The sheriff must have heard it, too, because he said, "I've enjoyed our little chat, but I better leave now."

I wondered how he planned to kill me and decided to ask. "What about me?"

The man calmly replied, "Well, the Hot Dish Heaven Café is about to burn down, and you'll be trapped in the fire."

"What?"

"You heard me."

As if propelled by a force far greater than me, I then lunged at him. I was determined to stop him from burning down the café. And determined to save Otto and myself. But, as I pushed against him, I caught a glimpse of a shiny metal object in his hand. I also heard my cell phone ring. Then, my world went dark.

Part IV

Eat It All Up

Chapter Twenty-Nine

PRESUMED I WAS DEAD. And because I smelled smoke, I doubted eternity was going to be very pleasant. I couldn't imagine what I had done to warrant a sentence to hell, but, obviously, I'd been sent there. In addition to being smoky, it was dark and smelly. And it scared me to death—well, you know what I mean.

I couldn't overcome the notion that there had been a mistake. That I'd been directed to this place in error. But, if that was true, how did I ask for a review? How did I request a do-over?

My cheek itched. Or was it a tickle? I couldn't rub it. I had no arms. Either that or they just wouldn't work. Figures. Hell was being unable to scratch an itch.

Another tickle. Although this one was wet. And it was followed by several more, all of them accompanied by whining.

Admittedly, I was an accomplished whiner. But I wasn't making these noises. No, it wasn't me. It was someone—or something—else. A dog, perhaps? Yes, a dog. My dog. It was Otto.

How cruel! That was my first thought. How could a little dog be sent to hell? The worst he had ever done was piddle against my indoor flower pots. Otto wasn't particularly smart. All the more reason to judge him with leniency.

More licking and whimpering until I forced my eyes open. They only fluttered, yet it was enough to see Otto sitting on my chest, watching me with deep concern. Once more I went to lift my arms, and this time I succeeded. Barely. I patted his back. "It's okay, little guy." My voice sounded like tires on gravel. "It's okay."

My dog didn't appear convinced. And surveying my surroundings, I understood why. While we weren't in hell or even dead for that matter, we were shut up in my room. And it was rapidly filling with smoke.

Of course we had to get out, but I wasn't sure how to stand up to make that happen. I rolled onto my side and pushed myself into a quasi-sitting position. My head felt like it was about to pop, and when I lifted my hand to inspect it, I discovered a bump the size of a hockey puck. The sheriff must have knocked me out with his gun. I thought I recalled something like that. Again I gently patted the lump, my fingers sticky from the blood matted to my hair. "Otto, we have to go."

I used the bed to leverage myself to my feet. Then, with my pup in my arms, I staggered to the bedroom door. This time I forgot to check the knob, and when I grabbed it, I burned my fingers. Even so, I pulled the door open and peered down the hall. The smoke caused my eyes to water, and I had to rub them a number of times before I got a clear picture of the flames licking their way up the staircase. It wasn't one of the sheriff's tricks. It was the real deal. The café was on fire. And Otto and I were trapped.

Bending over and barely clearing Otto's head, I threw up everything I'd eaten that day. And when done being sick, I collapsed on the floor, completely spent. I wanted to save myself and Otto, but I was too worn out to move. Besides, I had no clue where to go. The flames had ascended the staircase and were making their way down the hall. It wouldn't be long before they overwhelmed us.

My head was fogging up again. I knew Otto was nestled against my chest, and I assumed he was getting sleepy, just like me, but beyond that, I couldn't comprehend much. I needed rest. More rest. After that, I'd be able to . . .

As I fell deeper into the smoky abyss, I heard my furry little friend whimper. Then, he coughed. And even in my stupor, it sounded pathetic. But not nearly as pathetic as the sound he made when he began to gag. That was so wretched I pressed myself back to consciousness just to check on him.

Peering through my matted lashes, I saw him staring at me. By way of another whine, he asked why I wasn't helping him. I tried to answer but couldn't. My mouth was too raw. A coughing fit of my own then led me to scrunch my eyes shut against the pain. And that's when I heard him gag again. No doubt about it, he was dying. My little buddy was dying. If I didn't do something soon, it would be too late.

Calling on every last bit of strength, I wrenched my eyes open and shoved myself to my knees. After that, I crawled back into the bedroom, determined to save Otto or die trying.

℘   ℆

The only escape route was the sole second-story window at the back of my room, and I crawled toward it. Reaching the nightstand, I grabbed the lamp and inadvertently knocked my plate of desserts to the floor. Then, yanking the lamp's plug from the wall socket, I shuffled along on my knees.

At the window, between body-racking coughs, I lifted the lamp over my head, extending its base out in front of me. I was about to swing it at the glass when the fire siren blasted down the street, startling me backwards, onto my butt.

The blaring noise filled my head, while renewed hope overflowed my heart. Evidently, people were on their way. Yet, when I saw Otto's limp form in my arms and heard the staircase collapse behind me, much of that hope fell away.

The town of Kennedy was small, and the fire station was located just down the road from the Hot Dish Heaven Café. But, as was the case in many small communities, Kennedy's firefighters were volunteers, which meant they had to race from their homes to the fire hall to get their equipment before answering any calls. And that took time. Otto and I didn't have time.

No doubt, if we were to survive, I'd have to make it happen myself. So, with desperate urgency driving me, I buried Otto's face in my chest, shut my eyes, and smashed the lamp against the window. Peeking out from beneath my half-closed eyelids, I found I had broken through the inside pane as well as the old storm window.

Using the base of the lamp, I went on to poke away the stubborn pieces of glass. And, once that was done, I dropped the lamp and nabbed a pillow off the bed to wipe the shards from the ledge. I then leaned through the window and spotted a few cars headed into town, but I was certain the people in them wouldn't be able to help us. The smoke was getting thicker. I was having difficulty breathing. And the flames were all but racing into the room.

Barely able to see, I pulled what I hoped was the quilt from the bed and doubled it over the window ledge. Next, I positioned myself on the ledge, as if mounting a horse. Lifting my inside foot out, I contorted my torso until I was perched on the opening, one arm cradling Otto, the other braced against the window frame to keep me from falling. Another glimpse down the road, and I realized I had no choice. My only hope was to jump and pray I didn't die when I hit the icy sidewalk.

To improve my odds by getting five feet closer to the ground, I wiggled around until I was dangling from the window, my free arm clamped like a vise on the ledge. Another loud crash from inside. Probably the floor giving way. I tightened my grip on Otto, made a silent plea to God, and let go. It was then that my world once again faded to black.

ℬ   ℭ

WHEN I CAME TO, I was on a gurney, inside an ambulance. I was covered with blankets, an oxygen mask over my mouth. It was dark, but because of the moonlight shining through the open door, I was able to make out the shadowed figure next to me. It was Randy.

"Welcome back." He bent down and kissed my forehead.

"Otto?" I mumbled through my mask.

"He's fine." A smile lurked at the edges of his mouth. "The guys gave him oxygen, but they'll also have the vet in Greenbush check him out."

I had lots of questions, but I was in too much pain to concentrate on them. "I hurt."

He caressed my cheek with the back of his fingers. "I can only imagine. You have a concussion. In a few minutes, you're going to the hospital in Hallock. You'll spend the rest of the night there with Doc Watson. Remember him?"

I pulled my mask down. "I've spent more time with him than with you." During my first trip to Kennedy, I'd ended up in the hospital, under the care of Doctor Watson, a grisly, old man with a gruff manner but a soft heart. "I don't—"

"Emme, you'll hurt his feelings if you don't go." He was clearly teasing, although his countenance didn't match his words. He appeared worried and, perhaps, even a little scared. "Plus, you have to get checked out. It could have been a whole lot worse. Thankfully, Shitty broke your fall."

"What?" Shitty was a portly plumber who drove a van with a sign on the side that read, "Your Sh** Is My Bread and Butter." Yep, he was a class act. And, from the sound of it, my hero.

"He's a volunteer with the fire department. He was on his way to the fire hall when he spotted you climbing out the window. He stopped his van in the middle of the highway and ran to help. He got there just as you let go. You landed on top of him."

"Is he all right?"

"Yeah. Doc's going to take a few x-rays. But, he seems fine."

I coughed, and Randy returned the oxygen mask to its rightful place over my face. "Rest now. You've got quite an egg on your head and several lacerations. Doc says you'll need stitches."

"Randy."

He nervously fidgeted with my blanket. "You know, if you were that desperate for me to visit, you could have called." Obviously, he wasn't sure what to say and was doing his best to mask his unease. "You didn't have to start the building on fire."

I whispered, "I did call."

He dropped all pretense. "I know." His voice was raspy with emotion. "I got here as soon as I could."

"Did you catch 'im?"

He let go of an exasperated breath. "You mean Booger and Delmont? Well, I lost track of them, and that made me worried about you. I phoned, but you didn't answer. I thought that was odd, so I drove over to make sure you were okay." He sighed. "As I turned down the alley, I spotted the two of them. Booger and Delmont. They were standing next to Delmont's pickup, talking with the sheriff. I pulled up, and the sheriff closed Delmont's truck topper." He shrugged. "The sheriff then sent Booger and Delmont on their way and ordered me back to the office. Said that after questioning them, he saw no point in following them. Said he was positive they had nothing to do with Bair's death. He insisted we start concentrating all our efforts on building a case against Tom."

He took my hand. "I was almost to Hallock when Ed radioed me that the café was on fire. Right away I figured there was a connection to Booger and Delmont."

With his free hand, he brushed my hair off my forehead. "I couldn't get back here fast enough. Ed said he suspected you were trapped inside. He said he'd already called for an ambulance." He swallowed hard. "I was really scared, Emme. Scared that . . ." He didn't finish. There was no need.

Once more I pulled the mask down. "Booger and Delmont weren't there, Randy. Not when the sheriff was with me."

"What?" His hand tightened around mine. "What do you mean, 'when the sheriff was with you'?"

I cleared my throat. "He conned me into opening my bedroom door. Said he had to kill me because I was on to him. I wasn't, but he thought . . ." I touched the welt on my head. "I got him to tell me most everything before he knocked me out and left me to die."

Randy's body tensed. His muscles coiled against my skin. "The sheriff?"

"I thought you knew. You said—"

"I told Ed to pick up Booger and Delmont. He found a couple empty gasoline cans in the back of their truck. Not exactly hard evidence, but he still arrested them on suspicion of arson. They started spilling their guts before he even got them cuffed. Claimed they had nothing to do with the fire. Insisted it had to be the sheriff's doing. Naturally, Ed didn't take them seriously."

"The sheriff wanted me dead, Randy. He was going to make it look like an accident. Like I got caught in the fire."

He shook his head. "That doesn't make sense. He knows it'll take the fire marshal less than two minutes to determine that this was arson."

"So? With me dead, no one but Booger and Delmont could point the finger at him."

Randy continued along that same line of thought. "And, if the gas cans in the back of Delmont's pickup got tied to the fire, their statements would be worthless."

The wheels were spinning in his head. "Tiny and his fed buddies picked him up, Emme. The sheriff, I mean. They had to in light of Booger and Delmont's claims." He glanced over his shoulder. "He's expected to be released soon, though. I need to call Ed and bring him up to date."

"He killed Boo-Boo."

He pulled his head back, as if he'd been cuffed along the jaw. "The sheriff? He confessed to you?"

"Uh-huh. Though the way he tells it, it was more of an accident."

"Why? Did he say why he did it?"

"Boo-Boo had an affair with his wife."

He frowned. "I thought she was involved with the President."

"She was."

I stopped for a much needed breather. "Randy, the President was part of the fraud conspiracy."

"He's not in custody. No one can find him. When the fire started, Tiny dropped his surveillance. Thought he should be here, instead. Then, after Booger and Delmont started running off at the mouth, Tiny volunteered to pick up the sheriff. We decided it would be better for everyone if us deputies kept our distance."

The pain in my head was getting to me, and I may have winced.

"You need to get to the hospital." He gently kissed my lips before once again placing the oxygen mask over my mouth. "I have to go. But I'll check in on you later."

"Be careful," I mumbled.

He chuckled. "Says the woman lying on the gurney in the ambulance."

Chapter Thirty

*I*T WAS NEW YEAR'S DAY, and we were sitting around a table at the Kennedy Senior Center. Randy had picked me up at the hospital around noon. My face was battered, my knees were scratched, the palm of my right hand was burned and patched, and my right ankle was deeply bruised, necessitating crutches for the next week or so.

Before I was released, Randy and Ed interviewed me at length, after which, I borrowed Randy's phone and called my editor. I agreed to file a story about what had happened. I promised to e-mail it to him within the next twenty-four hours. He assured me I'd get a byline. He also wanted to talk to me about changing my assignment. Moving me to hard news. I told him we could discuss it when I returned to the office. But, first, I was taking a two-week vacation.

The nurses at the hospital helped me get the blood out of my hair, and Barbie promised to trim it to hide the bald spot, where stitches stretched for more than an inch. But there wasn't anything they could do to save my pajamas, so I was wearing one of Margie's old sweat suits. It was pink and pilled, with a pair of kittens embroidered on the top. As for the bottoms, they were so big I had to bunch them at the waist and secure the knot with a safety pin. And, if that weren't bad enough, because all my belongings were burned to a crisp, I was presently going commando.

Given that, Margie didn't want her sweat suit back. And while Randy agreed to take me shopping in Grand Forks the following morning, he only did so after laughing at my predicament, until I threatened to hit him with my crutch.

80   CR

BARBIE SERVED COFFEE and Breakfast Hot Dish along with rolls she'd picked up at the Farmer Store before making her way down to Kennedy. She said she was there, with us, as a friend first and a reporter second. But Margie confided in me that our friend needed our company as much as we needed hers. "Tom's sponsor took him to an in-house treatment center this mornin'," she explained. "She can't see him for a while, so she's feeling kind of lost, don't ya know. I'm not sure what she's gonna do."

I had my bad foot propped up on a padded chair. Randy was sitting next to me, his arm slung over my shoulder. Tiny was on the other side of him. While Ed and his wife, Sandy, sat across from him, alongside John and Margie.

"How are you two doing?" Ed asked John and Margie.

John stretched his legs out and folded his hands over his stomach. "We're hangin' in there like loose teeth."

"I can understand why. It had to be a shock. Getting a call on your wedding night that the café was on fire."

"What are you going to do?" Barbie asked the question as she made the rounds with the coffee pot.

"I don't know," Margie replied. "I guess I'll see what the folks at the 'V' have in mind?"

Barbie stopped, the pot hovering over Tiny's cup. "Would you actually consider staying closed?"

Margie glanced at John before shrugging. "It would give us a lot more free time, that's for darn sure. And, at my age, I'm not lookin' forward to goin' through the hassle of buildin' a new cafe." She patted John's arm. "Paintin' the interior of my house has been challengin' enough."

"What about keeping this town going?" I asked, my cup to my lips, the aroma of fresh coffee teasing my nose. "Won't you feel as if you're letting folks down if you don't rebuild?"

Margie tilted her head toward the ceiling and pursed her thin lips as she contemplated the tiles and, ostensibly, my questions. "No," she said at last. "I've given most of my adult life to this town. It's time some of the younger folks step up. It's easy for them to say we should do this or that. It's another thing for them to get off their duffs and do somethin'."

"Whoa!" Randy exclaimed. "You sound a little rough, there."

"Seein' your life's work go up in smoke will do that. It puts every-thin' in perspective. No sugar coatin'."

Ed groaned. "I don't know, Margie. What will we do without the Hot Dish Heaven Café?"

"Uff-da, you'll be so busy after becomin' sheriff, we'll never see ya anyways."

He chuckled. "I haven't won yet."

John turned toward him. "Dat may be. But da sheriff can't very well wage a campaign from jail. And dat's where he'll remain for a long time to come."

Randy let go of a giant sigh. "I still can't believe he killed a man. And tried to kill Emme." He kissed my temple, his whisker stubble scratch-ing my face. I didn't mind.

"Yeah." Ed rubbed his tired-looking eyes. "I always pegged him as dumb but harmless."

Tiny's chair was pushed away from the table, and prior to speaking, he leaned forward and propped his elbows on his thighs and clasped his hands between his knees. "Between good and evil, there's a lot of gray area. You play in it long enough, and you forget what side you actually came in on."

"Is that what happened to the sheriff?" Barbie placed the coffee pot on the table and slid onto the chair next to him.

"Probably. The President, too. They both played fast and loose with the rules for a long time."

"Well, they'll be held accountable now. State prison for the sheriff and federal prison for the President, Booger, and Delmont."

Margie waived her hand, a fork twined among her fingers. "That means there'll be three spots open on the city council. I'm gonna encour-age Burr to go after one of 'em."

"Really?" Ed twisted in her direction. "You think he deserves that?"

Margie didn't hesitate. "Oh, yah. He's a good guy. He just got put in a terrible situation."

Tiny shook his head. "I'll accept that he wasn't actually involved in the scam, but I'm still not convinced he knew nothing about what was going on. He can't be that dumb, can he?"

Everyone else at the table responded with a resounding, "Yes!"

"Ya know," John said, "I've known Burr my entire life, and I want to think da best of 'im, but I'm not sure our friendship will survive dis mess."

Margie gazed at him. "Well, I sure as heck hope it does. He needs his friends, just like the rest of us." She grinned. "Speakin' of friends, guess whose car's been in Burr's driveway ever since late last night?" She answered right away, "Janice's." No one said a thing. "Well, I think it's great. And I hope it's the start of somethin'. Both of 'em could use a good relationship."

Barbie piped up, "If it makes her nicer, I'm all for it." She snapped her fingers. "Hey, do you suppose that's why she's been dressing more con-servatively lately? Burr's a conservative guy."

"Could be," Margie uttered. "Could be."

Ed's wife, Sandy, spoke next. "Emme, are you gonna be okay?"

Everyone looked my way, and I felt my face grow warm from the attention. "Yeah, I'll be fine." I twisted my hair around my finger. "Though I'm still confused about a few things."

Randy leaned in. "Such as?"

"Well, for instance, why didn't the café's smoke detectors go off?"

"The sheriff disabled them."

"And who called in the fire?"

He snorted. "The Anderson sisters. Remember, they keep tabs on everybody and everything from their windows."

"But the fire started in the middle of the night. How did they—"

"When you're their age, I guess you get up a lot."

I had to close my eyes while attempting to make sense of what he'd said. "You mean to tell me I'm not only indebted to Shitty, I also owe Hen-rietta and Hester."

Randy chuckled. "Yeah, big time."

That would take some getting used to.

"Any other questions?" Tiny asked.

"Well, the sheriff said he practically led the President to you. How'd he do that?"

Tiny remained hunched over. "This was not my best work." He shook his head. "I dismissed any suspicions I had about the sheriff being involved in the murder because I thought he was a stand-up guy. Sure, he was full of himself. But he was helpful with the fraud investigation." He immediately amended that statement. "Well, not right away. But after the murder, he was extremely accommodating. It should have raised some flags. Yet, it didn't. Or, at least, I didn't pay any attention to them."

"What did he tell you?"

"Nothing specific. But he definitely nudged me along. Repeatedly told me how folks were concerned about the EDA loan the Kennedy City Council had awarded." He stroked his bearded jaw. "Looking back on it now, I think he wanted to give me more but was afraid I'd ask why he never came forward sooner. Although last night he did tell me that the President had confided in him. Evidently said he intended to split the EDA loan money with Booger and Delmont but had no plans to give Rogers a dime." He groaned. "Yeah, I missed a lot."

Randy nudged him. "Don't beat yourself up. You and your buddies caught the President before he made it to the Canadian border this morning. If you hadn't done that, we probably would have lost him for good." He sighed. "Besides, we all made mistakes. I never should have left Kennedy after I saw Booger and Delmont with the sheriff. I knew something was off. I felt it."

Ed dropped his hand on the table. "Take your own advice, Randy. We all did the best we could at the time. And that's all anyone can ask of us."

He glanced in my direction. "Does that fill in all the holes for you, Emme?"

"Almost." I adjusted my bad foot. "Was . . . umm . . . Boo-Boo . . . involved in the fraud scheme?"

Tiny answered. "From what we've learned, it was just as we suspected. He didn't want to get involved. He was scared. That's why he asked to talk to you, Emme. He wanted your advice."

A part of me still felt as if I had let him down, although I didn't get to wallow in self-pity because Barbie spastically waved her arms over her head until she drew everyone's full attention, mine included.

"Hey, now," she began, "not that I want to belabor the point or anything, but despite Owen Bair's fears regarding the fraud scam, he ended up dying because of his womanizing, which, if you will recall, was my theory all along, even though most of you poo-pooed it." She cast a superior look at each of us. "Therefore, at the very least, you owe me an apology, not to mention your ever-lasting devotion."

Tiny threw a crumpled napkin at her. "Okay," he said, "I'll admit you were right about that. But you didn't want to believe the two crimes were linked, and they were, in a way."

I peeked in her direction. "Barbie, at the risk of cutting short this whole gloating thing you have going, I have a few other questions. Like, why on earth did Booger and Delmont ever agree to put the sheriff's gas cans in Delmont's truck?"

Again Randy answered. "The sheriff knew those two idiots would do whatever the President wanted, so he told them the President had asked that they deliver the empty cans to him."

"But, didn't they see the fire? Didn't they put two and two together?"

Randy shook his head. "The sheriff sent them—and me—on our way before he set the fire. After he had poured the gas. But before starting the fire. Of course, when Ed picked them up and told them what was happening back at the café, they figured things out."

Ed joined in. "Yet, even when they insisted the sheriff was the guy we wanted, I didn't believe them. In truth, they probably would have ended up being blamed for the fire if not for you, Emme. The information you got from the sheriff was paramount to solving these cases."

I took a deep breath. "Now for the million-dollar question. Is there any chance the fraud victims will get their money back?"

Tiny groaned. "Rogers and his wife own some cars and houses and other assets, but because they're encumbered for the most part, no one will get much."

Barbie blanched as he spoke, and I couldn't help but feel sorry for her. She was in her mid-fifties, and her retirement savings were gone.

"But, who knows?" he went on to say in an obvious attempt to give her hope. "Maybe the prosecutors will come up with a way to use the President's assets, along with those of Booger and Delmont, to make partial restitution."

"And the EDA money?"

"Well, it actually looks as if we might recover that."

Barbie patted the table. "Now what?"

"What do you mean?"

She checked her Betty Boop watch. "It's getting late. What's everyone going to do?"

Barbie wasn't very good at subterfuge. It was obvious to the rest of us that she was primarily interested in Tiny's plans. And when we all stared at him, he actually got a bit flustered before he answered. "Well . . . ahh . . . I need to get back to Minneapolis in a few days. And in the meantime, I've got to tie up some loose ends." He hesitated. "I'll probably stay where I am in Karlstad. Probably spend some time in the Maverick tomorrow. I really like that place." He wasn't the least bit subtle. He wanted Barbie to know exactly where she could find him if she were so inclined.

"Hey," he continued awkwardly while casting glances at Randy and Ed, "it was great working with you guys." As far as cover-ups went, it was pretty lame.

"Yeah," Randy replied, his smirk only partially hidden behind his fist, "we'll have to keep in touch."

Margie stood up and arched her back. "Well, John and I need to get on over to Vivian's house. She thinks we need family support in our 'hour of need,' so she's hostin' a dinner for the entire clan."

Barbie snorted. "I doubt Buford or Buddy will be there. Wally and Little Val, either. All four of them were so drunk last night they couldn't have hit the floor with their hats." She winked at Margie. "As you often say."

"Well," John interjected, "I hope it's an early evenin'. I could use about three days in bed." He realized his mistake as soon as the words left his mouth. "I mean three days of sleep."

It was too late. Randy and Ed teased him about wedding nights and honeymoons until Margie raised her hands and said, "You guys make me wish I had more middle fingers."

At that, we all doubled over with laughter.

And only after everyone had settled down again did I ask, "Are you still going to Costa Rica?"

"We'd like to," Margie replied. "We're waitin' to see what kind of deal the airlines will give us under the circumstances. In the meantime, we have tons of paperwork to do for the insurance company."

"Yah," John added, "and, if nothin' else, we'll set up da ice house out on Lake of da Woods, dere. I could go for a little walleye fishin'."

"Oh, yah," Margie agreed, her eyes on me. "John has a real nice fish house, don't ya know. It's like a regular cabin. If we go out there for a few days, ya and Randy hafta join us for an afternoon. It's always a good time." She waved her finger. "Last year there were so many houses on the ice that an entire Girl Scout troop came out and went door to door, selling cookies."

John chuckled. "They made a killin'."

"Well, we'll keep you posted," Randy told them.

"And what about you two?" Margie asked. "What's on your agenda?" She winked at me, and I'm sure my face turned scarlet.

For his part, Randy gave my shoulder a squeeze. "I guess I have to take her shopping tomorrow." He had a silly expression on his face. "She has some foolish idea that she needs clothes."

I elbowed him in the side, as everyone guffawed.

Rubbing the spot, he continued. "I suppose I also have to get back to work at some point."

Ed merely said, "Yeah, at some point."

Randy then leaned in and murmured to me alone, "We also need some quality one-on-one time, if you know what I mean." He did the hula with his eyebrows.

And I responded in kind. "Sounds good to me."

The End

Recipes

℘ Potato Hot Dish ℘

Hungry Jack instant potatoes   1½ c. cottage cheese
1 c. sour cream with chives   Mild cheddar cheese

Make Hungry Jack instant potatoes for 12, according to the recipe on the box but reduce the required liquid by one 1 cup. Mix prepared potatoes with sour cream with chives and cottage cheese. Place in a greased, 9-by-13-inch casserole dish and sprinkle with a moderate amount of mild shredded cheddar cheese. Bake in a 350-degree oven (preheated) for 30 minutes.

℘ Chicken Crescent Hot Dish ℘

3 c. cooked chicken   1 8-oz. can crescent rolls
1 can cream of chicken soup   ²/₃ c. shredded Swiss cheese
1 4-oz. can mushrooms   ²/₃ c. slivered almonds
1 8-oz. can water chestnuts   2 to 4 tsp. melted butter
²/₃ c. mayonnaise
½ c. chopped celery
½ c. chopped onions
½ c. sour cream

Mix ingredients in left column and cook until hot. Pour into a buttered cake pan. Separate rolls and place them on top. Mix cheese, almonds, and butter and pour over rolls. Bake in a 375-degree oven (preheated) for 20 to 25 minutes. Let stand for 10 minutes before serving.

✏ Raspberry Squares ✑

Butter Crunch Crust:

    ½ c. butter (softened)   1 c. flour

    ¼ c. light brown sugar (packed)   ½ c. chopped pecans

Mix first three ingredients, then stir in pecans. Pat mixture in a greased 9-x-13-inch pan. Bake in a 375-degree oven (preheated) for 15 minutes or until lightly browned. Take out of oven and immediately break into crumbs using a wooden spoon. Then, pat firmly into pan again, reserving ¼ cup for topping. Let cool, then refrigerate while making the rest of the recipe.

Filling:

    1 large pkg. raspberry Jell-O   2 10-oz. boxes frozen

    2½ c. boiling water   raspberries

    2 T. lemon juice   ½ c. sugar

Dissolve Jell-O in boiling water. Add lemon juice, frozen berries, and sugar. Stir. Chill until thickened.

Topping:

    1 8-oz. pkg. cream cheese (softened)   1 tsp. vanilla

    ⅔ c. powdered sugar   2 c. whipping cream (whipped)

Combine softened cream cheese with powdered sugar and vanilla. Fold in whipped cream. On top of chilled crust, place one-half of cream cheese mixture, then all of the Jell-O mixture. Finally, top with the rest of the cream cheese mixture, followed by the reserved crumbs. Refrigerate. Best if made the day before serving so it has time to firm up nicely.

℘ Salted Carmel Brownies ℆

1 c. butter	1 tsp. vanilla
1 oz. (4 squares) dark or	1 c. flour
semi-sweet chocolate	½ tsp. table salt
2 c. white sugar	¼ c. caramel ice cream topping
4 eggs	1 tsp. sea salt

In a sauce pan, over low heat, melt butter and chocolate, stirring constantly. Remove from heat. Stir in sugar. Allow mixture to cool slightly. Beat in eggs, one at a time. Stir in vanilla. In a separate bowl, whisk flour and table salt together. Gradually add flour mixture to the chocolate mixture. Spread the batter into a greased 9-x-13-inch pan. Drizzle the caramel on top. Use a knife to swirl the caramel over the mixture. Sprinkle sea salt over the caramel. Bake 30 to 35 minutes in a 350-degree oven (preheated). Brownies are done when a toothpick inserted in the center comes out more or less clean.

℘ Nut Clusters ℆

1 12-oz. bag milk chocolate chips
1 12-oz. bag semi-sweet chocolate chips
2 12-oz. bag white chocolate chips
Approximately 30 oz. of lightly salted peanuts

In an electric skillet, melt all the chips over extremely low heat, stirring often. Add nuts and stir. Drop clusters by small ice cream scoop onto wax paper. Allow to set for a day. Store clusters in cool, dry area, but not in the refrigerator. To make the clusters shiny, stir in ½ cup of melted paraffin wax to the hot, melted chocolate.

℘ British Pasties ℘

Crust:

3 c. flour	1 egg
1 tsp. salt	½ c. water
1 c. shortening	1 tsp. vinegar

Mix the flour, salt, and shortening like for a pie crust. In a separate bowl, beat the egg, water, and vinegar together. Add this mixture to the flour mixture. Mix. Roll out four 8-to-9-inch circles.

Filling:

1½ pounds of ground beef	4 carrots, diced
4 potatoes, diced	1 large onion, chopped

Mix raw meat with vegetables. Season to taste with salt and pepper. Fill half of each crust. Top with a pat of butter. Fold crust over and seal, making slits for steam. Bake on cookie sheets in a preheated oven, for about one hour, at 350 degrees.

℘ Almond Bars ℭ

First Layer:
    1 c. butter, softened
    ½ c. powdered sugar
    2 c. flour

Second Layer:
    ½ c. sugar
    1 8-oz. pkg. cream cheese
    2 eggs
    1 tsp. almond extract

Frosting:
    ¼ c. butter, softened
    1 tsp. almond extract
    1½ c. powdered sugar

    1½ T. milk
    Sliced almonds (optional)

Mix all ingredients for the first layer and press into a 9-x-13-inch pan. Bake at 350 degrees in a preheated oven for 15 minutes.

While the first layer is baking, mix all the ingredients for the second layer (mix well). Pour onto baked first layer. Return to oven and bake for 15 minutes more. Cool.

Mix the frosting ingredients together and spread onto cooled bars. Sprinkle with almond slices, if desired.

ဆ Frosted Fudge Brownies ຕ

2 c. sugar	1¾ c. flour
1 c. vegetable oil	1 tsp. salt
4 eggs	½ to ¾ c. Hershey's cocoa
1 tsp. vanilla	

Mix above ingredients in order using an electric mixer. Bake in a bar pan (approximately 11-x-14 inches), at 350 degrees oven (preheated), for about 25 minutes. Don't overbake. (If using toothpick test, remove bars from oven as soon as toothpick comes out pretty clean.) Cool.

Frosting:

1 c. sugar	1 c. miniature marshmallows
¼ c. butter	½ to ¾ c. chocolate chips
¼ c. milk	

Mix together first three ingredients over medium heat. Mix in miniature marshmallows and continue to stir until mixture comes to a boil. (May have to turn up heat.) As soon as mixture starts boiling, remove from heat and add chocolate chips. Stir until smooth. Then spread over cool bars.

ℬ M & M Bars ℭ

2-1/8 c. flour	½ c. white sugar
½ tsp. salt	1 large egg
½ tsp. baking soda	1 large egg yolk
1½ sticks butter (12 T),	2 tsp. vanilla
melted and slightly cooled	1 12-oz. pkg. M&Ms, divided
1 c. brown sugar	

Preheat oven to 325 degrees. Line a 9-x-13-inch pan with foil, letting excess foil hang over the edge to help pull the bars from the pan. Also spray the foil lining the pan with nonstick cooking spray.

Mix the flour, salt, and baking soda in a medium bowl. Set aside. Whisk the melted butter and sugars in a separate large bowl until thoroughly combined. Then, add the egg and egg yolk, as well as the vanilla. Mix. Next, using a rubber spatula, fold the dry ingredients into the egg mixture until just combined. Do not overmix. Fold in 1 cup of M&Ms. Spoon the batter into the prepared pan, smoothing the top with the spatula. Sprinkle remaining M&Ms on top and press in lightly.

Bake until the top of the bars is light, golden brown and slightly firm to the touch, and the edges start to pull away from the sides of the pan (approximately 24 to 28 minutes). Cool to room temperature. Lift bars from pan by grabbing the excess foil and transfer the bars to a cutting board. Cut into squares.

❧ Rhubarb Bread ❧

3 c. light brown sugar	5 c. flour
1½ c. vegetable oil	2 tsp. baking soda
2 eggs, well beaten	2 tsp. ground cinnamon
2 c. buttermilk	4 c. chopped rhubarb
3 tsp. vanilla extract	1 c. ground nuts (optional)

Topping:
    ¾ c. light brown sugar
    2 T. butter
    1 tsp. ground cinnamon

Mix first set of ingredients in order listed. Pour into greased and floured loaf pans. (Batter ideally makes 7 small loaves.) Mix topping ingredients until crumbly. Sprinkle on top of bread mixture. Bake in preheated 350-degree oven for 45 minutes to one hour or until done. Bake longer in bigger pans.

❧ Gertrude's Hot Dish ❧

2 medium onions, chopped	1 can cream of chicken soup
1½ c. chopped celery	¾ c. white rice
1 lb. ground hamburger	1½ c. water
1 can cream of mushroom soup	1 T. soy sauce

Brown onions and celery with hamburger. Mix in remaining ingredients in order. Place in a large casserole dish and bake at 350 degrees, in a preheated oven, for 1½ hours.

ಖ Meatball Hot Dish ಜ

1 large can Pork and Beans	½ c. light brown sugar
¾ c. catsup	1 tsp. vanilla
1 c. warm water	

Mix above ingredients and let stand for 30 minutes.

1 lb. hamburger	½ c. milk
1 tsp. salt	1 T. cornstarch
½ c. bread crumbs	

While first mixture is standing, mix second set of ingredients and form into meatballs. Roll meatballs in greased pan and brown. Place browned meatballs in buttered casserole dish. Cover with bean mixture. Bake at 350 degrees in a preheated oven for one hour.

ಖ Cranberry Pudding ಜ

2 c. cranberries, cut up	½ c. water
1/3 c. sugar	1 ⅓ c. flour
½ c. molasses	1 tsp. baking soda

Mix all ingredients together and pour into 9-x-9-inch, greased pan. Bake in a preheated oven at 300 degrees for 40 minutes. Serve warm with the sauce below.

Sauce for Topping:

1 c. sugar	½ c. butter
½ c. cream	

Beat slowly over low heat to boiling point.

℘ Upside Down Hot Dish ☙

1 lb. lean ground beef	1 tsp. Garlic powder
½ lb. Italian sausage	1 15-oz. can tomato sauce
Salt and pepper to taste	1½ c. shredded mozzarella cheese
½ tsp. Basil	1 10-oz pkg. refrigerated biscuits
½ tsp. Oregano	

In a large skillet, brown beef and sausage. Drain grease. Mix in seasonings. Add tomato sauce. Cook over medium heat until hot. Transfer mixture to a greased, two-quart baking dish. Sprinkle with cheese. Flatten biscuits before arranging them side by side on top of the cheese. Bake at 400 degrees in a preheated oven for 15 to 20 minutes or until the biscuits are golden brown. Five servings.

ஐ Zucchini Cake ରେ

2½ c. flour	½ tsp. baking soda
2 c. sugar	1 c. vegetable oil
1½ tsp. cinnamon	4 eggs
1 tsp. salt	2 c. shredded zucchini
½ tsp. baking powder	½ c. chopped pecans, optional

In a mixing bowl, combine flour, sugar, cinnamon, salt, baking powder, and baking soda. In a separate bowl, combine the oil and eggs. Add egg mixture to the dry ingredients. Mix well with a spoon. Add zucchini. Stir until thoroughly combined. Fold in nuts, if desired. Pour into a greased 9-x-13-inch pan. In a preheated oven, bake at 350 degrees for 35 to 40 minutes or until a toothpick comes out clean. Cool before frosting.

Cream Cheese Frosting

1 8-oz. pkg. cream cheese, softened	1 tsp. vanilla
½ c. butter, softened	2 c. powdered sugar, sifted
1 T. milk	

In a small mixing bowl, combine cream cheese, butter, milk, and vanilla. Beat with an electric beater until smooth. Frost cake. Top with more chopped nuts, if desired. Store in the refrigerator.

❧ Heavenly Hash ❧

1½ c. water
¾ c. uncooked white rice
2 c. crushed pineapple, drained
1 10.5-oz. pkg. miniature marshmallows
1 4-oz. jar maraschino cherries, halved (save juice)
1 T. saved cherry juice
1 c. heavy cream (do not substitute Cool Whip)
½ c. confectioner's sugar

In a saucepan, bring water to a boil. Add rice and stir. Reduce heat. Cover and simmer for 20 minutes. Cool completely.

In a large bowl, combine cooled rice, pineapple, marshmallows, cherries and cherry juice. In a chilled bowl, whip the cream until peaks form. Fold in the confectioner's sugar. Then fold whipped cream mixture into rice mixture. Refrigerate for two hours.

❧ Rhubarb Custard Pie ❧

1½ c. white sugar	3 eggs
¼ c. flour	4 c. rhubarb, sliced 1" thick
¼ tsp. nutmeg	prepared 9" pie crust
Dash of salt	2 T. butter

Mix ingredients from the first column. In a separate bowl, beat the eggs smooth. Add the sugar mixture to the eggs. Beat again until smooth. Stir in the rhubarb. Pour into a 9" pie crust. Dot with the butter. Fit on the top crust. Bake in a preheated oven, at 400 degrees for 50 minutes. (You may want to wrap the edges of the crust with aluminum foil for the first 30 minutes of baking to keep the edges from burning.)

℘ Rhubarb Salad ଔ

3 c. fresh chopped rhubarb
½ c. white sugar
2 T. water
1 3-oz. pkg. raspberry Jell-O

1 c. cold water
1 c. chopped apple
½ c. chopped walnuts
Cool Whip

In a saucepan, over medium heat, combine the rhubarb, sugar, and the water. Bringing to a boil. Cook it for about 15 minutes or until the rhubarb is sauce-like. Next, in a medium-size bowl, stir the gelatin mix into one cup of the boiling hot rhubarb sauce. Keep stirring until the mixture is completely dissolved. Stir in the cold water. Add the apple and walnuts. Refrigerate for 2 to 4 hours, or until set. Garnish with Cool Whip. (You may have extra rhubarb sauce. It makes great topping for ice cream.)

℘ Cajun Chicken and Rice Hot Dish ℘

½ tsp. smoked paprika (this is what makes this recipe unique)

½ tsp. dried thyme

½ tsp. garlic powder

½ tsp. cayenne pepper

½ tsp. salt

½ tsp. pepper

1 lb. boneless, skinless chicken breast

3 slices bacon

2 tsp. canola oil

1 med. onion

1 med. red pepper

1 stalk celery

2 T. tomato paste

4 c. chicken broth (low sodium is fine)

2 c. long-grain white rice

1 c. frozen peas

Parsley

In a bowl, combine the paprika, thyme, garlic powder, cayenne, salt, and pepper. Cube chicken and toss it around in one-half of the seasoning mixture.

Meanwhile, cook bacon until crisp. Transfer to a paper towel. In the same pan, cook the seasoned chicken in the canola oil for 3 minutes, or until browned, stirring occasionally.

Transfer the cooked chicken to a kettle. Chop and add the onion, pepper, and celery. Cook over medium heat for 5 minutes, stirring occasionally. Add the tomato paste. Cook for just 30 seconds more. Stir in the broth, rice, and peas. Reduce heat to a simmer for 25 minutes, or until rice is tender and chicken is done. Stir in crushed bacon and parsley. Serve.

ಬ Telephone Bars ಚ

½ c. butter	1 ½ c. flour	1 c. dates
1 c. sugar	1 tsp. cocoa	1 tsp. baking soda
2 eggs	1 tsp. salt	1 c. hot water

You also need 1 c. of semi-sweet chocolate chips.

In a bowl, cream together the ingredients in the first column. In a separate bowl, combine the ingredients in the second column. Stir the flour mixture into the creamed butter mixture. Set aside. Mix together the ingredients in the third column. Finally, add the date mixture to the rest of the batter. Pour into a greased and floured 9-x-13-inch pan. Sprinkle with the chocolate chips. Bake in a 350-degree oven (preheated) for 30 minutes. Cool and serve.

ಬ Queso Mac and Cheese ಚ

1 16-oz. pkg. elbow macaroni
1 can (10 oz.) Ro Tel Diced Tomatoes & Green Chilies, undrained
1 16-oz. pkg. Velveeta cheese, cut into ½" cubes
½ c. 2% milk

Prepare macaroni according to package directions (omit salt). Drain. Meanwhile, combine undrained tomatoes and green chilies and cubed cheese. Microwave (covered) for 10 to 12 minutes, or until cheese melts. (Stir after 5 minutes and again after 8 minutes.) Add milk to the melted tomatoes-chili-cheese mixture. Gently stir drained macaroni into that same mixture and serve.

ஐ Cauliflower and Sausage Rigatoni Hot Dish ෪

½ lb. ground Italian sausage
2 T. olive oil
1 small onion, diced
2 cloves garlic, minced
¼ c. chopped basil
½ tsp. salt
¼ tsp. black pepper
1 qt. marinara sauce

1 lb. rigatoni
½ lb. cauliflower, cut into 1"
    florets (about 3 c)
5 Roma tomatoes, cut into ¼"
    pieces (optional)
1 c. grated mozzarella cheese
½ c. grated parmesan cheese

Bring a large pot of well-salted water to a boil and cook rigatoni until al dente (about 10 minutes). Transfer pasta to a large bowl, leaving the water in the pot. Return the pasta water to a boil. Add the cauliflower. Cook it until tender (about 2 minutes). Drain and add the cauliflower to the pasta.

Meanwhile, in a large skillet, heat olive oil over medium heat. Add diced onion and crumbled sausage. Cook until sausage is cooked through. Add garlic. Cook another minute. Drain excess fat. Add marinara sauce. Bring to a simmer. Turn to low heat. Add basil. Season to taste with salt and pepper.

Finally, add the meat sauce, the mozzarella cheese, and the diced tomatoes (if desired) to the cauliflower and pasta. Mix gently but thoroughly. Transfer the mixture into a 9-x-13-inch buttered casserole dish. Sprinkle the parmesan cheese on top. Bake at 375 degrees, in a preheated oven, for 30 minutes, or until the cheese is melted. Let the dish stand for 10 minutes before serving.

๛ Peppers Italiano ๊

6 sweet peppers, any color	4 cloves garlic, crushed
1 lb. Italian sausage	¼ c. olive oil
1 large onion, diced	2 c. mozzarella cheese, shredded
¼ tsp. oregano	10 fresh mushrooms, sliced
1 tsp. sweet basil	1 small jar spaghetti sauce or
¾ tsp. fennel seeds	marinara sauce

Pour olive oil into a medium-size frying pan. Saute the crushed garlic, being careful not to burn it. Add the diced onion. Saute until transparent. Add the sausage. Brown and crumble well. Add oregano, basil, mushrooms (reserving some nice slices), and fennel seeds. Add one-half the spaghetti sauce to the mixture and cook on low heat for 30 minutes. Let cool slightly. Add 1 cup of the mozzarella cheese. Mix well.

Cut peppers lengthwise in half. Clean out membranes and seeds. Cut lengthwise once more. Stuff the peppers with the meat mixture. Place on a cookie sheet. Top stuffed pepper quarters with the remaining spaghetti sauce and mozzarella cheese, along with a slice of fresh mushroom if so desired. Finally, seal cookie sheet with aluminum foil. Bake for 1 hour at 350 degrees, in a preheated oven.

৪০ Broccoli, Cheddar, Chicken, and Tater Tot Hot Dish ৫৪

2 cans cream of chicken soup
2 cans cheddar cheese soup
1½ c. milk
8 to 10 c. broccoli florets
2 large boneless, skinless chicken
    breasts (cooked and shredded)
1 tsp. hot sauce

½ tsp. salt
¼ tsp. black pepper
⅛ tsp. Lawry's Garlic Salt with
    Parsley
½ bag frozen Ore Ida
    Seasoned Tater Tots
½ c. shredded cheddar cheese

Place soup and milk in a large pot. Heat over medium heat for about 5 minutes, whisking constantly. Stir in broccoli. Cook for another 5 minutes. Add cooked chicken, hot sauce, and seasonings. Stir. Pour mixture into 11-x-7-inch casserole dish sprayed with cooking oil spray. Top evenly with tater tots, then cheese. Bake at 375 degrees in a preheated oven for 20 minutes. Cover with foil and bake another 15 minutes.

℘ Fabulous Fudge Bars ଔ

2 c. packed brown sugar
1 c. butter, softened
2 eggs
1 tsp. vanilla
2½ c. flour
1 tsp. baking soda
½ tsp. salt
3 c. quick cooking or regular oats

1 12-oz. pkg. semisweet or
    milk chocolate chips
1 14-oz. can sweetened
    condensed milk
2 T. butter
1 c. chopped walnuts
1 tsp. vanilla

In a bowl, mix sugar, butter, eggs, and vanilla. Stir in flour, soda, salt, and oats. Reserve 1/3 of mixture. Press rest of mixture into a 9-x-13-inch greased pan.

Heat chocolate chips, milk, and butter until melted, stirring constantly. Stir in nuts and vanilla. Spread over the bass mixture already in the pan.

Finally drop teaspoons full of reserved oatmeal mixture all over chocolate mixture. Bake at 350 degrees, in a preheated oven, for 25 to 30 minutes, or until slightly brown.

ꙮ Breakfast Hot Dish ꙮ

1 lb. ground pork sausage
6 slices white or light wheat bread
1 8-oz. pkg. mild cheddar cheese,
    shredded

8 large eggs
2 c. milk (2% or whole)
¼ tsp. salt
½ tsp. pepper

In a large skillet, cook the sausage over medium heat, stirring frequently, until browned and crumbly (about 10 minutes). Drain fat.

Cut and discard the crusts from the bread. Then, cut the slices in half and arrange them in a single layer in a 9-x-13-inch casserole dish that's been sprayed with cooking oil spray. (Cut the bread pieces to get them to cover the entire bottom of the pan in a single layer.) Sprinkle the bread layer with the meat, then the cheese.

In a large bowl, whisk together the eggs, milk, and seasoning. Pour over the cheese. Bake the casserole at 350 degrees, in a preheated oven, for 40 minutes. Let the dish sit for 10 minutes before serving. (Add ¼ c. diced onions and ¼ c. diced green peppers for some extra zing!)